Book Review

Two generations after *Narnia* appeared, Debby L. Johnston has given us a new and exciting glimpse of the future in her creative writing entitled *The Onyx Stones*. She has crafted a captivating story about Cricket (don't call her Christine) and Josh (whose name is quite similar to that of Joshua in the Old Testament) and their exploration of end times. This story is light and whimsical on one hand while dealing with the heavy and ponderous issues of rapture and tribulation on the other hand. I wish I had been introduced to eschatology with this book when I was fourteen years old. Ms. Johnston makes the topic attractive rather than off-putting.

Writing from the perspective of a pre-millennial pre-tribulation eschaton, Debby dances lightly through the topic with a twelve-year-old lassie who is quadriplegic. The author shows her versatility by occasionally launching into original music and poetry that should have a long shelf life in adolescent literature. *The Onyx Stones* is one of the two or three best teen books I have read in this new century.

JERRY B. CAIN
CHANCELLOR, JUDSON UNIVERSITY
JUNE 8, 2019

OTHER BOOKS BY DEBBY:

His Timeless Touch: Twelve Remarkable
Short Stories of Lives Changed by the Healer
The Cherish Novel Series:
Cherish: A Still, Small Call
Cherish: Behold, I Knock
Cherish: Create in Me a Clean Heart

THE ONYX STONES

THE ONYX STONES:

Mystery of the Underground People

Debby L. Johnston

ELM HILL

A Division of
HarperCollins Christian Publishing

www.elmhillbooks.com

THE ONYX STONES:
Mystery of the Underground People

Published in Nashville, Tennessee, by Elm Hill, an imprint of Thomas Nelson. Elm Hill and Thomas Nelson are registered trademarks of HarperCollins Christian Publishing, Inc.

Elm Hill titles may be purchased in bulk for educational, business, fund-raising, or sales promotional use. For information, please e-mail SpecialMarkets@ ThomasNelson.com.

Publisher's Note: This novel is a work of fiction. Names, characters, places, and incidents are either products of the author's imagination or used fictitiously. All characters are fictional, and any similarity to people living or dead is purely coincidental.

Scripture quotations are from NIV, unless marked KJV for King James Version.

Words to Hymn: *What a Friend We Have in Jesus.* Joseph M. Scriven, 1855 and Charles C. Converse, 1868 (in public domain)

Art Credits: DLJ logo designed by Kate Frick (Frick.chick.designs@gmail.com). All sketches, including cover image, by Debby L. Johnston.

Library of Congress Cataloging-in-Publication Data

Library of Congress Control Number: 2019914239

ISBN 978-1-400328604 (Paperback)
ISBN 978-1-400328611 (Hardbound)
ISBN 978-1-400328628 (eBook)

*Dedicated to Jesus, the One who will, one day,
catch us up into the air to be with Him, forever!*

And so, it begins...

CONTENTS

CHAPTER ONE

A Smashed Cricket

At my strangled cry, the disembodied beeping turned insistent. Voices rushed in, and hands fluttered about my head. Somewhere over my face I heard, "Good morning, Christine."

Morning? How can it be morning and be so dark?

"You're in the hospital," the voice continued, "and you have a breathing tube down your throat. Don't try to talk."

To someone, as if I couldn't hear, the voice said, "She can't see. I imagine she's scared."

When she (whoever she was) said my name again—*Christine*—I wanted to shout that my name is *Cricket*. Nobody calls me *Christine*, except for teachers on the first day of school.

1

In protest, I tried to sit up, but I couldn't feel me. *What...?*

Now the voice warned, "Don't move. You won't be able to. You have broken bones." A pillow shifted beneath my head.

No! my mind shouted. *No! This can't be. You're lying! Let me go! Let me sit up. I don't know you, and I don't know where I am. I want to see. I want to move!*

But although my mind shouted, my voice could not. The tube down my throat barely let me moan.

"You're at Mercy Hospital," the invisible voice said, "and Dr. Thrush will be here shortly to talk with you. Before he comes, I have a couple of questions. Do you feel any pain?"

I wanted to scream, *what about* my *questions? Am I truly in a hospital? How did I get here?*

The voice asked again, "Do you have any pain?"

I shook my head. But then I did have pain. The movement of my head made my throat hurt. The breathing tube interfered.

"Good," the voice said. "No pain."

No pain, except for my throat!

Then the voice asked, "Can you see any light?"

This time, I shook my head carefully. What else could I do? I could only breathe, shake my head, and move my eyelids.

I started to cry.

"That's okay," the voice said. "It's okay to cry. But we are taking good care of you. My name is Florence, and I'll be here all day." Florence wiped my tears as if she were dusting a table.

I'm not a table, I fumed. *Just because I can't move doesn't mean I'm furniture!*

I resented Florence. I wanted my mother! I wanted my father! I even wanted my aggravating little brother, instead of this cold,

2

invisible stranger. I imagined Florence as short and dumpy and with uncombed, colorless hair. I didn't like her. I wanted her to go away.

I blamed Florence for my predicament and would have lashed out at her if I could. But I couldn't move or shout. And I couldn't stop her from fussing around my face. I wanted her to leave. And then, she did.

When she reappeared, I gritted my teeth. And when she disappeared again, I gritted my teeth. And then I discovered that by huffing and breathing rapidly, I could make her come.

At last, something I can control!

I huffed and set off the monitor. The beeping interrupted whatever Florence was doing, and within seconds, I felt her hand brush over my face. Then I heard her turn off the alarms. When she left, I repeated my mischief.

After several episodes of blowing out air, I felt sure that Florence suspected my manipulation. But she came running every time.

Now a man's voice quizzed Florence outside my room. I tried to listen, but the only thing I heard clearly was his murmured, "Mm-huh."

"Good morning, Christine," Dr. Thrush said, at last.

My name is Cricket! I screamed inside.

Dr. Thrush said, "Florence tells me you don't have pain. Is that still the case? Blink once for *yes* and twice for *no.*"

I blinked once. Blinking was better than nodding.

"So," he said, "no pain. Do you see any light?"

I blinked twice.

"No light," he said. But he added, "Don't worry too much about that. It could change once the bump on your head heals. You'll have to let us know if you begin to see light."

Sure, Doc, I thought to myself. *I'll just call Florence and say,*

3

"Hey, Florence! I see light!" In my anger I snorted, and the monitor beeped twice.

Dr. Thrush said, "Florence tells me you're able to control your breathing. Can you give me three good puffs?"

Sheepishly, I complied. As I suspected, Florence had guessed my little game. The monitor beeped at my puffs.

"Good," said the doctor. "We can take that thing out." And then he disappeared. I heard no more from him.

Did I understand right? Are they going to remove the breathing tube? My heart beat with hope.

~ ~ ~

The removal of the tube was not without pain, however, and it left me in tears. My throat felt raw, and I could barely croak out a word.

"Thirsty," I squeaked. Florence let me suck on a small sponge soaked with water. I wanted more, and I was angry when she withheld it. *What could it hurt? Just a little water. Is she trying to make me dry up and blow away? Who can I complain to?*

But before I could tattle on her, Florence announced that I would be moving. I hadn't realized I was in post-operative recovery. "You'll be in intensive care now, in a room," Florence said matter-of-factly.

I sighed. *What difference will that make? One room or another is the same to me. I can't see—and I'm thirsty!*

But then I wondered, *Will I get a new nurse?* I hoped so.

~ ~ ~

As my bed moved, my head wobbled. Voices came and went. Elevator doors dinged. And when the movement stopped, the room was quiet. Then the staff reconnected the equipment and I heard the beeping and pumping I had hated in the recovery area. I clenched my teeth and blew out my irritation. This might be a different place in the hospital, but it wasn't different to me.

I want out. I want to go home. I want...

What did I want? My mind was too fuzzy to process more.

But I did get one thing I wanted, a new nurse.

Unlike Florence, Lucy was quick-talking, engaging, and funny. And Lucy talked *to* me and not *at* me.

"Hello, Miss Christine. Welcome to Fantasy Land. Your wish is my command—to a point, that is."

"Cricket," I corrected her with a croak, and I never heard *Christine* again.

"I love the name Cricket," she insisted.

"Me, too," I rasped with a smile.

"Thirsty?" Lucy asked, and when I said yes, she replaced Florence's stingy, little water-sponge with a straw. *Finally,* I thought, *I can drink.*

The ice water soothed my dry throat. *But now I'll probably have to get up and go to the bathroom fifty times,* I thought. And then I remembered that I couldn't get up. *So, how's that going to work?* I wondered.

I asked, and Lucy explained that I had a catheter and a bag that took care of my bladder functions. I frowned. *That's not normal.* But I couldn't formulate a good protest against it. My mind was too fuzzy. Try as I might, my thinking went no further than my immediate needs and frustrations.

I complained that I couldn't concentrate. "It's the medicine," Lucy explained. And I wondered, *why do I have to be all doped up?* I fought the grogginess, to no avail.

Sleep brought no relief. Nightmares haunted me. In them, I fell deeper and deeper into a black hole that echoed and flashed with faces and voices I couldn't identify. I wanted the dream to stop.

"I don't want to think or dream," I whimpered when I awakened.

"Let's try television," Lucy suggested. Before I could object, she said, "I know you can't see it, but I can find a channel you can listen to."

True to her word, Lucy found a movie about a girl and a horse. The story reminded me of a book I had read last year, in sixth grade. Lucy set the scene so the dialogue would make sense. Then, whenever she checked on me, she supplied details my sightless eyes were missing: the horse was chestnut with a white blaze on his forehead, the girl had violet eyes, etc.

I tried to follow the story, but the girl and horse faded in and out of my prescription haze. Other images tugged at the edges of my mind, but I could not pin them down. Faces I felt I should know floated in and out of my fog, and questions that formed on the tip of my brain remained just out of reach.

~ ~ ~

For two days (or was it more?), I hung in that fuzzy state. Only Lucy could cut through to offer me water or stroke my forehead. Otherwise, I remained in a stupor.

But then, slowly, my mind began to clear. I could sometimes concentrate on television or calculate when an aide might return to check on me. It was a relief to think. I laughed at Lucy's hospital gossip, and I critiqued her search for interesting programs on television.

Then one morning, I awakened to a scroll of TV channels. Lucy was searching for a Disney program or a cartoon I could listen to as I sipped my breakfast drink. Before she finished her scroll, however, a voice called from the hallway, "Lucy, I need a minute of your help." Lucy answered, and I heard her go.

I closed my sightless eyes and let the television drone on. It was not Disney or a cartoon, but rather the end of a local news story about a natural foods store. Just before the commercial break, a reporter announced the *news tease,* designed to keep viewers from changing channels. The reporter divulged: "Two local college professors and their young son died this weekend in a major traffic pileup on the north outer belt. A twelve-year-old daughter recovers from serious injuries at Mercy Hospital. State police are investigating the accident's cause. More on the tragedy after this…"

When I stopped breathing, my monitor beeped. Instantly, Lucy returned.

"Are you okay, Cricket?" she cried.

"No," I whispered, and my heart peaked on the pulse monitor. Shock surged through my brain.

Lucy couldn't find what was wrong. I felt her hand on my forehead, and I heard her reciting procedures as she checked the equipment.

Then the TV commercial ended and the news story about the car accident aired. Lucy gasped. "Oh, dear!"

In an instant, she replaced the details of the car accident with a game show and obnoxious dinging. Someone had won the grand prize, and the studio crowd cheered.

But my ears remained stuck on the news, and my mind burned with questions.

My voice trembled. "Lucy, I need to know. Are my parents all right? Are they in the hospital, too?"

Lucy didn't answer, and I whispered, "My parents died, didn't they?"

I felt Lucy's cheek against mine. Together, we cried. And when I asked if my brother, Scooter, had died, too, we sobbed.

~ ~ ~

I shut out everything. I refused to listen to or answer anything. In my blind waking moments, I replayed and relived a past I could now recall vividly.

I mourned that I would never eat Sunday dinner at the big table in our dining room. I grieved that I would never see my dad at work on his computer in the den or my mother correcting students' papers at the breakfast bar. I would never feel my parents' hugs or bask in their praise when I brought home good grades on my report card. I longed to hear their voices. And I regretted that I had ignored my little brother and sent him away countless times as I roamed the college campus where my parents taught.

I remembered long hours in the car on the way to the Grand Canyon. And I lamented my family would never make our trip to Disneyland.

As I mourned, various hospital aides intruded and performed their duties. Their well-meaning cheerfulness sent my grief deeper. Only Lucy let me grieve in peace. She swept about me like a tender ghost, whispering only if it was needful. Whenever she saw tears in my eyes, she pressed her cheek against mine, and I felt her tears mingle with my own.

Time stopped for me. I was sure it would be this way forever.

Lucy warned, "You've got to eat, Cricket, or they'll put in a feeding tube. You don't want that."

And even though I didn't care what happened to me, I did make myself sip the liquid breakfast or lunch she offered. I wouldn't have

8

responded if the suggestion had come from anyone else. Lucy knew my hurt. Without her, I would have willed myself to sleep, never to awaken. Lucy was keeping me alive.

But evidently no one cared, because suddenly, in the depth of my depression and at the end of my second week at the hospital, I was moved to a nursing home. And Lucy, my lifeline, was gone.

~ ~ ~

Also gone were the bustling hospital sounds in the hallways at all hours. Mustier smells replaced the sharp, antiseptic air to which I had become accustomed. The staff sounded younger than the hospital nurses, and they teased and tossed childish remarks to the residents in their care. Moving from room to room, they cajoled and scolded their charges as if the aged were toddlers. I was a kid, but I was nearly thirteen. And nobody was going to treat me like a baby.

I winced at an overly cheerful, "Christine, you have visitors!" and I overheard a mumbled exchange at the door. I tried to guess who might be visiting. *Neighbors? Someone from the church?* But it was neither.

"Hello, Christine," a man's voice said. "My name is Gary Tipple. You don't know me, but I knew your parents. I'm their lawyer. Please know how sorry I am for your loss."

My loss? My parents and brother aren't lost. They're dead! Lost can be found, but dead can never be returned.

Then Mr. Tipple said, "Mr. Gilson is with me. Mr. Gilson is from Children's Protective Services. The two of us have been assigned by the courts to oversee your care. We are charged with advising you and handling your financial affairs until you come of legal age. Do you understand what that means?"

I had a general idea. I nodded that I understood.

Mr. Tipple continued, "Your parents have left everything to you in their will. But until you reach twenty-one, in nine years, your inheritance will remain in trust. Current expenses will be drawn as needed by my authority on your behalf."

He paused, as if waiting for a response.

"Okay," I said quietly.

"Your hospital care is covered by insurance and by the trust," Mr. Tipple said. "And Mr. Gilson and I have agreed with the recommendation of your doctor that you be placed here, in The Arches Nursing Facility, until such time as you might be able to resume an active life. At present you are in need of extreme care, and The Arches is equipped to handle your needs for as long as necessary. We hope you will find the facility comfortable. We will visit you often, to check on your progress and keep up with your needs."

Now Mr. Gilson spoke. "You'll also have a visit from Mrs. Jamieson. Mrs. Jamieson is a counselor with Protective Services. She's a very nice lady. You will find her a good person to talk to and share with. Feel free to relate to her any needs you have. Mr. Tipple, Mrs. Jamieson, and I are all available to serve you as you recuperate. You can ask the nursing home staff to call us at any time for help or a special visit. Do you understand?"

I understood. And my anger boiled. *You—perfect strangers—have come here to tell me you are now in charge of my life. Even though I can't see your faces, I'm supposed to trust and confide in you. Who are you kidding? I'm just a kid, and you've stuck me in a nursing home, a place of no return. How could you?*

Once, when my mom's mother had grown ill, I had visited her in a nursing home. It was a sad place filled with old people waiting to die.

10

It scared me, now, to think I might never leave this room. *I'm paralyzed, and I can't see. Will I die before I reach* legal age?

In my blind helplessness, I wanted to yell, *what kind of life is this?* I tried to close my ears, to shut out the hum of the machines and the voices in the hallway.

I might as well go to sleep and never wake up.

~ ~ ~

But the next morning, I did wake up. And I was irritated. Someone rudely hollered from the doorway, "Hey! Are you awake yet?"

I didn't answer, and even though I could see nothing, I kept my eyelids closed. *What does this clueless aide want?* I wondered. *Whatever it is, I'm not interested.*

"Hey!" the obnoxious voice yelled again, "wake up!" Hands now patted my cheeks in quick little slaps.

What in the world? "Go away!" I growled.

"But I just got here," the voice protested.

"Well, go back to wherever you came from," I barked. I wanted this unwelcome intruder to get the hint and leave.

Instead, the voice offered, "I'm Josh. I think we're about the same age."

Same age? Nobody in this place is my age. This is an old people's place.

I kept my eyelids screwed shut. I hoped it was enough for *Josh* to get the message. But *Josh* ignored my every attempt to dismiss him. He did not go away.

Instead, he quizzed, "Is this your breakfast?" I heard him shake the nutrition drink an aide had brought for when I awakened. To my

11

amazement, I heard Josh insert a straw into the drink box and take a swallow.

"What do you think are you doing?" I demanded, with blind eyes now open. "That's my breakfast, not yours!"

"It's a good thing," Josh said. "This stuff is blah." Then he said brightly, "I had a pancake with syrup for breakfast. It was a lot better than this. Say, do you want me to get you a pancake? If I hurry, I bet I can still get one from the dining hall."

Before I could reply, Josh called out, "I'll be right back!"

I snorted. *Is this guy for real? I'm not even sure I'm allowed to eat, yet. Everything so far has been liquid. I probably can't digest real food.*

But the prospect of hot pancakes made my tummy gurgle, and I could almost smell them.

And then I did smell them. Josh was holding a pancake under my nose. "Smells good, doesn't it?" he said. "Here. Take a little bite." I felt the fork at my lips.

Maybe just a little bite, I thought. *Just enough to get a taste.* I opened my mouth, and Josh eased in a bit of pancake. I chewed, swallowed, and opened my mouth for more.

Josh laughed. "Tastes good, doesn't it?" I smiled. When there were no more bites left, Josh said, "I'll get more, tomorrow. I'll get enough food for both of us, and we can eat together."

While I contemplated that, I heard Josh stuff the empty paper plate into the trash. It sounded like he buried it. "You're a funny kid," I said. "Did you steal that?"

"Nah!" Josh said. But then he whispered, "I just don't want to get into trouble for feeding you pancakes if they're stuck on giving you those awful drinks."

I laughed. "You'd better wait to see if I keep this down and don't get sick."

"Aw! You won't get sick," Josh said. "I won't allow it."

I laughed again. *You won't allow it? That's a good one!*

But I giggled at the thought that we were getting away with something of which the staff might not approve. And I thought, *if I'm going to die, anyway, I might as well have pancakes.*

Now, Josh stood directly over my face. Although I couldn't see him, I could feel his breath as he said, "Well, I've got to go now. But I'll be back tomorrow, with pancakes!"

Then he called out, "See ya!" and he was gone.

~ ~ ~

I wondered, *was Josh for real?*

I asked one of the aides if there were other young people in the nursing home. Did anyone know a young person named Josh?

"No. There's no Josh or anybody here under seventy, except for you," one girl said. And then she raised her voice and slipped into her *perky* routine about how special it was for me to be here and what a lovely day it was outside.

I wanted to shake her and say, *wake up! Can't you see that the world isn't all sunshine for everybody? I'm only twelve years old. And being stuck in here is not a life! I don't want to grow old and die here.*

But I doubted she would have understood. After all, she wasn't blind and paralyzed.

CHAPTER TWO

JOSH RETURNS

As I dropped off to sleep, I dreamed the kitchen staff nabbed Josh in the breakfast line with two trays of food—or even just one tray of food. Surely, somebody would stop a kid who didn't belong here.

Or maybe Josh was just a figment of my imagination, the result of grief and having no one to talk to. Maybe that's what happens when you become useless and lie around waiting to die.

~ ~ ~

"Don't pancakes smell good? Of course, bacon smells better, but pancakes are good. I think we'd better wait on the bacon, though," Josh said before I even opened my eyes.

I sighed. *It must be morning.* And I did smell pancakes and maple syrup.

"Didn't anybody see you carry two breakfasts into my room?" I spouted.

"No. I don't think so," Josh answered.

And before I could ask anything more, I felt a bite of pancake at my lips. I hadn't got sick yesterday, so I decided it was okay to live dangerously and eat the sweet, sticky breakfast. I heard Josh eating, too.

"Do they always have pancakes in the dining hall?" I asked.

"Yup! Every day," Josh said. "And other stuff, too."

I finished every bite Josh offered me. He laughed. "You're a big eater, aren't you?"

I fired back, "Got to keep up my strength, you know."

What a joke! I haven't an ounce of strength. My body is a blob of nothing.

All at once, it occurred to me to ask, "Josh? Am I all here? I mean, do I have both arms and legs and everything?" I had never thought to ask the staff.

"What? You want me to look?" he asked.

"Yeah," I said. "Look. And tell me what you see. But no peeking under the nightgown."

"As if I would!" Josh snorted.

On my face, I felt the breeze of the blanket being lifted and replaced.

"Hmm!" Josh said. "Just as I suspected. Nothing there."

"What?" I yelped.

"Just joking," Josh said. I imagined the grin that filled his freckled face. (Surely, he had red hair and freckles, I reasoned.)

"Some joke," I declared, pretending to glare at him with blind eyes. "So, what did you really see?"

"Well," drawled Josh, "I saw a body and two arms and two hands and two legs and two feet."

"So, I'm all there?" I repeated, to be sure.

"Yeah. I'd say you're all there," Josh said. "But you're not going anywhere soon. You're all bandaged up and have several casts. It looks like you've broken just about everything you could break."

I sighed. "That's pretty much what they told me at the hospital. They said I'd been in a bad accident." Then I ventured, "And I'm the only one who survived."

"I'm sorry," Josh said. And from the way he said it, I knew he meant it.

After a few moments, I asked, "Are *you* all there?"

I had wondered if Josh was like me, someone stuck here because of a handicap.

Josh laughed. "Yeah. I'm all here—my arms and legs and all."

"And you're not in a wheelchair?"

"Nope."

Now the question, *then why are you here?* was on the tip of my tongue. But suddenly Josh was in a hurry.

"Oh! I've got to go!" he blurted. And I wondered where he was off to.

Before he left, I heard him bury the breakfast plates in the bottom of the trash can. He said, "I've hidden the evidence. I'll bring you more pancakes, tomorrow. See ya!"

And he was gone.

His departure left me wondering where Josh went each day. If he wasn't a resident, did he live nearby? Did he sneak in each morning? Why didn't anyone ever see him? *Was Josh real?*

But he must be real. At least the fullness in my tummy was real, and I could still lick sticky, sweet pancake syrup from my lips. Furthermore, I was sure that if someone checked the bottom of the trash, they would find empty plates and plastic forks.

But I didn't want them to check. I didn't want them to find the evidence. I didn't want Josh to stop coming.

~ ~ ~

That afternoon, Mrs. Jamieson, the Protective Services counselor, knocked on my door.

"Good morning, Christine," the woman began, and I corrected her.

"My name's *Cricket*," I said firmly. "Nobody calls me Christine."

"Ah," said Mrs. Jamieson. "*Cricket*. I like that. May I come in?"

I didn't answer, and she came in anyway.

She asked if I was doing all right.

I laughed on the inside. *How do you suppose I'm doing? How would you be doing if your family had been killed and you were trapped in a body that couldn't feel or see?*

I answered in monosyllables. I repeated the words "I don't know" at least a dozen times.

To her credit, the woman didn't become irritated or turn pushy. After half an hour, she announced, "It's okay to keep your thoughts to yourself, for now. But I hope we can get to know each other better soon. I'll be around a couple of times each week. You may think of questions you'd like to ask me. How would that be?"

"Fine," I murmured. (If I said no, she'd probably quiz me about it, and I wanted her to leave.)

I heard her push her chair away from the bed. "I'll see you in a couple of days, Cricket," she said, and she left.

Now, an aide breezed through to see if I needed anything. Her feigned pleasantness grated on my nerves.

I told her, "No, I don't need anything," and I closed my sightless eyes, as if to block her out.

Without asking, she turned on the television before she left. *Another stupid game show.*

I clenched my jaw. Everybody seemed intent on cheering me up and making me talk. I didn't want to talk. I didn't want to be cheery. And I didn't want constant TV noise.

~ ~ ~

I must have napped, because a new voice awakened me.

"Cricket?" a man said. "It's Pastor Howard." I opened my eyes to let him know I was awake. "Everyone at Bethel Community has been asking about you and praying for you," he said.

"Thanks," I said. I know he saw tears fill my eyes.

"We're sorry you've lost your parents and your brother," he said. I sobbed, and he let me cry.

Finally, my anger overtook my sobs. I said, "Next time you pray, be sure to tell God I'm not talking to Him anymore."

18

"Oh?" Pastor Howard said. "Why not tell Him yourself?"

I snorted and answered through my teeth, "I told you, I'm not talking to Him anymore. I'm not sure I even believe in Him."

Pastor Howard said, "I take it you blame God for what has happened?"

"What do you think?" I retorted. "Who else? He could have kept it from happening—if He was real. But He didn't, did He? He's a fake."

Pastor Howard said nothing, and I continued, "Everybody always says *God is good, God is good.* No, He's not! He's cruel and heartless—IF He exists. Why else would He kill people who believed in Him and then leave me all alone and unable to see or sit up or walk or feed myself or…? It's not fair. It's not right. It's—it's awful!"

Again, silence.

Finally, Pastor Howard said, "I know you don't see it now, but God hasn't abandoned you, Cricket. He knows you're hurting, and He wants you to know He loves you."

"He has a funny way of showing it!" I nearly shouted.

Pastor Howard said, "Don't tell me. Tell Him."

"No!" I spat. "I'm not talking to Him."

I heard Pastor Howard sigh. "I'm not here to argue with you, Cricket."

He tried to change the subject. "The children's choir sang last Sunday," he said. "They sang the song I heard you practicing with them before your accident. It was…"

In harsh bitterness, I interrupted him. I imagined his surprise when he heard me say, "I don't want to hear what people are doing without me. If I can't be there, I don't want to know what I'm missing!"

I could tell that Pastor Howard hadn't thought how it might feel to hear how the world was going on without you. I doubted he would make that mistake again.

When Pastor Howard recovered from my rebuke, he said, "That makes sense. I'm sorry." Then he declared, "I do want you to know, however, that I came because all of us at Bethel Community love you. If you need anything, you can count on us to help. I've given the nursing home staff my number. In case you think of something, you can have them call me."

He asked, "Is it okay if I come back to visit you?"

I didn't want him to think I was mad at him, even if I didn't want to hear about God or what was happening at church, so I said, "Sure. You can come."

"Thanks, Cric," he said, "I'll be back." He patted my head and said goodbye.

I didn't want any more visitors. *What's the point? No one can help me. Life goes on for everyone, except me.*

CHAPTER THREE

THE STONES

I heard the television click off before Josh's announcement. "Breakfast is here!"

A paper plate scraped across my nightstand, and I took in the forkful of food that met my lips. I wasn't sure if Josh ate off my plate or his own. I could hear him chewing.

"The only food I like better than pancakes," Josh said, "is fish. I love fish, especially those I've caught myself."

After I swallowed, I nodded. "I love to fish, too." And my mind's eye took me to Shadow Lake.

I could feel the cool air on my face and hear the slap of water on the sides of the boat. I pictured Grandpa Noffer sitting opposite, our lines cast in toward the shore. Sunlight filtered through the leaves on the bank, and a turtle slid off a downed branch. Granddad and I reeled in our lures and cast again. This time, an explosion shot a water-spray high into the air, and my line nearly jerked from my hands. Granddad barked orders and reached for the net to draw my fish into the boat.

"Don't lose 'im!" Granddad called out.

I played the fish, wearying it and making sure I didn't allow slack or any chance for the fish to spit out the lure. And soon, it was safely on board. We hooted and laughed at my success, and I couldn't wait to show off my trophy when we returned to the dock. That day of fishing is my favorite memory, one I still treasure, even though it has been a long time since Granddad died.

When Josh said, "We'll have to go fishing once you get out of here," I frowned. *Not likely,* I thought. *I'll probably never leave here.*

Instead, I asked, "Where do you fish? I always fished at my grandpa's cabin in northern Minnesota."

Josh's voice grew dreamy, and he said, "I used to fish at a lake east of here. I went with friends who had big boats. But sometimes I would just sink a line from the shore and catch enough for everyone's lunch."

"Did you get big fish?" I asked.

"The biggest!" Josh said. "Bigger than any you've ever seen."

"Oh, yeah?" I challenged. "I've caught some pretty big ones!"

Then Josh said, "I fish now in the waters at the bottom of the great mountain at my home. You'd really like it. It's a perfect spot. Lots of people fish there."

"Your family owns a mountain?" I asked. I doubted it was a real mountain; probably just a big hill. Besides, there were no mountains in this area.

"Only God can own a mountain, silly," Josh corrected me. "But we live there. It's a giant mountain, and beautiful."

"Ah," I said. I wondered how much of Josh's story to believe. Was his family wealthy? But then, what would a rich kid be doing hanging around here?

"If lots of people fish there, isn't it crowded and fished out?" I persisted.

"Nope. There are always lots of fish. The trick is to catch them!"
I rolled my sightless eyes. I had heard fish tales before.

~ ~ ~

In the afternoon, the nursing home doctor, Dr. Ellerman, introduced himself.

I assumed he checked under my covers and shined a light into my eyes. (I could only assume, because, of course, I couldn't feel anything.) He murmured several *mm-huhs,* and I wanted to shout, *is that all you doctors ever say?*

After Dr. Ellerman scratched the findings on his pad, I expected a report, but he said nothing. Because I feared he would leave without telling me anything, I blurted out, "Am I getting better?"

He murmured a noncommittal, "Some better; your bones are healing."

Now, I wanted to ask my big question, but I was afraid. So, instead, I asked him when I could start eating regular food. (I figured I might as well find out if Josh was killing me with pancakes or if I could safely continue eating them each morning.)

Pages rustled as Dr. Ellerman thumbed through my chart. He stopped reading my history (I assumed), and said, "We might try you on some soft foods to see how you do. I'll put in the order. You can start with supper, tonight."

I smiled. Evidently, Josh's pancakes weren't killing me. After all, they were *soft,* weren't they? And I hadn't died, so far.

Now, I asked my big question; I didn't want Dr. Ellerman to leave before I heard his best guess. I said, "Can you tell me when I'll be able to get up?"

I sensed his hesitation. Finally, he said, "It's early, yet. But as your bones heal, the staff should be able to sit you up."

I knew he was hedging. He knew that's not what I was asking. I wanted to know when I could leave my bed and walk out of here. I wanted to know when I could feel my body and see again. I forced an answer by repeating my question.

Now he said bluntly, "Your spine has been severely damaged, young lady. You may never walk or have feeling again."

My chin quivered. He softened his statement with a skeptical, "A miracle could happen. But, except for your sight, it is more likely that it will not."

He said now, "Enjoy your soft diet, and keep your chin up. I'll be back to see you soon." With that, he escaped out of the door.

How I hated that I had made him tell me the bad news. It sounded so final. My despair deepened. *What's the point of anything? If I'm never going to leave my bed, what does anything matter? Even if I recover, I have no place to go. My family is gone, and Mr. Tipple has probably sold our house. I have nothing. I know nothing. I am nothing.*

I refused my soft-food supper. I wasn't hungry. I assumed the soup and pudding they had brought remained on my tray until someone finally took it away.

~ ~ ~

"Poached eggs? Somebody brought you poached eggs for breakfast?" Josh said the next morning. "And they aren't even warm. Ugh!"

"It doesn't matter if they're cold. I don't want them," I said flatly.

"Well, I hope you're hungry for something," Josh said. "I've brought you a waffle with strawberry syrup."

I knew Josh wouldn't take no for an answer, so I took the bite he offered. And in spite of my resolve to not eat, I ate the whole thing. It tasted too good to pass up. And I found myself smiling when I heard Josh bury the plate in the trash. *If the staff only knew!*

I told Josh about Dr. Ellerman's report. "I'm never going to walk again or leave this place," I said glumly. "I know it for sure, now."

"Stop that!" Josh said with a force that surprised me. "You will be walking and running and climbing trees better than ever before. Trust me!"

Trust you? I thought. *Who are you to dispute the doctor's findings?*

Plus, how did Josh know I used to climb trees? Maybe he just assumed that since I fished, I must be an all-around tomboy—which I had been. I had, indeed, climbed my share of trees, some at home and some in Minnesota.

"There's a really BIG tree in our yard," Josh said. "It's so tall there are clouds in the top of it. And you can see all over the world from there. You'll see."

Sure, I will, I thought sarcastically. *I can fish in your family's lake and I can climb your fabulous tree.*

Even though I thought these things, I kept them to myself. What tall tales!

"I suppose there are apples at the top of your tree," I teased.

"Not apples," Josh said, "but there are tasty fruits. You can pick some when you get there."

I allowed the image to form in my mind of Josh and me sitting on a branch so high in a tree that we could see across the state and maybe further. And we shared a tasty yellow fruit with purple seeds. And a silver bird with ruby eyes flew past and sang so sweetly a lump formed in my throat.

What a daydream!

The picture faded, and I shook my head. Maybe when you can't see or move, your mind paints these vivid thoughts to make up for the loss.

But I wondered, *why does Josh have to stretch the truth and tell such lies? They are beautiful lies, but they are lies, nevertheless.*

Instead of confronting him, I said, "You make your home sound like a wonderful place." Then, I prodded, "So, why aren't you there?"

His answer was immediate and simple. "Because I'm here with you."

"Okay," I said. I knew I might as well give up. Josh was a game player.

I frowned. *I'm weary of games. You, Josh, have some serious issues. Are you really so hard up for a friend?*

Now I sighed. Perhaps Josh was ugly or deformed. I had not imagined that. I had formed a completely different picture of him in my mind. But if he was an outcast for some reason, I could be a friend. There wasn't much else I could do in my state, but I could be a friend.

Josh must have seen my frown because he suddenly said, "I've brought something for you."

Expecting it to be more food, I said, "I'm already stuffed."

But it wasn't food. Instead, Josh touched my cheek with something smooth and round.

"It feels like a glass drop," I said. "What is it?"

I scoffed when he answered, "It's a kind of magic."

Here we go again, I thought. *More stories.*

"It's a stone," he said. "It's like polished agate, but it's black onyx. I have another just like it. That's because we need two to make the *magic* work."

Josh pushed a ribbon bearing the stone over my head, and I relished the cool glassy weight in the hollow of my throat.

I remembered my rock collection and the small onyx stone I kept next to my quartz crystal. *Onyx: a semi-precious igneous rock, formed when silicate magma from a volcanic eruption cooled. Striped with alternating white and black bands and with properties like quartz.*

I had possessed my stone for a couple of years, and it had never exhibited magical properties. *Hmmph! Magic! I don't believe in anything supernatural. Including God.*

"So," I muttered, "when do we call on the stones to make me well?"

"Oh," said Josh, "they're not that kind of magic."

"Then they're not much good, are they?" I spat.

Josh insisted, "They are good. You'll be surprised."

"Right. Surprise me," I challenged.

"Okay, I will. Tonight. You'll see."

CHAPTER FOUR

FLYING!

A fter Josh left, one of the aides announced that Miss Donaldson, from Wing school, was here.

I had never had so many visitors in my life.

"Hi, Cricket," Miss Donaldson said brightly.

I gave her a fleeting smile. *Why does everyone think they have to sound so cheerful? Don't they know I'm in mourning?*

"Hello," I murmured. I hadn't thought of Miss Donaldson or my classmates since the accident. That part of my life seemed years in the past. And school was out of the picture.

I used to like school, and I had liked Miss Donaldson. She had told my parents I was her star pupil. She liked that I possessed an incredible vocabulary for a seventh grader and read books far beyond my grade level. I supposed it was because I had my parents' genes. Both of my parents were brilliant in their fields, Mom in philosophy and Dad in mathematics. In addition, our home sat on the edge of the Golden Plains Christian College campus and had been a favorite gathering place for students. Over Cokes and popcorn, I had sat in on scores of great debates in our living room. And I knew every college building and walkway. My favorite haunt had been the library, where I had checked out books on dozens of topics, including my long-term interests in butterflies and rock collecting. Miss Donaldson had encouraged my rock collecting, and I wished I could show her my latest acquisition, a polished Petoskey Stone from Lake Michigan, named for Chief Rising Sun (*Pe-to-se-ga*). The surface of the fossilized coral looked like dozens of little rayed suns. Miss Donaldson would have liked it. But the stone sat locked up in my room—*if Mr. Tipple hasn't sold the house*. It was unlikely I would ever see my Petoskey again.

I wondered if Miss Donaldson had brought homework for me. Probably not. She had to know I couldn't see. *I might never read or write for the rest of my life.*

"I miss having you in class," Miss Donaldson said. *And I miss being there,* I wanted to say, but I was afraid I would cry.

When I didn't answer, Miss Donaldson said, "We finished studying the solar system. Do you remember the names of the planets?"

Of course, I knew them. Memorization had always been easy for me. Miss Donaldson was waiting, and I finally recited, "Mercury, Venus, Earth, Mars, Jupiter, Saturn, Uranus, Neptune, and Pluto, in order of distance from the sun."

"Very good, Cricket! I knew you would remember."

I warmed in her praise. Miss Donaldson was a good teacher— better than my sixth-grade teacher, who had treated her class like infants. Miss Donaldson had challenged us. She had expected more from us than good behavior. Miss Donaldson had set up learning centers around the room on different subjects. Under her supervision, I had grown rock sugar crystals on a string in a glass of sugar water; copper-plated several coins; exploded a volcano of vinegar, water, dish soap, and baking soda; and built a small electric generator from scratch. Her classroom had featured an aquarium of garter snakes that we took turns feeding, and my classmates and I had collected caterpillars and butterfly chrysalises and watched them hatch. Each hatching had been the closest thing to *magic* I had known.

Miss Donaldson now said, "I had hoped to have you back for our last experiments in making *diamonds* from charcoal." And I imagine that my sudden outburst of weeping alarmed her.

"I'll never be back," I cried. "I can't see, and I can't move. My life is impossible!"

"Nothing is impossible," Miss Donaldson said firmly. In her classroom voice, she added, "You haven't lost your good mind, and you can hear and you can speak. That's more than some people have ever been able to do. Never give up, Cricket. Never!"

I pushed back my depression, if only for a moment. I wanted to believe her. I wanted to learn and explore the world again. I wanted to be alive! But, how could I?

Even with my doubts, I answered her with, "Yes, Miss Donaldson."

I felt her kiss on my forehead before she left.

And then I cried. I wallowed in my unhappiness for the rest of the afternoon and into the evening. Now I not only missed my family, I also missed school.

~ ~ ~

As supper came and went, I wondered if Josh would, as promised, show up. Josh had never come at night.

The television droned maddeningly until bedtime. When the night aide finally turned it off and tucked me in, she called out, too loudly, "Good night, Christine! Sleep tight!" And then, the entire nursing home settled into quiet.

I hated the quiet even more than the interminable noise of the television. The silence was supposed to signal sleep for the residents, but for me, it did not. Instead, in the dark of my blindness, combined with the deprivation of daytime sounds, I heard my pulse, my breathing, and my blind eye blinks. The sounds of my body's functions were what my life had become.

And then, I heard Josh whisper, "I said I'd be back. Are you still awake?"

"Yes," I answered quickly. "I'm awake."

"Are you ready?"

Before I could reply, I felt Josh's breath on my face, and I heard the sound of the onyx stones clicking against one another.

Instantly, I was flying!

~ ~ ~

I rose, weightless, from my bed, and I gasped to see that Josh had been wrong: the stones *had* made me well. I could both *feel* and *see!*

My arms spread from my sides like wings, and my nightgown floated gloriously about me. And instead of flattening against the ceiling as I feared, we passed right through the roof and into the clouds of the night. My skin relished the coolness of the breeze, and I gulped in my first breath of fresh air in weeks. Up and up we flew, and everything below us grew small.

I looked back but could no longer see the nursing home or the town. My house and school were lost in the mist of the stratosphere. I could see Josh, however, and I was satisfied that he looked exactly as I had pictured him. He was close to my age—maybe thirteen instead of twelve. Red hair flew about his face, and his eyes glittered with excitement. His shirt had come untucked from his jeans and flapped at his waist. And his grass-stained tennis shoes pumped the air, as if that would make him fly faster. I laughed, until I discovered I was doing the same thing.

"Isn't it grand?" Josh cried.

And I asked, "Where are we going?"

"I can't say," Josh yelled back, which left me unsure if he knew or if he didn't.

In any event, Earth shrank to a pinpoint, and we sped through stars set in a deep expanse of jet blue. On and on we flew toward a partially lighted sphere that expanded in size with every second. We hurtled at a frightening speed through lavender-tinged clouds toward the planet's surface. The ground threatened. I drew in a breath.

But just as I had calculated our demise in a momentary splat like a bug on a windshield, we curiously stalled and hung suspended in slow motion. My dizzy mind struggled to catch up with the change. And before I knew it, we were deposited as gently as butterflies onto the sidewalk of an empty city street.

What a strange place—a ghost town or the set for some movie after the cast and crew had left for the day. Where were the planet's people?

Josh and I looked up, and our shadows fell long. It had been night on Earth when we had left, but now, on this planet, a setting sun glistened off the tops of the sleek, earthlike skyscrapers that rose above us.

Where are the people? I wondered again. *What are they like? Why have they gone? Will they return?*

My answer came with a sudden shrill blast that shattered the peace and threatened to break our eardrums. The whistle reverberated off the concrete canyon's floor and walls. We shrank against the building just in time to avoid a stampede of overly dressed people who spewed from every doorway. Elbowing and cursing, the charging herd trampled one another in a mad dash to fill a line of empty train cars on a siding a couple of blocks away. Josh and I cowered against the blows and abuse of those who slammed into us in their headlong rush.

Their curses intensified when, with a loud clang, the full train pulled out and left multitudes still milling near the boarding platform. As the filled cars retreated, the runners stumbled at a slower pace, but that didn't stop them from rudely pressing one another to gain a better advantage for boarding the next train.

As they growled and shoved, they noticed Josh and me. Wary eyes narrowed in their assessment of us. "Children in the business district!" someone sneered.

Not only were Josh and I mere kids in a sea of adults, but I, in my nightgown and bed socks, and Josh, in his T-shirt and blue jeans, looked nothing like these people. All around us, layers of gaudy fabrics and heavy jewelry screamed for attention. And cosmetic masks hid faces under garish colors and false smiles.

"Who are you, my pretty?" a lewdly painted woman leered. Her jeweled, clawed finger poked me, and I backed away.

Then a wildly wigged woman grabbed my onyx stone and yanked its ribbon, throwing me off my feet. The woman declared, "I'll take that trinket. It's lovely and you're too young to…," but before she could finish her sentence, she released the stone and pulled her hand away with a scream.

"You've burned my hand, you awful little girl!" she shrieked. "You cruel child! You knew that stone would burn me and you didn't stop me. You can't get by with this!" Then, as an afterthought, she demanded, "And where is your mark? Look everyone, she has no mark!"

A cry went up, "No mark! She has no mark! Officers! Apprehend this girl!"

Arms stretched out to grab me, but Josh grabbed me first and pulled me between the legs of my accusers.

"Run!" he cried, and we left the braying pack churning in place as we fled. No one gave chase because the selfish mass refused to give up their places in line. They simply pointed in our direction when the police arrived.

I was sure we would be apprehended, but the clanging approach of another train impeded the police. The officers were caught in the surge of those pressing toward the newly arrived, empty rail cars.

Josh roughly shoved me out of the pandemonium and into an alley. Here there were no people, and we ran a great distance to crouch behind a dumpster. Within seconds, the beam of a flashlight scanned the alley entrance and voices approached. My heart leaped to my throat. We were going to be caught!

But the squawk of a cell phone on the hip of one of the officers brought the pursuers to a halt.

"Come on!" the policeman shouted. "This way!"

At once, the direction of the chase changed. In less than a minute, our alley was abandoned. I let out a whimper of relief and buried my head in my hands.

"Don't move," Josh cautioned, and I stiffened. We heard the police check the alley entrance again, on their way back to the train platform.

Josh kept a warning finger at his lips, and we barely breathed for several more minutes. My knees ached from crouching, and I was grateful when Josh cautiously rose and pulled me to my feet.

"Now what do we do?" I whispered, still afraid to make noise. But as I turned, a soda can slipped from the pile of garbage in the dumpster and hit the ground with a clatter. Startled, I swallowed and jumped to the back of the bin. There, I hit something in the shadows.

"Quiet! You'll get us caught!" a strange voice hissed.

I held my breath. It wasn't Josh. Who else was behind the dumpster?

Josh heard the hoarse command, too, and he leaned into me protectively, but none of us made a sound.

After what seemed an hour of silence, we stood, and the stranger asked, "What are you two doing here?"

"Hi-hiding," I stammered. "We're hiding because a woman tried to steal from us."

The stranger, dressed in nondescript grays, stared skeptically. "People on the street don't bother to steal from the likes of us," he said. "We have nothing worth taking. Or have you?"

"We don't have anything," Josh hurried to say. "The woman

mistook a rock for a valuable stone. In any event, she claims we harmed her and she called the police on us."

The man asked, "So, did you harm her?"

"No," said Josh. "She made it up."

"Sounds likely. Nobody believes us!" the stranger spat in disgust.

Still doubtful of us, the man asked, "Why are you out in the daylight, and why are your clothes so clean and without holes? Did you steal them?"

Josh replied quietly, "No, they're our clothes. But we're new here. We've just arrived in town and don't know much about the area. We've been lucky, so far. But we don't know this place, and we aren't sure how to avoid trouble."

I wondered if the stranger would respond with help or harm.

"Do you have any food?" the man asked.

"No," Josh answered.

At the mention of food, my tummy rumbled. I dismissed it. How could I be hungry?

"Do you promise not to call more attention to yourselves?" the man insisted now.

We nodded. "We'll try."

"Then take this and come with me."

We hugged to our chests the thrust garbage the man had pulled from the bin. He loaded a large bag with more trash and tugged Josh and me to the wall behind the dumpster. There, a rectangular iron grate sat on end beside a matching foundation hole. The man pushed, and I toppled into the hole with a yelp.

"Shush!" the man commanded, and then Josh collided with me.

Now, the stranger crowded into the hole, too. He reset the grate and gave us a shove. As one, we tumbled toward the bowels of the earth, along a dark metal chute. After sliding, sometimes upside down, for what seemed a black eternity, the chute abruptly dumped us in a mixed-up pile of arms, legs, and garbage.

"Don't lose the stuff I gave you!" the man's voice commanded. "And stay close."

In the shadowy darkness, we gathered our trash and followed the stranger's footfalls away from the metal shaft. I lost track of right and left turns and marveled that the man could navigate without light. Josh and I would never find our way out of here without him. In the back of my mind, a new fear formed. *Is our guide a murderer, or worse?*

I feared we might die down here, and no one would ever know.

CHAPTER FIVE

THE UNDERGROUND

After many dark minutes, I heard a murmur of voices and saw a dimly lit doorway. We were led inside a gray room of makeshift tables and shadowy figures, figures now grown silent. Dozens of eyes blinked in the dim glow of flickering lamps—tin cans lit with tiny wicks.

"It's all right," our guide assured everyone. "They've brought supplies."

Supplies? I thought. *Josh and I have nothing but the garbage held tightly in our arms. Surely, no one would be excited about this stuff.*

But the man off-loaded our burdens and laid out our trash on one of the tables. When he said, "Let's see what they've brought," the shadows drew nearer.

Most of the items on the table were indecipherable but seemed to be food. I made out part of a cast-off sandwich, a banana with one bite left, a few drops of liquid swishing in a paper cup, and the remains of a Chinese dinner. Another cup held a red drink. Two peanut-like items shook in the bottom of a white, stenciled sack. And I became fixated on a couple of still-wrapped after-dinner mints.

"Let us give thanks," our stranger intoned, and everyone bowed their heads.

"Thank you, God, for Your provision, and that You have loved us with Your everlasting love," the praying man said without a hint of sarcasm in his voice. His words ended with a corporate, "Amen."

They prayed! I marveled. *They prayed to thank God for* garbage!

In my current dislike of God, I thought, *sounds about right. These people will learn the truth about God soon enough. From the looks of them, I'm surprised they haven't already.*

Now, our guide said to Josh and me, "Since you brought these things, you take your pick first, and the children will choose next."

I balked. Technically, the items on the table weren't ours, and I didn't want to take anything from these pitiful people. But Josh nudged me forward. He whispered, "We have to take something or they will suspect us."

I finally took one of the dinner mints and the bite of banana. Josh took the two peanuts and one of the cups of liquid. Then we backed away.

Our guide seemed to approve, and then he called the children forward.

In the dim light, I saw small hands pick out items, one per person. I marveled at the order and politeness among the little ones.

Then, the teens and adults came. Like the children, each took one item. Some had to do without, but no one complained.

After the picking, families retreated into groups against the walls, and everyone talked quietly among themselves. I felt their glances and guessed that much of their whispered conversation was about Josh and me. *What must they think?*

I managed to overhear one mother shushing a small child with the words, "They're okay. They don't have marks."

It was the second time I had heard someone say that Josh and I had no *marks*. I wondered what that meant. What were the *marks?* And why did they matter?

"Foley. My name's Foley," our guide said with an extended hand. "And you can sleep here."

He pointed to a small space along the wall near his family. Josh and I settled there on the floor. A disfigured teen, who looked nothing like Foley or his wife, ignored us (perhaps he was shy?), but a little boy Foley's wife tended made no bones about staring at us.

Josh sank to the floor and pulled a sheet of newspaper over himself. I realized I was exhausted, too. I pulled a piece of the paper under my chin and dropped off to sleep.

~ ~ ~

In the middle of a vague dream, Josh roused me. Foley and several others waited at the door.

"We need to go with them," Josh said. "They've invited us."

I blinked off my sleep and accepted a large empty bag to carry. Like the others, I stuffed it under my arm. Josh and I took our places at the back of the entourage.

I knew it must be night, and I knew we were going scavenging. This camp needed more food than the little bit we had brought from the dumpster. Were there more dumpsters to raid? Surely there were in a city this size.

Thankfully, our path led to stairs (instead of the chute) and took us to a different alley. The earlier turmoil on the sidewalks was gone. Only a few people, laughing like partygoers, strolled under the street lamps, and we hid from them.

"Stay close," Foley whispered, and our group made its way forward in the shadows.

Without a word, we crossed streets, a few at a time in widely spaced intervals, and as we progressed, some of our members peeled off to disappear down alleys. Once, we walked a good part of a block with only the building shadows for cover. Rising above us, the skyscrapers presided, like blind and unblinking giants staring their black, empty windows at each other. An old church looked the saddest. Apparently long abandoned, only one window remained unbroken—it was the stained-glass rose window located high above the front door. A brass plaque on the building front read: St. Andrew's Church.

When it was our turn to peel off from the group, we followed Foley to the back of a restaurant. I smelled Italian food, or did I? Did this planet have Italian food? I could almost taste lasagna or tortellini.

"Watch out for rats," Foley warned. "And keep quiet."

We worked silently to remove as much edible garbage as we could carry. It was impossible in the dark to know exactly what we were gleaning; sometimes our noses informed us and sometimes not. We would discover what we had when we spilled our bags onto the tables back at the shelter. I wished we could take all the food from the bin, but even after we three had filled our bags, we had barely made a dent in the dumpster contents.

"Ready?" Foley finally whispered. "Let's go."

My bag had become heavier than I had expected, and the closure bands cut into my hands and arms as I hoisted the load over my back. Because of the weight, I lagged several paces behind, but I pushed forward. In my mind's eye, I saw the faces of the hungry children our bags would feed. I wanted them to eat well and not be restricted to one small item from our stash. I wanted to earn our keep.

As I labored under my bundle, I thought about the people of the shelter. *Who are they? Why are they living underground? Why are they scrounging for food? Why are they afraid of the police? They don't seem to be criminals. They're kind to us. They believe in God. And their company is definitely more desirable than the soulless throng who pushed and shoved their way to the trains this afternoon.*

And I wondered, again, about the *marks. What do the* marks *mean? What do they look like? Who has them, and who doesn't? And why?*

Suddenly, in mid-thought, I was yanked backward. I tried to scream, but a hand covered my mouth. I watched in dismay as Josh and our guide moved on without me. A greasy rag replaced the hand over my mouth, and I gagged, but I could not spit it out. Nor could I keep my hands and feet from being roughly bound. I was pushed to the ground and shoved against a building, so that I lay in its deepest shadow on the sidewalk. I could only watch as my bag disappeared with the men who had assaulted me.

Now, alone in the dark, I couldn't move or cry out. It would have been bad enough if this had happened back home, but it was worse here because this wasn't my world and these weren't my people. I feared this planet's police as much as I had feared robbers and thieves on Earth. No one but Josh knew me, here, and Josh was now far away.

My heartbeats pounded in my ears. Tears of fear coursed down my cheeks. *Josh! Please turn around and come looking for me!*

The rough bindings cramped my muscles, and they cut into my wrists and ankles as I fought to free myself. I did manage to spit out the rag, but I was too afraid to call out. Who might come in answer to my cries? I couldn't take the chance. What was I going to do?

God! Please don't let me die here, I prayed, before I realized what I was doing. I was praying to the God I had sworn I would never speak to again. Now I back-pedaled. I wondered if God would even hear me in this place. But as my fear grew, I let myself pray. I knew no one else could hear me. Maybe God could. I begged, *God! Nobody but You knows where I am. Please help Josh find me.*

My tears spilled onto the pavement, and I tried to loosen my bindings. But my wriggling and struggling only resulted in more scrapes and bruises.

How long will I lie here? Will I be here all night? Will I be arrested in the morning and put in jail by awful people like that woman who had tried to steal my stone?

My imagination painted terrifying possibilities. And then, reality trumped them all: a rat emerged from the sewer.

Drawn by the garbage smells on my clothes and skin, the rat twitched its nose as it drew near. Would this vile creature gnaw on me? I was powerless to swat it away.

I protested. *No, God! Not rats. Please help me, God!*

To make matters worse, the rat was not alone. Another rat nosed its way out of the sewer, and then another. Were there more?

As the creatures closed in, I imagined teeth nibbling on my fingers and nose. I knew I would scream at any moment. A single, choked cry escaped, and I drew in a breath.

It was then that something burst from the shadows. A flash of fur raced to attack one of the rats. I saw the vile sewer dweller shaken savagely and flung into the air to land inches from my face. The rat's dead eyes stared, and its greasy fur lay matted in blood. The rat's lifeless tongue hung out between razor-sharp, yellow teeth. I recoiled from its face, as my rescuer continued to work. A snarl and a pounce sent the second and third rats flying. Thankfully, their twisted bodies landed near the curb. I prayed there were no more. The rat attacker sniffed the storm drain. Then he nosed each rat body to make sure it was dead.

A dog. My rescuer was a dog—a street dog, and a hungry one. His ribs said he could not have eaten much in days. I felt sorry for him. But then I wondered, *will* he *attack me now?*

I cringed and sucked in a breath when the animal sniffed my ear. But then a warm tongue licked the tears from my cheeks. A terrier face peered into mine, and the dog cocked his head as if to question why I wasn't petting him. I decided the creature wasn't going to eat me, and I ventured to whisper, "Thank you, boy. Good dog, good dog."

The eager-to-please canine wagged his tail and licked my face again, and I laughed. *God had sent a dog!* It hadn't been what I had expected. But then, God and I weren't exactly on good terms.

With the terrier sitting between me and the dead rats, I ventured to pray again. *Thank you for the dog, God. But please send Josh now. Please send Josh.*

I lay still, since my struggling did no good. My hands and feet had grown too numb to work the bindings. Only the terrier's warmth comforted me. The skinny little dog curled himself tightly into my side, and he did not leave. Every minute we lay there felt like an hour, and I cried and prayed, and prayed and cried.

And I'm not sure when I fell asleep, but I must have. In my dream, Josh was whispering in my ear, "Time to get up, lazy bones. I have pancakes."

I laughed at the dream. *Pancakes! What I wouldn't give to be back in the nursing home with Josh feeding me pancakes. I could even smell them.*

"Okay, then don't wake up," Josh said. "I'll eat them myself."

In the groggy, slow motion of sleep, I protested, "No! Those are my pancakes!"

And then I felt the forkful of pancakes at my lips. I opened my mouth.

At once, I knew I wasn't dreaming. I was, indeed, back at the nursing home, and I was again blind, paralyzed, and hungry.

CHAPTER SIX

HERO

"The pancakes taste good, don't they?" Josh said as I chewed. Then he declared, "I already ate mine. That trip of ours worked up an appetite."

"That trip of ours almost killed me!" I protested. "I thought I was going to die there. If it hadn't been for a little dog, I might be dead."

"Uh-huh," Josh replied. "This dog?" A lick on my cheek and a nibble on my ear told me the terrier was on my bed.

"How?" I exclaimed. "How did...?" Another forkful of pancake interrupted my question.

Josh said, "The little dog had snuggled so close to you that when I clicked the stones to bring you back, he showed up, too. He was as surprised as you are. But he's recovered well."

Between bites of pancake, Josh told me how he and Foley had realized I was missing and had backtracked to find me. "Foley said robbers sometimes steal from his people, and he was sorry they had targeted you. At least you're still alive."

I frowned at the memory of being yanked to the ground and my bag stolen. And I shuddered to recall the threat of the rats. "But how did I get back here?" I asked.

"No problem," Josh said. "When we found you, we untied you, and I clicked our stones together to bring us back."

I felt my stone, now, in the hollow of my throat. It lay cool and heavy, the only thing I could feel below my face. I asked with a half-chuckle, "What do you suppose Foley thought when we disappeared?"

"It probably scared him. I can't imagine what he's told the people in the shelter." Then Josh confessed, "I'm sorry I had to frighten him. I wouldn't have brought us back this way if things had been different."

"I'm glad you did," I said. "I've never been so scared." Then I said, "I even prayed."

"Praying is good," Josh said. "Praying is always good."

I had to admit that, for once, the results of my prayers had been good. But I was still unwilling to give God all the credit. He might have helped, but sooner or later Josh would have figured out I was gone and come looking for me. Even the dog could be explained away. He had probably prowled those streets on a regular basis and was a natural ratter.

God was still on trial, in my estimation. I still didn't have a family or a body that worked—except in dream adventures. Who would call that good?

I felt paws on my pillow and a nose on my face, and I recalled how the dog had saved me from the rats. I remembered, too, how thin he had been, and I asked Josh if he had given the animal anything to eat.

"He likes pancakes!" Josh answered with a laugh. Then he added, "And I'll get him some dog food after I leave this morning."

"Good," I said. "He deserves it. He killed three rats, you know. He kept them from eating me."

"I know," Josh said. "Foley and I saw them. Nasty things! Foley said sometimes the rats attack when his people are raiding the dumpsters. Their bites are awful and take a long time to heal."

I shuddered.

"And I should tell you," Josh said, "that you created quite a stir around here, first thing this morning."

"A stir? At the nursing home?" I asked. "What do you mean?"

Josh drew close and said quietly in my ear, "When the aide checked on you, she saw the scrapes and bruises on your arms and legs and your torn nightgown and dirty bed socks. She raced to get the supervisor, and they've been wondering all morning how this could be, since you never left your bed or this room; the hall nurse saw no one come or go throughout the night. They're still talking about it. You, Cricket, are the mystery girl of the nursing home!"

"Really?" I laughed. But then I paused. *Was Josh saying that our adventure hadn't been a dream?* I still hadn't sorted out what was real and what was not. I had held a healthy skepticism that I had dreamed Josh and had dreamed up the adventure. But now I shivered. *If it was true that the nursing home staff had seen my messed-up clothes, it might mean I could truly have died in that other world!*

"Josh," I asked suddenly, "are you real? And did we truly journey to another planet? Or is this all a trick of my mind?"

Josh dodged my question. In that maddening way of his, he announced it was time for him to go.

"See you in the morning, Cricket," he said.

I felt the terrier lick my face before Josh snatched him up. And then Josh and the little dog were gone.

~ ~ ~

That night, I dreamed. I know it was not another adventure with the onyx stones, because in the dream I was still paralyzed. And although I tried to visit the world of our strange journey again, I couldn't make it materialize. I could only dream things I had experienced with my family in this life. I heard my parents' voices and saw my mother working late at her desk preparing a test to give in the morning. I heard my dad tuck Scooter into bed. The memories made me cry. I wanted to wake up.

As I shook off my dream, I heard voices whispering over me and an aide saying, "Except for the tears, she seems all right. Nothing out of place this morning."

"Good!" another voice said. "I'd hate to have to report another incident to Mrs. Grouch."

"Be careful," the first voice warned. "One of these days you'll forget and call her that. Old lady Crouch won't like that!"

The second aide chuckled. "You've got that right!" And the two of them giggled.

I kept my eyes closed while the two women finished their tasks in my room and left. Seconds later, I heard Josh.

"I thought they would never leave," he declared.

"Yeah," I said. "I pretended I was still asleep. I heard them talking about how relieved they were that I wasn't *messed up* this morning."

Josh laughed. "They'll never figure out that mystery."

I thought to myself, *neither will I.*

A lick on my cheek told me the terrier was back. I wished I could pet him and pull him into my arms. "My little hero," I sighed.

"Say!" Josh said. "That would be a good name for him. *Hero.* It's a good dog name."

"Hey, Hero! Come here," Josh called. And the little dog abandoned me.

"He likes it!" Josh said. "He likes his name. Why don't you call him and let him stay with you while I go get our breakfast?"

Before I could object (after all, how could I keep Hero from leaving?), Josh was gone.

I needn't have worried. Hero snuggled next to my ear, and his fur tickled my neck until Josh reappeared.

~ ~ ~

Over the next couple of days, I found myself thinking about Earth's solar system and how our planet was different from and yet similar to Foley's planet. And I wondered where Foley's planet sat in the universe. Even though I had flown there, I couldn't identify our direction or the constellations we had passed. *How different it was to fly* through *the stars than to observe them from the Earth.*

And I thought of Foley and the shelter families. *Will I see those people again? What is going to happen to them? How long will they hide underground? And from what, exactly, are they hiding?*

I wondered most about the children. *How often do they go hungry? Have they ever seen their sun? Do they ever leave the labyrinth? Will they die in their underground prison?*

I contrasted how, even in my helpless state on Earth, I had never had to worry about running out of food or being neglected. I lived in a bubble of plenty while Foley's children lived in constant want. I yearned to help them.

~ ~ ~

Mrs. Jamieson showed up again, and I resented her prying into my thoughts. As before, I gave only the briefest, least revealing answers to her questions. She never took notes (I never heard pen and paper), but

I was sure she wrote down everything once she left. To my relief, she stayed only a half hour. I couldn't have stood another minute of her poking at the wounds of my heart. I saved my tears for when she left.

That's how Pastor Howard found me, angry and crying. "Bad time?" he asked.

I thought, *at least he asks. Everyone else just comes in, plops down, and expects me to be ready to talk.*

"No. It's all right," I said. I had cried enough to take the edge off my grief. I would finish my tears later.

"I've brought a card from your Sunday school class," Pastor Howard said.

"I can't see it," I muttered. But he said he'd read it to me.

We miss you, Cricket. And we're sorry you got hurt. Our class prays for you to get better, soon. Jillie drew the flowers. Even though you can't see them, they're pretty. Sending our love, prayers, and best wishes. Love, Mrs. Anderson and the seventh-grade Sunday school class.

"They've all signed their names," Pastor Howard said. "It's a nice card."

"Yeah," I said.

Pastor sat for a moment without speaking. Then he said, "Lorna Hopkins offered to come and read the Sunday school lesson to you."

I pictured Lorna. She was the quiet one. It would cost her a great deal to overcome her shyness and come to read to me. But I didn't answer Pastor Howard. I didn't want to tell him I wasn't interested in hearing God stuff at the moment. I was sure he wouldn't like that, being a pastor and all. It was enough that God knew it.

"Maybe later," I finally murmured. It was the only way I could say no without giving away my continuing bitterness against God.

"Sure," said Pastor Howard. "I'll tell Lorna, *not yet.*" Then he asked, "Anything you want me to share with the rest of the class? Or anything I can help you with?"

I didn't want to talk about church anymore. I said, "Tell the class thank you for the card. And, no, there's nothing else I need." Then I said, "Thanks for coming. Say hi to the people who know me."

Pastor Howard didn't miss the hint that I was done talking. He said a few more things about people I knew and how they were praying for me, and then he asked, "May I pray with you before I leave?"

I couldn't very well say no, so I closed my eyes when he laid his hand on my forehead and prayed, "Lord Jesus, thank you for Cricket. Continue to strengthen and heal her body. Encourage her heart, and comfort her in her tears. Guard and keep her from any other harm. Amen."

CHAPTER SEVEN

EMPTY HOUSE

Over the next few days, get-well cards, including dozens from Golden Plains Christian College, arrived with the mail. Each card was read by an effusive nursing-home aide. Many were from people I barely knew.

Flowers came, too, although I wondered why people bothered. One particular bouquet, a large one from Mr. Tipple and Mr. Gilson, drew *oohs* and *aahs* from the staff. But I pursed my lips and thought, *so that's how my guardians are spending my money. Don't they get that I can't see?*

The only good news I received was when Dr. Ellerman ordered one of my casts removed. I don't know why that elated me, since I still had no feeling. But I guessed it was a sign I was experiencing even a small degree of healing. Dr. Ellerman also ordered the staff to begin inching up the head of my bed—another sign of progress. Slight, but progress. I would take whatever I could get.

~ ~ ~

Josh commented on the removal of the casts. "Finally, half a ton of plaster gone." He chortled.

I sniffed. "I should be up and running in no time, right?"

"Not," Josh said.

He was the only person who could have gotten away with that negative remark.

Over pancakes, Josh and I talked about hiking and walks in the woods. I had loved the out-of-doors. I enjoyed telling of my discoveries of various birds' eggs and plants, like jack-in-the-pulpits. I told him how I had uncovered salamanders and newts under rocks by the stream at the college campus. I wished I could explore again.

It dawned on me that perhaps the onyx stones could take us to the woods. "Could the stones take us on a hike?" I asked.

Josh's answer left me wondering, as always. He said, "Maybe, at some point."

I gathered that we weren't going on a hike any time soon. So, I asked if we were ever going back to Foley's planet.

"We'll see Foley again," he answered, and I grew excited.

"When?"

"Soon."

I wanted to go today, but I could tell it wasn't going to happen. So, I changed the subject.

"Where in the universe is Foley's planet? On our last trip I tried to get a fix, but the constellations seem so different when you're flying through them."

"I couldn't tell you," Josh said, which frustrated me. His answer could be taken two ways: one, he didn't want to tell me; and two, he might not know.

I finally said, "I'm getting antsy, Josh. When we go to the planet, again, I have an idea. It may be impossible, but…"

"Go on," he said.

"Well," I ventured, "I've been thinking about how Hero was able to stow away with us. And I've been wondering if we could use the same principle to help Foley and his people. It's a crazy idea, but it might work."

It probably won't work, I thought. *Josh is going to say it's impossible.* But I forged ahead.

"I've been wondering if we could take food and supplies to Foley, to supplement what his people get from the dumpsters and to provide better nourishment for the children."

Josh didn't interrupt me, and I couldn't tell from his silence what he thought of my idea.

At last, he said, "Theoretically, it might be possible. It's a tall order, though. There are about three dozen people to feed. That's a lot of food."

I nodded. It was an impossible dream. *Silly of me. Of course, Josh was right. Transporting Hero is one thing, but hauling several boxes of food is another.*

But just as I decided Josh had rejected the suggestion, he said, "You know, if we're going to make such a trip, we need to take more precautions."

In excitement, I hurried to ask, "What kind of precautions?"

Josh chuckled. "The kind that keep you from adding to the mystery of the nursing home! You need a change of clothes."

"Okay," I said. But then I asked, "And how do you propose I do that? I can't very well tell the nursing home staff to fit me out in blue jeans and T-shirts for no reason."

"And tennis shoes," Josh added.

"Where would I get clothes?" I asked.

"I could raid your closet," Josh suggested. "But I don't know what clothes you like."

In dismay, I pictured Josh going to my house and rummaging through my things. I imagined the awful outfits he might come up with. So, I hurried to say, "Why not let the stones take both of us to my house and I could pick them out?"

Then I murmured to myself, *if my house is still there.* I feared that Mr. Tipple and Mr. Gilson had cleaned everything out and sold the place. After all, it would be a long time before I turned twenty-one, and they held all the purse strings.

When Josh said, "Sounds good," I wanted to jump out of bed and hug him. *(No chance of that, of course.)* A visit would allow me to get clothes *and* check out my house.

"When can we go?" I asked, and Josh suggested we try later in the day.

I could hardly wait.

~ ~ ~

That afternoon, during nursing home naptime, the stones deposited us inside the front door of my house. It was a wise transport. If we had landed outside and had to let ourselves in with the spare key, someone would likely have noticed.

I stood motionless in the living room. It was my house, but I felt like an intruder. Except for our breathing and slight movements, there was no sound. The rooms seemed asleep.

I wanted them to wake up.

I wanted to shout, "I'm home from school, Mom!"

I wanted to walk past my dad's study and see him at work on an assignment.

I wanted to yell at my brother for leaving his bicycle in the middle of the driveway.

I wanted...

Josh broke the spell. "Is your room upstairs?"

"Yes," I said, pulling myself together. "First room on the left."

Josh led the way, and I followed.

The evening sun poured through a stairway window and lit up the hallway. I could see out over the campus when we reached the first-floor landing. Students moved along the walkways, probably heading to or from the library.

My steps slowed as we climbed. I made myself look left, and not down the hallway to the right. *Keep your eyes on the floor,* I told myself. *The floor is safe.*

And then I saw one of Dodger's stuffed toys. My breath caught. I had almost forgotten that Scooter's dog, Dodger, had died in the crash, too.

Josh saw what had frozen my attention. He picked up the toy and suggested, "Why don't we take this for Hero? I think Dodger would have liked that."

I swallowed in an attempt to keep tears from getting the best of me, and I nodded. "Good idea."

Josh put the dog toy into his pocket, and we continued down the hall.

When we arrived at the bedroom, I let out the breath I had been holding. The only ghost in this room was mine. My bedroom was a safe spot.

And, here, for the first time since the accident, I felt like me.

Everything was as I had left it. My bed was made, my desk was clean, and my books lined the shelves along the wall. My hairbrush and comb sat on the dresser.

When I looked up, I saw myself in the dresser mirror. I'm not sure what I expected, but I was relieved to see that, except for the strange nightgown, I looked much as I had looked before the accident. And the necklace, with its onyx stone and loop of ribbon, appeared inconspicuous. To a casual observer, it might be dismissed as a simple trinket.

I walked to my desk. A large silk cocoon, folded inside a dry maple leaf, sat where I had put it before my world had changed. Sadly, in my absence, the moth had hatched.

I was disappointed. I had planned to identify the moth by its cocoon in my caterpillar field book. But now, it had already emerged and probably lay dead somewhere in the house. I didn't want to hunt for it. Anything outside this room was more than I could handle emotionally.

And besides, we weren't here to catch moths. We were here to pick up clothing.

I focused on a search for my second-best pair of tennis shoes. (I refused to think where my *first-best* pair had ended up.)

Josh put the shoes and a jacket I had pulled from the closet into his satchel. Then I selected a pair of blue jeans and a light-blue T-shirt from the dresser drawers. That should be enough. I had no place to keep extras.

I moved across the room. At my desk, I hovered over my rock collection. Although I knew I couldn't pocket the stones to take with me (how would I explain their sudden appearance at The Arches?), I could do a quick examination.

With my back to Josh, I compared the collection's onyx to the stone hanging around my neck. *Are the two samples alike? Is Josh's magical onyx different?* I couldn't tell. And I couldn't very well click the stones together to see what might happen. Reluctantly, I set my collection sample back in its tray and turned around.

Josh said, "It's time. We need to get back." He led the way to the door.

I would have preferred to click our stones and leave from here, but Josh was already halfway to the stairs. I had no choice but to follow.

In the hall, I had to face what I had dreaded. Two bedrooms lay before me: my parents' and Scooter's. Unless I closed my eyes and took a chance on falling down the stairs, I could not avoid seeing them. It was impossible to pretend they weren't there. I took a deep breath and kept walking.

Then, when I was nearly to the stairs, a movement caught my eye. Something fluttered out of my parents' bedroom door. In my surprise, I forgot my resolve to keep my distance, and I rushed forward. It was my moth! And it was magnificent.

The creature's wings batted against the curtain at the end of the hall, and the barrier of the window gave me a chance to capture and examine the beautiful six-inch male Polyphemus moth. I had never seen one outside of books.

Its unique tan scales, markings, and feathery antennae were perfect. Transparent spots on the forewings opposed the huge eyespots on the hind wings. I don't know why, since the moth's wings have *two* eyes, it had been named for the one-eyed giant of Greek mythology. But that matters little now.

What thrilled me more was that I got to see him. I cupped him in my hands to let Josh admire him, too.

"Isn't he beautiful?" I exclaimed.

And Josh murmured, "Perfect!"

"I need to let him go," I said, and I started down the stairs.

At the bottom, Josh led the way to the front door and opened it wide. I stood on the porch just long enough to thrust the moth up toward the sunset. The weightless creature pressed his wings against the invisible air and floated several feet away. There, my freed captive settled on a low tree branch, and if I hadn't seen him land, I wouldn't have noticed him. His protective coloring served him well.

In the wonder of the moment, I caught myself whispering, "Thank you, God, for the moth; something alive from my past."

Had God sent the moth? I now wondered. But Josh interrupted my musing.

"We need to go," he reminded me.

I pulled the door shut and stood for one last moment. I closed my eyes and pictured the living room as it used to be—alive with plans and hopes and dreams. I didn't like it empty. But I also didn't want it to change.

I whispered, "I wish I could be sure that Mr. Tipple and Mr. Gilson wouldn't sell the house and get rid of everything. I want things to stay as they are—at least for now. I want to be able to visit my memories and not have them gone."

"So, tell them," Josh said. "Tell Tipple and Gilson you don't want things touched. It's your house."

"But will they listen?" I asked.

"I think they will," Josh assured me.

Yes, it is my house, I thought. *I will tell them! Although I can't change the past, I can try to preserve the present at 1205 E. Meadow Lane.*

The nursing staff would help me place the call.

~ ~ ~

Mr. Tipple sounded surprised to hear from me. "Yes, Miss Dalton," he said. "How may I help you?"

I had seldom been called *Miss Dalton.* It made me feel grown up. I told him what I wanted.

"I see," he said. "I can understand your concern. But you needn't worry. Please know that on decisions of this nature, we will always consult you. Personal possessions are different from financial accounts. Rest assured that we have no plans to clear out or sell your family home.

"We are bound, however, to keep the place from falling into disrepair. To that end, we have contracted with a lawn service to mow and trim in the summer and remove snow in the winter. We have a housekeeping staff that dusts and vacuums once a month. And we also have an agreement with the police to do occasional drive-bys to discourage thieves. I, personally, visit the house once a month to check on the house cleaning and to make sure the plumbing hasn't sprung a leak or vermin haven't taken over.

"The only items we've removed, to date, have been perishable goods from the refrigerator, freezer, and pantry. Otherwise, everything is as you last saw it. I hope you believe me."

"Thank you, Mr. Tipple," I said. "I do believe you. I feel better knowing that my home will stay untouched. It may sound silly, since I can't see it or visit, but it is important to me to know that it is there."

Mr. Tipple made reassuring sounds and said I should feel free to contact him if anything else came to mind.

Satisfied, I smiled. *Mr. Tipple has no idea that I have been in the house and know he is telling the truth. Would he be surprised if he knew of my visit there!*

Even so, I wondered if I would ever get to visit again.

~ ~ ~

Josh didn't come for breakfast for two mornings. And just when I had decided I had imagined everything, I smelled pancakes.

"Hungry?" Josh said.

"Where have you been?" I demanded.

"Well, aren't we in a good mood?" he retorted. "While you've been lying here, Hero and I have been gathering all kinds of supplies. That takes time, you know!"

I sighed. *Of course. You've been spending all kinds of money and shopping all over town. Ha! Ha!* Would I ever know what was real and unreal about Josh?

Hero licked my ear, and I couldn't stay frustrated.

"How's my favorite dog?" I asked, and Hero licked my face. I wished I could toss a ball or run with him.

I asked Josh, "Did you give him Dodger's toy?"

"Of course. He's buried it in his dog bed and sleeps with it every night."

Josh removed Hero from my pillow. "He's already had his breakfast," Josh said. "And you need yours if we're going on our trip tonight."

"Tonight?" I asked in excitement.

I was ready. I only wished we could go now.

Josh stuffed a forkful of pancake into my mouth. "Eat up," he said. "You'll need the energy. Everything is set, just as we planned it. I'll have the stuff here later."

As I ate, I ran through our plans. "Are you sure we'll end up at the same place as before?" I asked.

"We'll see, won't we?" came Josh's answer. It wasn't a reassuring response, but one could never tell with what I call *Josh answers.*

After I finished my pancakes, Josh buried the evidence in the trash, Hero licked my ear, and Josh called out, "See ya tonight!"

~ ~ ~

Why did God create anticipation? My day dragged by, and I was irritable.

"My, but we're impatient today," one of the aides remarked. I had asked for the third time what time it was. I found myself willing the teen comedy show on the television to end, wishing lunch to hurry, resenting the pace of the mystery movie someone had set for me in the afternoon, and barely tolerating the necessity of suppertime.

I practically cooed when the night aide turned off the television and said, "Sleep tight, Christine!" I didn't even bother to correct her with, "My name is Cricket, not Christine!" The only thing that mattered was that Josh would be here soon. I felt the weight of the onyx stone in the hollow of my throat, and I ached to set out on our adventure.

~ ~ ~

"I have your shirt, jeans, and tennis shoes," Josh assured me when he finally came.

"Great!" I said. "I can pull them over my nightgown once we get there."

Josh set something on my bed and offered, "I've brought a very large shoulder bag for you, too." Then he explained, "I thought it might come in handy for carrying Hero."

"Oh, yes!" I cried. "Let's do take Hero with us. The children will love him."

At the mention of his name, Hero barked, and I imagined his tail wagging.

Now Josh said, "I've tied the boxes of food around my waist. I sure hope this works!"

"Me, too," I said. And I worried that the boxes might be too heavy.

"If they don't fly," Josh laughed, "I'll be grounded."

Oh, please let them fly, I breathed.

Suddenly, Josh asked, "Ready?" and I heard the stones click together. I felt the sky rush into my face, and I opened my eyes to see that we were on our way!

I looked back to make sure Josh was flying, too. Were the boxes of food cooperating?

To my relief, the supplies seemed as weightless as we were. The freight trailed behind Josh on a long rope tied to his waist, and it looked like the tail of a kite. Nothing slowed our flight. We shot past the moon and out among the stars.

Until we reached the stillness of space, Hero's ears flapped in the breeze. He reminded me of Dodger with his head out the window of our car whenever my family took a drive.

Now, Foley's planet came into view. I experienced the familiar sensation of approaching with too much speed and the likelihood of our disintegrating on impact. But just inches from the surface everything stalled into slow motion. We slipped feetfirst onto the surface as lightly as autumn leaves. Even the boxes tethered to Josh settled softly, one by one.

Unlike our last visit, we arrived at night, and I recognized the dumpster in front of us. It was the dumpster behind the Italian restaurant. Obviously, Josh had expected Foley to return to this spot. I wondered if he would.

I hurriedly pulled my shirt and blue jeans over my gown, and I pulled the tennis shoes over my bed socks. When Foley came, I wanted to be ready.

Foley will come, won't he? I worried. It seemed likely that he visited this dumpster each night; there was so much food here. But what if Foley didn't come? What if Josh was wrong? Would we be able to drag all of these boxes to the shelter? Could we even find the shelter?

A movement at the end of the alley drew a whispered "Hide!" from Josh, and we ducked out of sight. We didn't want to scare Foley away before he saw who we were.

We crouched and waited. Only after Foley and his men had started picking through the leavings in the bin did Josh slowly emerge and whisper, "Don't be afraid! It's just me!"

In his fright, Foley tipped forward and fell headfirst into the bin. His companions froze, ready to flee.

"Foley, it's me, Josh," Josh said more loudly. "Let me help get you out of there."

Thankfully, one of Foley's crew recognized Josh and reassured the others. "It's okay," the young man said. "It's the kid who was here a few weeks ago—the one who disappeared."

The others helped Josh pull Foley out of the bin.

"We've come back, with presents," Josh told them, and Foley clasped Josh in greeting.

"Good to see you," Foley said.

Josh repeated, "These boxes are filled with stuff for the shelter. Can you carry them?"

Foley asked, "Food?"

"Yes," said Josh. "Fresh food and canned goods."

At this news, the men and teens with Foley excitedly abandoned their scavenging and tested the weight of the boxes. Finding them easy to handle, they hauled them onto their shoulders and began the walk back home. I carried one of the smaller boxes, and I shouldered the satchel containing Hero. I stayed close, this time, and didn't lag behind.

We slipped in and out of alleys and followed the streetlight shadows of buildings. I said a sad hello to St. Andrew's Church and was glad to see that the rose window above the door remained unbroken.

CHAPTER EIGHT

FOLEY'S HISTORY

Underground, I marveled, again, at how these people could find their way through the dark passageways. I found it impossible, as before, to memorize the right and left turns along the way. Hero, however, knew exactly where we were going. His nose led him.

When we passed through the lit doorway of the inner room and our eyes adjusted, I smiled to the wan women and thin children who pressed around us. Hero scampered from person to person for pats on the head.

"Our friends have returned with gifts," Foley announced, and he set the boxes on the tables. "Let's see what they've brought." Foley backed away and said to Josh, "You should open these, son."

Josh did not hesitate. He whipped out a pocket knife, cut through the box tape, and turned back the flaps. When he pulled out loaves of bread, the group rushed forward. "Bread! *Fresh* bread!" several women exclaimed in astonishment. "Our babies have never had *fresh* bread!"

The contents of the next box drew similar exclamations: "Powdered milk!"

Bags of nuts, jars of peanut butter and jelly, cans of vegetables and fruit, fresh potatoes and apples, tins of various meats, and boxes of cookies drew excited cries. And the box of soap—bars, liquid, and shampoo—generated weeping among the adults. At a box of diapers, one woman swooned.

Once all the boxes had been opened, Foley raised his hands. "We must give thanks. Bow with me."

I bowed my head with the group as Foley prayed.

"Thank You, most faithful Heavenly Father, for these provisions and for the angels who have brought them. We rest in the assurance of Your everlasting love through the Lord Jesus, and we are grateful for Your daily care. Our tongues fail in offering adequate praise. Words cannot begin to express all that our hearts feel! Thank You, again, Lord. Thank you! Amen!"

When I opened my eyes, I saw that most of the fellowship had fallen to their knees. Sometimes the people in my church had prayed on their knees, and I had seen my dad among them. I said to myself, *at least this time, the prayers aren't for garbage.*

I helped stack the canned goods cleverly to hide the bread, potatoes, and apples in the center of a little mountain.

"The cans will keep the fresh food safe from mice and rats," Foley's wife explained. "And as we empty cans, we can flatten the tin to form a better keeper."

Some fruit and cans were kept out for supper. An eager crew served them up as if they comprised a great banquet. The bread was especially savored, like slices of soft gold.

Then, when the cookies were distributed, the children were beside themselves. Even though their tummies were fuller than they had ever been, the children nibbled on their dessert. Hero gleaned what few crumbs he could find under the table.

"I've never seen my daughters so contented," one of the women said. "How can we thank you?"

"It was Cricket's idea," Josh said, and I hung my head.

"It was the least we could do," I murmured.

"We are grateful," repeated the woman, and she moved from the table to an area along the wall that I guessed was her family's spot. She settled her little girls on blankets to play quietly. Other adults did the same with their children in their family spots. And then, a group of teens and adults returned to the tables.

Now Foley stood. With an open book set on a box on the table before him, I thought Foley looked like a preacher. And I wasn't far from wrong.

"Tonight," said Foley, "we are going to study the parable of the lost sheep."

My head shot up. I had learned a similar parable in Sunday school. I looked at Josh to see if the similarity should mean anything, but he ignored me. Josh focused his attention on Foley as Foley read from his book.

"In the Scripture," Foley began, "we read that Jesus said, 'Suppose one of you has a hundred sheep and loses one of them. Does he not leave the ninety-nine in the open country and go after the lost sheep until he finds it? And when he finds it, he joyfully puts it on his shoulders and goes home. Then he calls his friends and neighbors together and says, "Rejoice with me; I have found my lost sheep." I tell you that in the same way there is more rejoicing in heaven over one sinner who repents than over ninety-nine righteous persons who do not need to repent.'"

I sat, astonished. There was no doubt that this was the same story I knew.

I wondered how this could be. How could Foley's planet have the same Bible and the same parables as my planet? Or was it just a coincidence that this particular story was similar to one from my world? Was the Jesus of Foley's Bible the same as the Jesus I knew? Had my Jesus visited this planet, as well as Earth? Nowhere in my lessons had I ever heard such a thing. My Bible said that Jesus came to *Earth,* to save *my* people. I didn't begrudge that Jesus might also have visited Foley's planet and saved them, but I had to let my mind get used to that idea.

When the lesson and prayer ended and the adults joined their children in their separate family areas, Foley asked Josh and me to remain at the table. Foley and the teenager he called Eli sat with us.

Foley asked quietly, "Are you angels?"

The teenager with the badly scarred face leaned in to hear our answer.

"We're friends," Josh said.

"But how do you appear and disappear?" Foley persisted.

Josh simply said, "I can't explain it now. Perhaps later, I can."

"But where do you come from?" Foley asked.

Again, Josh hedged and said, "I can't give you the answer right now. But one day, you'll know."

I wondered why Josh didn't tell Foley about the onyx stones and about Earth. Why was it a secret?

"I know you are sent by God," Foley said. "But I can't get over your visits and how God is using you—a couple of children—to supply our needs."

As I was thinking how incredible our visits felt to me, too, Josh said, "Our God is faithful. And Cricket and I are honored to be used in whatever way He chooses."

Foley smiled. "I feel the same. Never would I have thought I'd be the leader of an underground people and that I would be teaching them the Scriptures. But God has a way of accomplishing things of which we never would have dreamed."

"So, you weren't always a preacher?" I asked.

"Heavens no!" Foley said. "I never darkened the door of a church until I was in my mid-twenties. And that was only by accident."

"Tell us about it," Josh encouraged.

Foley warned, "It's a long story."

I was ready. Hero settled on my lap.

With eyes focused on days in the past, Foley murmured, "Before most of the adults, here, were born, our families lived outside. No one hid. Everyone lived in decent homes and purchased the things they needed from stores or over the communications exchanges. Everyone enjoyed fresh bread and goods like those you've brought us. And everyone thought their lives would be like that forever.

"But they were wrong. Changes were underway, changes that started in the city but soon spread to the entire planet. And the changes came about subtly and over a period of years.

"First, all the neighborhood stores closed and families had to shop farther away. And then an alarming number of larger stores closed, all across the nation. Food and goods became available only through communications exchanges. Everything anyone needed had to be ordered, and all orders were delivered by mail or courier, which could take days. My parents and others complained, but they had no choice, so they slowly adjusted.

"Then cash was banned. Everyone paid with credit accounts,

including those who lived on government support. Paperwork became a thing of the past, even for taxes. And, again, people adjusted.

"Then credit theft began, and it created an uproar. People sometimes found their accounts cleaned out, their credit zero.

"The authorities scrambled to catch and stay ahead of the credit robbers, but the exchange-criminals were everywhere: in every city, every country, and every government across the globe. And there was not a fail-safe the thieves couldn't crack.

"Businesses were especially targeted, and, soon, employees couldn't count on paychecks. Working families lost their homes and ended up in shelters. My family was among them.

"To make matters worse, war broke out. I was a small child when my dad was drafted. Our family worried about him, because new, unspeakable weapons were being unleashed and leveling hundreds of cities and towns around the world. We watched reports on our cell phones and wondered when our city might be next.

"In the fourth year of the war, my dad was killed.

"Then the planet, itself, seemed bent on destruction, with earthquakes and tsunamis and volcanic eruptions. Food production ground to a virtual halt, and people all over the globe began to die from disease and hunger. Only the rich managed to ride out the storm.

"When I was fifteen, my mother and sister grew ill and died, and I was left orphaned. I ended up living on the streets.

Before I learned to prey on the rich, I rummaged for garbage in dumpsters and stole food from shelters. But eventually, I learned how to steal wallets and break into cars. And I joined a gang for a couple of years, before I realized they only took from me and cared nothing about me. I could just as easily steal for myself.

"Somehow, I managed to make it into my twenties without being killed or jailed."

Foley paused. With a sad smile of remembrance, he shook his head. I tried to imagine what he looked like back then.

"Then, one day," said Foley, "I followed a woman into an empty church. I thought she had food hidden in her jacket, and I planned to steal it.

"I ducked low and followed her down a set of cement stairs. Imagine my surprise when I arrived at the bottom and saw several families around a large table sharing a meager meal by candlelight. Cans of vegetables had been opened and were being passed. First, it was green beans, and then corn. Another can I couldn't identify made its rounds, and another.

"Then the woman I had followed produced a sleeve of crackers which she crumbled so that each person could receive a piece. I realized that it wouldn't have been worth stealing from her.

"Suddenly, I felt a hand on my shoulder. I had not heard the person who now stood behind me. I whirled to face a man larger than myself. The man caught me in an iron grip. 'You're welcome to join us,' he said. 'Come.'

"The man dragged me toward the circle of people I had been watching. 'Here,' he announced to the group, 'is another soul God has brought us. Please make room for him.'

"At once, a place opened, and the man sat me down. I expected snarls and resentment from those next to me, but each face held only smiles. Now, I focused on a half-empty can on the table. Before anyone could stop me, I snatched it and tipped it into my mouth. Pieces of diced fruit in a thick juice tasted sweet as I gulped them down. Then

I gripped the can like a weapon, ready to jam its edges into any hand that defied me for what I had taken. But no hands were raised.

"Instead, attention had turned to a loaf of bread. Every person, in turn, took a small handful and passed it along. When the bread came to me, I tore out a large hunk and stuffed it into my mouth.

"The young man next to me seemed amused. 'Nobody's going to take your food,' he said. 'We share what we have, here, and you're welcome to it.'

"I snorted. Surely, there was a catch, some ulterior motive at work. Nobody shared food, not even in a gang.

"But the sharing continued with a can of grape juice. I swallowed mine immediately, but the others waited until the *gang leader* told them to eat the bread and drink the juice. Then, they sang a song.

"Now, the leader invited me to stay for *Bible study*. 'And you should plan to spend the night here,' he said. 'It's safer than on the streets.'

"I didn't tell him I wasn't afraid of the streets, and I didn't tell him I didn't need his ragged little gang. He probably thought I had come here because I had wanted to join up. *Fat chance!* I was a loner, and I would be making my escape, soon.

"During what the man had called *Bible study*, I kept my eyes peeled for hidden signs, and I carefully evaluated the various *gang members*. They were a weak-looking group, except for their leader. I decided that if I could give the leader the slip, I wouldn't have trouble getting away.

"But neither the leader nor the gang seemed bent on preventing my leaving. Instead, their attention focused on a story I had never heard before.

"The leader, who they called *Pastor Peter*, told about a man named *Jesus* who was the *Son of God*. Peter said that God sent Jesus to be born as a man and to live among the people on this planet so He could heal the planet's people of *sin,* that common flaw or *sickness* that hinders mastery of life, relationships, and closeness to God. As part of God's plan, Jesus, a perfect, innocent man, was to be charged as a criminal and put to death for the sin-sickness of everyone else. And Jesus willingly allowed Himself to be killed. But Jesus did not stay dead. When He came back to life, it showed that He had accomplished His task. He had overcome the sin-sickness, and He could extend His health to others if they would believe and accept Him into their hearts."

Foley said, "I thought Peter's Jesus story was beautiful, but I didn't understand why the people gathered in the basement were so attached to it. It sounded like a fairy tale.

"When the story ended, the group broke up and everyone left— except for Pastor Peter and me.

"Peter insisted that I lie down on one of the padded pews in the room upstairs for the night, and I did as he directed. But I planned to slip away after a few hours of sleep.

"My plan didn't work, however. I didn't awaken until the sun streamed through the stained-glass windows and onto my face.

"When I sat up, I saw Peter at the front of the room on his knees. I eased to my feet and headed silently for the door, but I was stopped by his words. Although he wasn't addressing me, Peter was mentioning my name.

"'Help Foley to learn about You, Lord,' Peter was saying. 'Help him to grow strong in Your Word. Help Foley become a leader of others for You, no matter what the world may do.'

"His words stung my brain, and I could not leave. *Who was this man? And why was he concerned about me? What did he want me to learn and become?*

"When Peter finished his prayer, I made a noise as if I had just awakened. I pretended I hadn't heard his words, and I faked a bored indifference when he noticed me. I felt guilty to receive his genuine greeting, so unlike my old gang leader's false joviality. I mumbled a *good morning* and announced that I had something to do and had to leave.

"Peter did not stop me. As I left, he simply called out, 'I hope you'll come back for Bible study, tonight. We'd love to have you.' With a noncommittal nod, I strode out the door.

"I don't know why I came back. But that night, and many nights for weeks, I returned to the little rag-tag group for Bible study. They were unlike any gang I had ever known.

"Night after night, as I listened to Peter, I pieced together more and more of the Jesus story. And I began to become acquainted with the people who gathered to listen with me. I learned their personal stories, and I helped wherever I could. I was young and strong and had no qualms about stealing medicine or food. It seemed the right thing to do, since Pastor Peter's lessons stressed how Jesus wanted us to love and care for each other.

"And at first no one asked where I got the things I provided.

"But one day, Pastor Peter pulled me aside and said, 'Foley, I don't want you to think we are ungrateful for your gifts, but you need to stop stealing. We have benefactors who donate to us, and we don't resort to thievery.'

"I scoffed at the idea of benefactors. I hadn't seen much in the church larder beyond a few canned goods and some old loaves of bread. Only once in a while would there be meat or fresh produce.

"*Why so stingy?* I wondered. The wealthy I saw and stole from every day on the streets looked healthy and smug, and they frequented dozens of restaurants in our area. It was only the poor who suffered.

"I struggled with not stealing, and I didn't give it up, completely. I also struggled with the concept of sharing, instead of hoarding. But I tried to comply.

"Meanwhile, our little group remained faithful. And for over six years—yes, *six years*!—I continued to meet with them. They became my family. And I suffered when age and death reduced their numbers.

"At my first funeral, I saw Pastor Peter celebrate as well as cry. It confused me. Even though I knew Peter believed the person had gone to Heaven, I couldn't understand celebrating their death.

"As Peter spoke words over a makeshift casket, he explained that Heaven was for those who had invited Jesus into their hearts. And at this, and at each subsequent funeral, Peter asked if anyone present wanted to accept Jesus as their Savior. I always looked away and ignored his invitation. I didn't have much use for fairy tales.

"And then, one day, nearly seven years ago, I changed my mind.

"On that day, I awakened to a commotion. I leaped from my pew and rushed to look out the church door. In the streets, I saw women wailing and men screaming: 'Where's my wife?' 'Where's my baby?'

"I didn't understand. I hurried to report to Pastor Peter, but I couldn't find him. He must have gone out at the sound, too. I stayed inside and ended up answering the questions of dozens of searchers who came to check out the building: 'No, your son isn't here.' 'No, your wife didn't come here.' 'You're welcome to look.' 'No, I haven't seen anyone today.'

I wished Peter would hurry back.

"Throughout the morning, I wondered what had happened. Where had all the missing people gone? The images on my cell phone were confusing, and I gathered that this was more than a local phenomenon.

"Reports suggested that two and a half billion people—nearly one-third of the population—from all over the globe had vanished. They had simply disappeared. Thousands of airline pilots had vanished and their planes had crashed. Drivers of cars had disappeared and their automobiles had piled up on the highways. Doctors and healthcare workers had vanished, and hospitals overflowed with sick and injured people and less staff to care for them. A handful of astronauts in space labs had vanished. World leaders had disappeared from meetings and offices. Parents and children had vanished, leaving other parents spouseless, childless. Strangest of all, mortuaries reported missing a number of bodies that had been prepared for funerals.

"And churches of Jesus-followers had suffered the most—some churches had suffered one hundred percent losses.

"In a panic, I wondered if Pastor Peter and our little group had been affected. Was that why Pastor Peter wasn't here? Was he comforting someone—or was he gone, too? In an attempt to reassure myself that Peter was only temporarily away, I headed for his office. Reading upside down, across his desk, I checked his note pad and saw nothing scheduled that would have taken him away. Then, I walked around the desk to look further. And that's when I recoiled.

"There, on Peter's chair, were his clothes! His T-shirt looked as if he had evaporated right out of it and let it drop to the seat. His blue jeans were draped over the edge where his legs had rested, and his socks and shoes sat below, on the floor. Even his watch had been left behind.

"I couldn't breathe. *What could possibly do this? And why?* I now understood the multitude of frightened people in the streets who were screaming in terror.

"I stood trembling. This church had been my home for six years, and Pastor Peter had been a father to me. I couldn't bear to think he was gone.

"And what about our little group? Would anyone come tonight so we could console one another? What would I do if my friends were gone, too?

"I left the church and roamed the streets for hours. I shared the shock of everyone's loss, and I moved woodenly through the afternoon.

"At night, as I always did, I returned. As usual, because the church couldn't afford electricity, the upstairs was dark and empty. But by this time, candles had always been lit in the basement and people had gathered and were talking. Tonight, there was silence. I lit my way down the stairs with my cell phone, which I had illegally charged in the neighborhood library without paying.

"In the basement, I lit the candles. I drew out and opened two cans from the pantry, and I sat at the table, alone, and ate.

"When the time came for Bible study and no one had shown up, my mind began to play tricks. I pretended that everyone was here, but that Pastor Peter had forgotten to bring his Bible from the office. 'No problem,' I said to no one, 'I'll be back in a minute.' And I hurried up the stairs.

"In the office, I refused to look at the chair. I reached over the desk and slid the Bible into my arms. Downstairs, I pretended Peter had a problem with his eyes and couldn't read.

"'That's okay,' I said to an invisible Peter. 'I can read the words, and you can explain.'

"I let the Bible fall open to wherever it might, and it landed on a page that Peter had bookmarked. My eyes were drawn to an underlined passage, and I started there to read aloud: *'For the Lord himself will come down from heaven, with a loud command, with the voice of the archangel and with the trumpet call of God, and the dead in Christ will rise first. After that, we who are still alive and are left will be caught up with them in the clouds to meet the Lord in the air. And so, we will be with the Lord forever.'*

"Then I read the handwritten note Peter had left in the margin: *'Two men will be in the field; one will be taken and the other left. Two women will be grinding with a hand mill; one will be taken and the other left.'*

"My voice trailed off. Suddenly, I knew. I knew that Pastor Peter and all of our little group of friends were in Heaven. And I was left behind."

Oh! I cried, and Josh glanced at me. I didn't mean to cry, but I couldn't help it. *Everyone Foley loved has been taken from him.* I felt his pain, and I wasn't surprised to hear Foley say, "I sobbed for an hour. Everything Pastor Peter had been teaching suddenly rang true. And I regretted that I had refused to accept it. I wailed. Now, I would never see Peter or my friends, again.

"I must have cried myself to sleep. When I awakened in a puddle of tears, I remembered the verses I had read, and I wailed again and shouted at God, 'Why didn't you make me believe? Why?'

"I shoved the Bible away from me, across the table. As I did so, a piece of paper slipped out sideways. I would have ignored it, except that scrawled across the top was my name: 'Foley.'

"I reached over to pull the paper out. It was in Peter's handwriting. And … I still have it here in my pocket."

As Josh and I watched, Foley pulled out a tattered piece of paper and lovingly unfolded it. He started to read:

Dear Foley,

If you are reading this, I know you are looking for answers. No doubt, the Great Disappearance has occurred.

Do not be afraid. This has been predicted. God's prophets have said a day would come when all Jesus-followers would be removed from the world in a single instant. I am sorry you have been left behind.

Although it may seem so, the Great Disappearance is not the end of the world. Nor is it the end of your chance to be reunited with us.

You have heard me tell how God's Son, Jesus, came to this planet many years ago to make God's love plain and to conquer your sin and your death with the sacrifice of His own life. He gave His life on the Cross to save your soul, as He has saved mine and your other friends'. By accepting Jesus' substitutionary gift, even now, you can become a Jesus-follower, and you can be assured that God will not forget you.

Sadly, you will have to remain in the world until a succession of terrible troubles passes. Life will be nearly unbearable. But God is faithful and will preserve your soul, either in Heaven through death or in His presence when He comes again.

You see, at the end of the next seven horrific years, Jesus will come. He will arrive personally on the planet and restore it for a thousand years. And after a thousand years, He will do even more: He will wipe away every remaining trace of evil and brokenness, and He will create a brand-new, forever world.

And so, Foley, I pray you will turn to Jesus and hold fast, no matter what awful things may occur.

How do you become a Jesus-follower? How do you ask Jesus to make you His? There are no magic words. Simply ask. Agree with God that you were born broken and unable to make yourself whole and holy. Tell Him you want Jesus in your heart and you want Him to break the barriers between God and you.

It's that simple. And once you belong to Jesus, even if the mountains crumble and the sky rolls up like a scroll, your forever-life will not be lost—you will be with Jesus. And in His company, you and I will see each other again!

Believe, Foley! Believe and live.

Pastor Peter

P.S. Foley, I believe God has sent you to this church for a reason, and I believe you will one day come to accept Jesus into your heart. I also believe you will become a leader for others who finally understand and begin to follow Jesus. I want you to have my Bible, and I hope you will read it. Share its words with others who become Jesus-followers after the rest of us are gone. Tell everyone the stories of Jesus and how to accept His gift. Show them the prophecies about the Great Disappearance, and assure them that Jesus is coming again. Stand fast, my friend! And one day when Jesus comes, you and I will worship Him, together. Until then ...

When Foley came to the end of the note, his eyes had watered, and he carefully refolded the paper and put it back into his pocket.

How remarkable! I thought. How had Peter known to write the letter? Had God given him a vision of the nearness of the Great Disappearance?

I shook my head in wonder.

"My life changed that day," Foley said. "I stayed and lived at the church. And little by little, people who suspected the truth about the Great Disappearance came looking for answers. Together, we searched the Scriptures and prayed.

"Soon, four dozen new Jesus-followers met every night for Bible study. And although no more donations of food came to the church (I assumed that our benefactors had been taken in the Great Disappearance), we weren't in need. The property and pantries of the 2.4 billion believers who had vanished were available for relatives. And because of inheritance, four of those who met with us were well off. And until other troubles came and we ended up here, they supplied the basic needs for those in the group who had not been as fortunate."

Foley passed his hand around the room. "These are the remnants of the people who met with me at the church. We are a family of believers, and we are waiting for Jesus to return."

Foley smiled at Josh and me. And I looked once more at the little group gathered in this underground shelter.

I had listened to Foley's story with a jumble of emotions. Because of my own experiences, I understood the loss of family, and I wondered which family members and friends these people had lost in the Great Disappearance. I marveled at how the shock of their loss had brought them to the church and to Jesus so they could be together. I only wished they were still living above ground and meeting in their church. It sounded like their lives had been better, freer. They had been able to enjoy the sun and fresh air.

What, I wondered, *had driven them underground? How had they come to leave the church building and move to this dark labyrinth beneath the city?*

Before I could ask about it, Foley stood.

"Would you excuse me for a moment?" he asked.

When we nodded, Foley moved from the table to where his wife and son waited in their spot along the wall. I saw him tuck his little boy under the covers of his rag mattress on the hard floor and kiss his wife.

Then he came back to Josh and me. Foley extinguished all the tin-can candles on the tables but two, and taking one of them, he said, "Come. There is more to our story, but I don't want to disturb the little ones."

Foley led Josh, the teenager named Eli, and me into the hall where we sat cross-legged.

~ ~ ~

Hero sat at my feet, and Foley cleared his throat as he prepared to tell more of his story.

"After the Great Disappearance," Foley said, "chaos reigned everywhere, and everything on the planet was turned upside down. The world stormed through a desperate scramble to reestablish order and stability. The worldwide financial market crashed, and businesses and government offices were in shambles because so many key personnel had vanished.

"Only a half-dozen companies had been untouched by the Great Disappearance. One of those was a multinational business called Tannin Industries. Greg Tannin, son of the company's founder, suddenly appeared on television screens around the world and seemed to be the answer man.

"Tannin was a brilliant orator and thinker, and people hung on his words and latched onto his ideas and promises to restore the systems that made things run.

"Tannin gathered the remaining world leaders and businessmen together. When these elites emerged from a secret, month-long session, Tannin had been elected their leader.

"Tannin began, at once, to implement solutions to every problem, starting first with global financial restructuring and establishing a congress of world government. He ended wars and made alliances, including a seven-year alliance with an ancient God-people who had been the focus of much global unrest. As part of an uneasy truce, these God-people were allowed to reclaim a disputed mountain and rebuild their Temple there. This ancient people had always rejected Jesus as God's Son, but in light of the Great Disappearance and a fresh search of the Scripture prophecy, they were now reviewing that decision.

"Under Tannin, people from all over the globe worked together for three and a half years as they never had. A worldwide police force ensured peace and safety in every neighborhood. Gangs and looters no longer operated in our cities. And the government took possession of all abandoned properties and all unclaimed financial accounts. These acquisitions considerably enlarged the government's treasury. And then, Tannin announced his new financial platform.

"People cheered! Tannin's plan seemed brilliant. All debts and mortgages, no matter how small or large, were to be canceled. Whatever homes or goods one possessed at the moment would remain theirs. But current credit was wiped out. Jobs were assigned, and everyone, whether rich or poor, was to be given the same generous annual personal credit to draw from.

"As you might expect, people who had been fabulously wealthy before the world crash complained about their job assignments and diminished accounts, but the masses went wild with their new buying power.

"All went well, at first—until those who poorly managed their accounts ran out of credit before the year's end. Then, those with nothing robbed from those who still had buying power. Soon, no one was safe on the streets. Homes became fortresses, and riots and theft were rampant. And this financial instability, coupled with rounds of what seemed to be never-ending natural disasters, made supplies of everything more and more difficult to come by, even on the black market.

"Once again, Tannin announced a solution.

"This time, he ordered each person's account to be refilled with credit—if they would receive a universal identification mark—an implant in their forehead or forearm. The implant would assure that credit could not be drained by non-essential purchases and that one's credit identity could not be stolen. Furthermore, the implant could pinpoint the location of anyone who engaged in violence, robbery, or black-market exchanges. No one could hide.

"As the plan's implementation began, people applauded it. It seemed a perfect solution. Because no one could escape the law keepers, financial peace would reign at last. Headlines screamed, *Utopia is at hand!*

"But," Foley said with a deep sigh, "paradise was not to be for everyone."

Aha! I thought. *Here it comes. Here's where we learn why Foley is underground.*

"Almost immediately," Foley said, "Tannin began to rewrite the code of ethics. In addition to the usual legal dictates, Tannin set up new rules. He decreed that people who disagreed with him on even the smallest things could be thrown into prison.

"And he discouraged those who had become God-followers from gathering and praying. Tannin announced that such activities could turn subversive. After all, didn't the Bible teach that God was above the laws of men? Such teachings were dangerous.

"To reinforce his decrees, Tannin appointed a cruel accomplice who targeted anyone who spoke of or taught about God's *Kingdom of Heaven*. Tannin's accomplice ruthlessly enforced the new law. After all, Tannin's peace required unity and one kingdom: *his!* Allegiance to any other kingdom was punishable by death.

"Tannin also revoked his treaty with the ancient God-people and desecrated their Temple with an image of himself. Tannin claimed to perform great and terrifying miracles, and he insisted he was the only god that people needed. If someone wanted to worship a god, they could worship him!

"As the identification implant centers proceeded to process citizens, some brave people held back. They—including our group, of course—refused the mark. We feared the unchecked power of Tannin's rule. With the implant, our every move would be monitored, and freedom for us would be meaningless.

"Tannin already held Jesus-followers on record as enemies of the state. Although he promised that if we recanted, our past religious choices would be overlooked, we knew that our past could be dredged up and used against us any time Tannin might choose.

"Besides, we will never recant. We trust God. While Tannin might kill our *mortal* bodies, God will save our *immortal* souls. To avoid enforcement of Tannin's decree, we fled from our church building. By chance, we came here, and we have been an underground people ever since."

Foley sat tall and proud.

"Here," he said, "in the safety of the labyrinth, we continue to study the Scriptures, and, through them, God gives us words we can trust.

"We have read that Jesus, and God's prophets before Him, predicted the Great Disappearance. And God's prophets predicted that three and a half years after the Great Disappearance, a godless ruler would rise to power. *Because we have lived it, we know that precisely three and a half years after the Disappearance is when Tannin came to absolute power.*

"Then the prophets foretold that the godless ruler would demand his mark be placed on every person who wanted to buy or sell. Again, we have seen these prophecies come true. *What could be more descriptive of the prophesied mark than the universal implant Tannin has devised?*

"Scripture also predicted that the godless ruler would bring persecution and tribulation-suffering on the world for three and a half years before Jesus would return. The godless *beast* would persecute and murder everyone who followed God and resisted taking the mark. *How better could God's prophets have described our situation, today, than this?"*

"But," cried Foley triumphantly, "the Scriptures also say the return of Jesus will bring the godless ruler's evil to an end, and everyone who has stayed true to God and resisted the mark will be rewarded."

Foley said, "Our little underground group hopes to live to see that day! I and my people believe God will send Jesus, soon. It has been close to seven years since the Great Disappearance; three and a half years before Tannin took power and three and a half years of Tannin's evil reign. We have been in hiding since Tannin took over, and we're getting excited for Jesus to come!"

"Yes!" exclaimed the teenager seated next to Foley. Then the young man caught himself. He didn't want to awaken the children in the next room. He repeated, this time in a whisper, "Yes! We're ready!"

~ ~ ~

When it became clear to me how long Foley's people had been living underground, I exclaimed, "You've been hiding here for more than three years?"

"Yes, Cricket," said the teenager.

And Foley concurred. "We've been living in the labyrinth for over three years. And so far, we've been safe. But we know that at any time we might be found and killed. We have a price on our heads."

At this, the teenager hissed, "But we will fight if we have to. And we know hiding places of which they've never dreamed!" The young man's eyes glowed defiantly in the fire of the candle, and the flame's flickering shadows exaggerated the wound on his cheek.

Foley smiled, but not without sadness. "Many have resisted and died. And many remain in hiding. We are not alone in suffering persecution. There are pockets of Jesus-followers everywhere.

"Tannin has especially targeted the ancient God-people who have become Jesus-followers. Before Tannin broke his treaty with them, thousands of their number came from around the world to live near their Temple. Now, Tannin has sworn to kill them all. At last report, the God-people have escaped from their Temple city to a secret place that has not yet been discovered. We hope they will survive until Tannin's rule ends. That godless beast will find he is no match for the God of Heaven when Jesus returns!"

I looked at Josh. I wondered, *could the ancient God-people and Foley's people outlast Tannin's pursuit?* I hoped so. I prayed they would not be discovered by Tannin or his armies. I had experienced only the tiniest example of the coldness of people who bore the mark. I recalled, again, the unscrupulous woman who had tried to steal my onyx stone and the accusing crowd who had tried to turn Josh and me over to the police. I also thought about the faceless people who had robbed me in the dark and left me to die on the street.

But wait! Those robbers had not been the same as the bold-faced crowd we had met in the daylight. And, although the robbers had operated at night like Foley's people, the robbers were nothing like Foley's people. *Who are those thieves? Why are they in hiding? Do those robbers not have the mark, either?*

I asked, "Am I right that there are other people, besides Jesus-followers, who don't have the mark? For example, the night people who attacked me and took my sack were nothing like you or your group. Who are they? Why are they in hiding?"

"Ah," said Foley. "You are right. And you're lucky those people didn't kill you. Many of them are vicious beings who have refused the implant because of their past. They are not Jesus-followers. They are criminals who escaped from prisons during the upheavals before Tannin took power. They fear being locked up again, or executed by Tannin—with good reason. They've persisted in their criminal activity, including attempting to steal people's implants. Only after several thefts and murders did they figure out that an implant's removal results in the death of the host and the deactivation of its credit. These criminals are diligently hunted. And their crimes have given all of us a bad name. We not only fear being captured and mistaken for one them, but we fear them. If our paths cross, someone from our group usually dies."

Foley added, "They left you to the rats, which is just as bad."

Hero felt me shudder and licked my chin. I petted him.

Josh said to Foley, "Thankfully, God preserved Cricket, just like He's preserving your people."

~ ~ ~

As I listened to Foley and Josh, I felt guilty. *God has helped me, hasn't He? When I prayed, God sent Hero and Josh to my rescue. And, if Foley is right, God's plans are bigger than I have imagined—on Foley's planet and mine. Have I spent too much time on my anger because of my losses and not enough on trusting God?* The faith of Foley's people in the midst of their hurts amazed me. I wanted to be like them. *But ...*

Foley said, "My experiences and the experiences of those with me have been nearly unbearable at times, but we continue to feel God's love. And we hope and believe in the words of the prophecies. Those words tell us that we will be reunited with everyone we have lost. We are assured in Scripture that Jesus will not be returning alone. He will bring with Him all those who are in Heaven—angels and all His followers. If we are still alive when they come, we will see them. If we die before they come, we'll be part of that returning assembly. Either way, we will be together again, and we will rejoice!"

Foley's face beamed to imagine the reunion he had described. But his smile was interrupted. A commotion arose inside the living space. It sounded like every child had suddenly awakened and started to cry.

Foley leaped up and raced into the room.

Mothers sat rocking their little ones and drying their tears, and Foley asked his wife, "What's wrong? Why is Joey crying?"

Sabrina said, "He's had a nightmare. And from what I gather, the other children have had the same dream. Joey said he dreamed the skyscrapers all fell and trapped everyone in the shelter. And the ground wouldn't stop shaking. And all the candles went out, and it was dark."

Foley frowned. "More of the prophecy," he said. "The time is drawing near."

CHAPTER NINE

GOD HASN'T FORGOTTEN

F amilies were still reassuring their children and tucking them into their rag beds on the floor when Josh motioned for me to follow him into the hallway.

"We need to go," Josh said. "You should take off your shirt and jeans, here."

My shoulders drooped. I didn't want to go. How could we leave these families to face falling skyscrapers? I had no idea what we could do, but…

Reluctantly, I started to change. It wouldn't do for the nursing-home staff to find a T-shirt and jeans drawn over my nightgown.

I pulled off the outer clothing and shoes, and I asked, "Is there nothing we can do to help them?"

Josh busied himself with rolling my shirt and jeans into a ball around my shoes and stuffing them into his bag. Then he put Hero into my satchel and fingered his onyx stone.

"Don't," I said. "Don't click the stones just yet." I backed against the wall and crossed my arms over the necklace. "I have to know if we will see these people again."

"Yes," Josh replied, but I wondered if he was humoring me so we could leave, or if he really knew.

"I don't know how you know these things," I told him, "and I want to believe you. Do you know how much time they have?"

"Less than a month," said Josh. "It will soon be seven years since the Great Disappearance."

"And we'll come back before then?" I asked.

"Yes," Josh promised. "And we will bring more supplies."

"Are they going to die?" I asked.

This time, Josh hesitated. "Some of them might," he murmured.

I wept. Death. I had never given death much thought until my family had been killed. And now I thought about it every minute.

"It's not right!" I cried. "Why doesn't God protect them? Why didn't He protect my family?"

I sank to the floor and held my knees. My tears soaked into the fabric of my nightgown, and I felt Hero's tongue on my cheek.

Josh knelt and put his hand on my arm. "I'm sorry, Cricket," he whispered. "Many things are hard to understand. That's what trust is all about."

"I'm trying to trust," I insisted. "But how can I trust a God who allows death and pain? He just sits up there and does nothing! He has no idea how it feels!"

"That's not true," Josh countered. "God isn't uninvolved. You forget that He sent His Son to Earth. And you forget that, to save people, God gave Jesus a mission that resulted in His death. God knows pain."

I rubbed my forehead in an attempt to take in Josh's words. I knew that it had meant great pain and loss to God to send Jesus to Earth. It must be true that God was not indifferent. In fact, He had *loved us to death.*

I finally said to Josh, "I guess God does understand, doesn't He? God has been hurt, too. He let Jesus die."

Josh nodded.

I whispered, "But why do we have to hurt so much?"

When Josh didn't answer, I dried my tears, and with a purposeful sigh, I said, "Let's go home."

~ ~ ~

As we flew, I wondered how soon I could pick out Earth from the wash of stars.

When I spied our planet, I marveled at how similar it was to the purple-cloaked planet behind us. We hurtled toward the Earth's surface at a dizzying speed, and as always, our descent threatened to be catastrophic. But in the second that followed our passage through the nursing home roof, we stalled into that strange cushion of slow motion, and the covers of my bed rose to enfold me.

The familiar darkness of my blindness and the lack of feeling of my paralysis drew down on me like a curtain. As hard as I tried to push it away, I could not.

An overwhelming drowsiness filled me, and I slept.

~ ~ ~

In the days that followed, I might have rejoiced when the last of my casts came off, but, instead, their removal brought new depression. I had wanted to be *healed.* I had wanted to *feel* again when the casts came off. But it didn't happen.

I still felt nothing of my arms and legs. I could only imagine they were there. I remained paralyzed from the neck down.

The aides chattered on about how I would now be able to sit up. But I resented their celebrating. Sitting up meant little to me. I had no sensation of sitting when the aides raised my bed higher—except that, at first, I suffered periods of dizziness.

I mourned my blindness and that my body still refused to respond with feeling and movement. And I despaired of my future.

Funny things go through your mind when you are helpless and have little hope of getting better. Not funny *ha-ha,* but funny *odd.* Although I was not yet thirteen, I mourned that I would never fall in love or get married or have a family of my own. My family's genes would die with me when my useless body finally gave out.

For some reason, I mentioned my thoughts to Pastor Howard on his next visit. As I lamented my worthlessness, I muttered, "I can only lie here and breathe. I'm no good to anyone."

"Is that right?" Pastor Howard countered.

I challenged him. "Name one thing I can do for someone else— just one thing!" When he answered, I groaned. *I should have known!*

"Pray," he said. "You can pray."

Right! The very thing I had not long ago sworn off and hadn't completely returned to with confidence. "I'm not good at praying for other people," I declared. "Prayer assumes that God will answer."

"And you don't think He does?"

"Sometimes, yes. But not often," I said. "He doesn't do what I pray for."

"God isn't Santa Claus," Pastor Howard said. "He's not in the business of giving every gift we ask for. And He hasn't guaranteed us a trouble-free life; He's never promised that. Instead, God promises two things: one, that He loves us; and two, that He sent Jesus to be with us no matter what we face. When we pray for others, we're praying for God to *walk with them* through their difficulties. That means He either steers them into calmer waters and brings healing, or He carries them through the storm so they can handle it. But either way, He's there. Don't let yourself believe otherwise."

I knew that Pastor Howard was right. Troubles did follow everyone. But I still wondered why that had to be. And I continued to pity myself.

Pastor Howard knew my thoughts and said, "Our biggest temptation is to think only of ourselves and throw tantrums when life doesn't happen our way. But that's not healthy. It's not the way God designed us."

As he talked, I felt a twinge of shame. I realized how little I had thought about, much less prayed for, anyone besides myself. Only in my otherworldly adventures had I left my grief and broken body behind. Without those things weighing on me, I had been able to feel sympathy for people who had nothing. But now, back in my real world of grief and a useless body, I had prayed for no one.

"Let me think about it," I murmured. "I need time."

"Sure," Pastor Howard said. "But be sure to spend some of that time talking to God."

CHAPTER TEN

MARLENE GRACE

F ew things, besides that first visit from Josh, startled me at The Arches. But Marlene Grace startled me. The new aide came in like a bulldozer with attitude and changes.

"Child, you need sunshine!" she said, and she threw open the window. I heard her draw in a deep breath.

"Don't bother," I grumbled. "I can't see."

"But you can feel!" she pronounced. "Feel that breeze?"

She was right. The breeze on my face did feel good. It reminded me of flying with Josh.

Marlene Grace (both names were her first name, I soon learned) kept up a flood of positive talk. And she practically shoveled my breakfast eggs and toast into my mouth.

"You need to keep up your strength, girl," she declared.

I didn't bother to point out that I didn't have the strength of a wet noodle, so why did I need to keep up my strength?

Nevertheless, I liked her. I pictured Marlene Grace as pleasantly plump. She was definitely African American, and there was no doubt that she had taken me on as a project. Unlike the other aides who barely remembered my name was *Cricket* and not *Christine,* Marlene Grace always got it right. And, unlike anyone else, she fussed over my hair.

"You gotta look beautiful, honey," she stated. "Those curls are a blessing, for sure. You just gotta tame 'em a little."

I pretended I didn't like all the new attention, but in truth I ate it up. Marlene Grace reminded me of Lucy, my intensive care nurse. Both women talked *to* me and not *at* me.

And when Marlene Grace gave me my sponge bath, she sang hymns.

"Don't you love those old songs?" she'd ask. And sometimes, if I knew the song, I would sing with her.

"My, my! You've got the voice of a bird," she'd say.

And I'd always retort, "A vulture?"

She'd laugh and scold. "What are we gonna do with you, child?"

"Whatever you like," I'd say. "I can't stop you!"

And we'd both laugh at that.

I chuckled now when she went off to do her other errands.

Day after day, Marlene Grace succeeded in making me laugh. I no longer awakened with a cloud hanging over my head. I listened for her voice, and I basked in her care.

With Marlene Grace as my sunshine and breath of fresh air, it was days before I realized I hadn't seen Josh.

And then, as if on cue, I heard Josh ask, "Miss me?"

I quipped, "I don't believe I know you, do I?"

"That bad?" he joked. "It's only been a couple of weeks."

"That's a long time," I said. Then I asked, "What do you do when you're not here?"

I wasn't surprised when Josh gave me one of his typical answers: "Wouldn't you like to know?" Then he asked, "What's new?"

I told him about Marlene Grace.

"You like her?" he asked.

"Yeah. She's fun. She teases me, and she takes good care of me."

"I can see that," Josh said. "She's managed to do something with that crazy hair of yours."

I gave him what I hoped was a look that even with blind eyes said, "Thanks for the compliment, I think."

"I hope she makes you eat," Josh said.

"Oh, yeah. If I didn't down my eggs and toast, she'd shoot 'em in my veins! But I miss my pancakes. I haven't told Marlene Grace that I like them. I'm sure she'd order them. But I only like yours."

"Pancakes are pancakes," Josh said.

"I know. But you're the pancake man," I insisted.

Josh sounded pleased. "Good. And don't you forget it!"

"So, are we going to take more supplies to Foley's people?" I asked. (I had no idea where Josh got the things we took, and I didn't bother to ask.)

"Tomorrow," Josh said. "After pancakes. I have all the stuff gathered, and I still have your clothes."

"Great!" I cried. "Can't wait!"

"Okay, Miss Dalton. See you later!"

I stalled him to ask, "Can you get toys for the children?"

"Boy, you don't expect much, do you?" he teased. And then he said, "I'll see what I can do. Bye!"

~ ~ ~

That night, I awakened to Marlene Grace comforting me.

"It's all right, child," she was saying. "Just a bad dream. Take a drink of water and let Marlene Grace sing you back to sleep."

I took a sip on the straw she placed at my lips, and Marlene Grace crooned a lullaby that I had never heard. (She repeated it later for me so I could memorize it. She called it *Miriam's River Lullaby*.)

Dream as you float
In your small wicker boat
To the whisper of crickets
From green, leafy thickets
Across the still waters
Not far from your crib.

In shadows of rushes
The breeze gently shushes
The dragonflies flitting
As moonlight is sitting
On cool, lapping waters
That rock your wee crib.

Then dawn paints the skies
In delight for your eyes
While the treetops are ringing
With joyful birds' singing
To celebrate morn'
As you 'wake in your crib.

[MIRIAM'S RIVER LULLABY, BY DEBBY L. JOHNSTON]

Marlene Grace stroked my hair as she sang, and I thought the song was the most beautiful thing I had ever heard. I remember floating on her music, and then I remembered no more. I slept soundly and peacefully, until Josh awakened me.

CHAPTER ELEVEN

IT BEGINS

"Hurry and eat your pancakes," Josh said. "We need to go soon."
"Is it morning, yet?" I asked thickly, still willing myself awake.

"Not yet," he said. "But if we wait, your Marlene Grace will be here, and we won't be able to go."

I heard his words and nodded, and before I was even fully conscious, I let him stuff his pancakes into my mouth. Then I heard the stones click and felt the wind take me through the ceiling and into the skies.

I kept my eyes closed and lifted my face to the breeze. And I felt Hero under my arm in the satchel.

At last, I was awake enough to look back and see Josh trailing his string of boxes. I wondered if he had remembered to pack toys.

"I've missed the children," I called over my shoulder.

Josh called back, "Yes, there's a box of toys."

Satisfied, I imagined the smiles of little ones who had never had anything but makeshift toys for birthdays or Christmas. I wanted to hear them laugh and play.

The stars danced as we hurtled past their clusters, and the purple-clad planet grew from a dot to a softball, and from a softball to a vast horizon. I marveled that we passed right through the planet's surface and into Foley's room in the labyrinth. Our slow-motion cushion came only feet from the cement floor. After the room's occupants, barely visible in the dim light, recovered from their surprise, we were enveloped in hugs and kisses.

"Cricket! Josh! You're back!" the children chanted, and they danced around our boxes. Hero barked to be set free.

"Hero!" Foley's son Joey cried out, and I extracted the dog from my satchel. All the children joined Hero and Joey to race in happy circles around the floor. No one paid attention to me as I slipped my T-shirt and jeans over my nightgown.

Eyes were focused on the boxes Foley and his men had hauled onto the tables. Josh slit the packing tape and unpacked carton after carton, and it sobered me to watch the canned goods disappear into individual backpacks and not into the pantry along the wall. *This was the sign of a group preparing for an exodus.*

I wondered where they would go and how soon their flight would begin.

At least we will have supper tonight, I thought. The women set out a portion of the food, and we ate.

Then, after dinner, Josh enticed Foley's son, Joey, to open the last box. The boy squealed when balls and toys spilled onto the floor. Every child scooped up and danced in delight with a prize. It was better than Christmas morning!

Foley breathed a thank-you. He said, "I don't care what you say, you two ARE angels!"

~ ~ ~

"We aren't likely to make many more visits," Josh said after supper.

His announcement caught me off guard but seemed expected by Foley.

Foley nodded. "The time is very short now. We are packed and ready to leave the shelter. The men and I have done a dry run in the night. It will be a delicate thing to gauge when to flee. If we go too soon, we could be apprehended and killed. But if we don't leave soon enough, we could be crushed or trapped. We trust that since God has forewarned us, He will also give us a sign for when to flee."

I had a hard time imagining a flight from the shelter. Everything seemed so normal at the moment. *What dangers and changes lie ahead for these people?*

As we watched the children play with their new toys, Foley confided, "Most of these little ones don't remember life outside the labyrinth. Many were mere toddlers when we came here."

It saddened me to think these youngsters and teens had little or no memory of a sunset or running in clover. They had not hiked in the woods or caught a fish. They had missed flocks of geese honking and the hatching of a butterfly from a chrysalis. They had never hit a softball in a vacant lot or tossed a bowling ball. They had never swum across a pond or carved out a snow angel. Without access to electricity, they had never possessed a cell phone or a laptop, so they had not even vicariously experienced these things online.

But they did play. It pleased me to see Hero race from child to child and then lead them on a merry chase after a ball he had stolen. When the players cornered him, they shrieked and giggled and smothered him with hugs. And then the game started over again.

But in the middle of the third keep-away, Hero froze. The little dog dropped the children's ball and cocked his head. I sensed his ears heard something beyond the noise of the children's cries. When Hero stiffened and let out a deep howl—a primal wail—shivers ran up my spine.

It was a warning. There was danger. Hero raced to the door and barked. His message was clear: Follow me! And hurry!

Foley reacted at once. He shouted, "Children! Grab your packs! Now! Just as we practiced. It's time!"

CHAPTER TWELVE

Run!

In a controlled frenzy, the children snatched up small bags and huddled at the door. The women followed with larger packs. And the men, who shouldered great packs, led everyone down the hallway on a run. Josh and I followed close behind.

The walls and floor now shook. I thought of the children's prophetic nightmare. The skyscrapers were going to fall!

Fear drove my feet. And Foley's voice boomed continually, giving direction for our flight. Without his commands, I would have despaired in the dark.

As we ran, dust sifted from the ceiling. I felt it on my head and shoulders, even though in the blackness I couldn't see it. Would we be crushed in a cave-in?

Because Josh and I brought up the rear, we stumbled often over those who fell. We helped them to their feet and then raced on. There was no time to waste.

Hero's howls echoed off the walls. I had read that zoo and farm animals have often predicted earthquakes. Now I knew Hero had the gift.

Perhaps it was the animal's acute hearing that let them hear the rumbling before anyone else could. Or perhaps it was a sixth sense that gave them warning. In any event, Hero had set off the alarm, and I hoped we weren't too late. The tunnels were long, and we had to get clear.

The thundering above us deepened. Everything shook—even my bones and teeth. We didn't dare stop. The towering cement jungle above us would soon be falling.

Please, God! I prayed as I ran, *please help us reach safety!* And in that instant, I saw a street lamp topple and go out. We were at the door!

But we didn't stop. We pressed forward through a hail of bricks, tiles, glass, and more. On we raced, down littered sidewalks and streets.

"This way!" Foley cried over the deafening roar. And as if performing a fire drill in grade school, we forged ahead, obediently observing the commands the group had practiced.

"Where are we going?" I panted to Josh.

He pointed ahead. "It's a park!" he shouted. "No buildings!"

Behind us, an explosion told me a skyscraper had fallen. A thirty-foot cloud of dust rolled our direction and threatened to overtake us.

"Don't stop!" Foley bellowed. And Hero kept barking.

The ground now shifted from side to side, sometimes throwing us off our feet. But we didn't stop.

I stumbled over someone, and I struggled to help them up. *A child. Is he hurt?* With a strength I didn't know I possessed, I yanked him from the ground and slung him over my shoulder. And I ran. The voices ahead of me had grown fainter, but I could hear, and I kept moving.

And then I tripped. The cement under my feet had given way to grass. We were at the park. I wanted to stop. My lungs were bursting, and my eyes stung. But I heard Foley's voice urging us on.

"This way!" Foley cried. "Don't stop!" And the adrenaline of fear lifted my feet.

Even though we were away from the buildings, the dust thrown up by the crashing skyscrapers continued to thicken. I feared that soon I wouldn't be able to breathe, not even through the shirt I had pulled over my face.

Somewhere up ahead, I heard Foley shouting for the men to use their crowbars. "Break the lock!" he commanded, and I wondered what they were breaking into. I got my answer when I caught up and rushed under the overhead door of the park's one-story maintenance garage.

"Inside, everyone! Hurry!" Foley bellowed to me and other stragglers who were still behind me.

Dodging the vehicles sheltered in the building, we flooded in, and Foley pulled the door down. The quaking continued, and so did our fear.

Crash! Rumble! Thunder! Crash!

Like dominoes, one by one, all of the skyscrapers hit the ground. At each explosion and tremor, on top of the ongoing quake, we shuddered. *Will the garage hold together?*

On and on the violence persisted until we thought our minds would break, too.

Only after a long half hour did the thunder and shaking subside. Now, smoke from fires added to our collective coughing. Cement dust had followed us indoors, and I pictured a suffocating cloud hovering over the city's ruins. No doubt, we all would have died inhaling its choking particles if we hadn't made it to the garage—a garage that remained whole and unbroken. Foley had chosen well.

As the quake's rumble dulled, I heard children crying and women weeping. There were no windows in the garage and no way to see one another. Like a good commander, Foley pulled our concentration into a headcount. Husbands, wives, and children were mingled throughout the dark garage, and the headcount served to assure that all family members were accounted for. Foley yelled out surnames, and the head of each family ran the roll call and gave a report.

"Thomases all accounted for."

"Bakers all here."

"The Lewis family is safe."

And so on.

The list rang out until only Foley's family remained. Sabrina shouted her name and Foley shouted his, and they waited to hear Joey call out. But there was no response. Sabrina screamed for her son, and the child sleeping on my shoulder roused. "It's me, Mommy," he cried out.

I had not realized that Joey was the child I had picked up and carried. "He's safe!" I hollered. And in the dark, Joey was passed from person to person until mother, father, and son were reunited.

Now, I called out, "Josh! Where are you?"

And Josh answered from the blackness. "I'm here, Cricket. And so is Hero. Don't worry."

Josh's voice reassured me, but it was unnerving to be *blind* in this dark place. To my relief, someone lit a tin-can candle, and faces began to appear. With more candles, the interior of the garage took shape. Our shelter wasn't much. I despaired that it differed little from the labyrinth we had just left.

And then we heard the rain. It was a violent downpour, not a gentle rainfall. Torrents of water pelted the roof.

Parents attempted to calm a new panic in their already traumatized children. "The rain is a good thing," I heard repeated over and over.

I had forgotten that these little ones had never seen or heard rain, and certainly not a thunderstorm. The pounding above us and the great claps of thunder and strobes of lightning unnerved us all. *Would peace ever return?*

At last, Foley's calm voice announced, "If we can settle the children, we need to sleep. We can assess things better in the morning." Then he said, "Thank You, God, for giving us shelter and our lives. We are grateful to be safe. Thank You for Your everlasting love and providence. All praise to Your Name! Amen."

In our exhaustion, and despite the howl of the storm and our endless coughing, we did manage to sleep.

~ ~ ~

Although it was impossible to tell by the darkness inside the garage, morning must have come. Thunder and quake aftershocks kept our hearts pounding, and the rain continued. But Foley's wife, Sabrina, lit the tin-can candles and rounded up grain bars from the women's backpacks. Foley prayed, and we ate.

Cement dust and smoke ash darkened the sober faces in the dim light, and I assumed my face looked the same. Dust caked everyone's hair, and I wanted a shower. But I was glad I was alive.

Cough! Cough! The hacking sound echoed throughout the garage.

I wished I could breathe and talk without coughing and tasting cement. Everyone had suffered damage, and I worried most about the lungs of the little ones.

Josh had joined me for breakfast, and Hero was snuggled in my lap. "Good boy," I said as I kissed Hero's ear and broke off some of my grain bar for him. I reflected that Hero had saved me twice.

Thank You, God, for this dog, I prayed. *And thank You for getting us to this safe place in time.*

My words echoed those of Foley's prayer during devotions after breakfast.

~ ~ ~

As the morning wore on, I struggled with what constituted *safe.* The garage had not fallen in or been crushed, and it offered safety away from the labyrinth. But it seemed to me that we had just exchanged one prison for another. And this one was worse because there would be no food to scavenge. The restaurants had been obliterated. There would be no garbage to pick through. And the water bottles would soon be empty.

Water seemed to be on Foley's mind, too, because he called for everyone to collect pans and buckets from the corners of the garage to set out in the rain. Mothers removed their children's clothes so the dirty items could soak, and I decided that the rain might be a blessing, after all.

Then, before the door was opened and the buckets set out, Foley lifted his voice. I had never heard him sing, and his rich baritone resounded in a rallying cry to the God of Heaven:

Surround me with Your holy band,
And guard me with Your sword;
And challenge all who seek to maim—
Repel them with Your Word.

Fight for me with clash of wings
And cherubim on high,
And with Your glory blind my foes
And lift Your banner high!

Help me to know Your force is near;
Let me hear You in the trees,
To know the sound of battle gear
And rams' horns in the breeze.

Open the blindness of my eyes
To see Your bright array,
To count Your warriors on the hills
And Your watchers on my way.

For greater are they that guard my ways
Than those that clang and roar.

For the battle is already won—
With victory, evermore!

[RAMS' HORNS IN THE BREEZE, BY DEBBY L. JOHNSTON]

By the third stanza of *Rams' Horns in the Breeze,* everyone joined him. The words filled the garage, and some (a cohort of teenage boys) lifted their hands like an army charged for battle. Smiles remained on the group's faces after the strains faded. It was comforting to sing.

But suddenly, Hero left my lap and stood barking at the garage door. One of the children called out, "Stop! Listen."

I closed my eyes, as if it would help me hear better. And that's when I heard voices on the other side of the door.

"Please, let us in. Help us!" someone pleaded.

Until that moment, I had thought we were the only survivors from the earthquake. It startled me to think that there were others. How had they managed? The dust, alone, would have defeated anyone on the outside. And with all the fallen buildings there was no shelter.

Foley challenged, "Who are you?"

"Reverend Beech," came the reply. "And several parishioners."

"How do we know we can trust you?" Foley persisted.

The reply sounded to me like Scripture:

"Immediately after the distress of those days 'the sun will be darkened, and the moon will not give its light; the stars will fall from the sky, and the heavenly bodies will be shaken.' At that time the sign of the Son of Man will appear in the sky, and all the nations of the world will mourn. They will see the Son of Man coming on the clouds of the sky, with power and great glory. And he will send his angels with a

loud trumpet call, and they will gather his elect from the four winds, from one end of the heavens to the other."

With eyes glistening to hear the prophecy, Foley instructed his men to raise the door.

CHAPTER THIRTEEN

NOT ALONE

Rain splattered in, and we peered at a drenched and bedraggled band of seven or eight people. They hesitated before entering. Their spokesman said, "Until we heard your singing, we had thought we, alone, had survived."

The first in from their party was being carried, and he thrashed in great pain.

Foley pointed to the bed of one of the maintenance trucks and said, "You can lay him there. How was he injured?"

Blood from the wound on the man's head flowed profusely and soaked the rags that Reverend Beech's people were using to staunch it. The man's cries filled the garage.

Sabrina offered an ointment, but Beech shook his head. "It will do no good," he said. "Don't waste it."

"We have nothing to stop pain," Sabrina apologized.

And Reverend Beech assured her, "He will not live much longer. He can use only our prayers now."

Reverend Beech, an imposing gray-haired man, now prayed over the injured man. "Merciful Father, forgive my brother, a sinner like us all. He has seen his error and has returned to the fold. Lord Jesus, cover him with Your grace and prepare to raise him up with You in the heavens. Amen."

"I'm sorry about your brother," Foley murmured.

Reverend Beech corrected him. "He is not my brother by blood, but he is my brother by faith. His is a remarkable story."

I wondered how anyone's story could be more remarkable than that of every person in this garage, but I soon learned otherwise.

~ ~ ~

Reverend Beech explained: "I had gone to seminary with this man, decades ago. Gregory had been a brilliant student and a pillar of the *faith*—a *popular style of the faith* that glossed over Jesus as Savior and instead enshrined the Golden Rule that Jesus taught. After graduation, Gregory rose through the ranks of clerical leadership. As a high council member, he advised political leaders as well as clerics, and in the name of peace, he worked to resolve doctrinal conflicts. Then, when the global catastrophes began, Gregory brought encouragement and selective words from the Scriptures. He always knew what to say. Everyone respected and looked up to him.

"I began to suspect problems, however, when Gregory sided more with the political element than the clergy. Gregory advised more leniency in our spiritual teachings. And even though, at that time, I lacked a true commitment to Jesus, my alarm grew. Gregory's support by the clergy waned in direct proportion to his fanaticism over Tannin. Then the Great Disappearance occurred, and most of the planet's clergy vanished. Like several others who were left, I realized my mistake in not having seen who Jesus truly was. Gregory, however, remained unchanged. In the midst of the world-wide turmoil, he rallied the remaining flocks and became a champion for them to get Tannin's implant. 'It will solve all of our problems,' he insisted. 'There is nothing to fear,' he promised. 'See?' he said, 'I have the mark, myself!'"

Foley suddenly leaped to his feet and roared, "No!" As Foley's makeshift stool toppled and crashed to the floor, he bellowed, "I've heard enough! Are you telling me that this man is Gregory Dunn, the toady of the Deceiver Tannin? And you have helped him?"

"Wait, my friend!" Reverend Beech pleaded. "You have not heard the rest of the story. If, after you have heard it, you insist on driving us out, I will understand. But I don't think you will."

Through gritted teeth and with clenched fists, Foley growled, "You have two minutes. That man is responsible for the deaths of thousands of true Jesus followers, including dozens of my family and friends! I will not have his carcass under my roof!"

"Two minutes is all I ask," said Reverend Beech, and he hurried to relate the rest of the story. "As I have said, Gregory believed Tannin had the answers, and he faithfully supported Tannin's policies—until one day. That's the day Tannin ordered the execution of a Jesus-follower named Ralph Grupp. Grupp had been a fellow student at seminary and was a friend of Gregory's and mine. Gregory visited the prison to reason with Grupp and persuade him to recant and live. But Grupp refused to be swayed. Instead, Grupp's joyous witness impressed Gregory and kept him awake that night. When Gregory returned the next morning to talk again with his friend, Ralph argued powerfully from the Scriptures with the truth about Jesus. 'Only Jesus has the power to give souls access to God,' Grupp told Gregory. And Ralph reminded Gregory of the many Scriptures predicting the rise of false prophets in the Latter Days. Ralph pointed out the predictions of the *beast* and the *mark of the beast*. And, for the first time, Gregory saw who Jesus and Tannin were. The truth of God's Son burned through the deceits Gregory had let overtake his heart.

"From that moment, Gregory hated the mark he had taken and the evil that Tannin was imposing on the world. At news of Ralph's execution, Gregory tore his clothes and stormed out of his office building. It was when he entered the streets that the earthquakes began. Gregory found himself in front of the sad, old church under which we hid, and he ran inside. There, with knees trembling from the quakes outside and inside his soul, Gregory knelt at the altar and begged God to forgive him. 'Please, God! Please let it not be too late! I trust in Jesus and will never again abandon Him. Even if You kill me, I will still trust in You.'

"One of the younger men from our group heard Gregory's impassioned plea to God. And, in the middle of the earthquake, he dragged Gregory down to our room. Tory had no idea who he was dragging or the danger this man with the mark might bring upon us. But no one was thinking clearly in the quake's rumble. To make matters worse, when I saw that it was Gregory, I began to smash in his face. 'Traitor!' I cried. Gregory did not defend himself. Instead, he cried, 'Yes, kill me! Please kill me! I have sinned greatly against the Lord of the Universe. I do not deserve to live.' Then he cried, 'Jesus, I have been wrong! I pray it is not too late to repent. Help me, even in death!'"

On his knees, Gregory wailed his confession, saying, 'I'm responsible for innocent deaths. Because of me, even our friend from seminary was targeted for execution. And despite my inability to save him, he has saved me. Ralph reminded me of the truth, that Jesus is God's Son who loved me enough to die in my place. And Ralph pointed out the Scripture that no one with the *mark of the beast* will be found in Heaven. Ralph's words burned into my soul. The fog of Tannin's deceit lifted from my eyes, and I saw the evil I had been doing. I recognized the implant for what it was. I cried from the depths of my being. And then the earthquake began. As everyone ran to escape the falling debris and toppling buildings, I ran to this church—one of the few churches Tannin had not yet demolished, even though it stands empty. I knew the building would soon give way under the quaking, but I wanted to die here. Your man found me repenting.'"

Reverend Beech now said, "At that moment, Gregory began to claw at his forehead. His fingernails dug deep beneath the skin, and I realized what he was doing. I didn't stop him, nor did I help him. I don't know how he managed it, but Gregory clawed until he uncovered the implant, and he tore it from his head. Then Gregory cried, "As you now see, I have torn the devil's mark from me. I will live with it no longer, even though it means my death.'"

Reverend Beech stopped now. To Foley he said, "I cannot condemn this man, but if you do, and you still wish to banish us from your presence and the safety of your shelter, we will go."

Foley stared at the ceiling.

Would Foley banish Beech and his people? I wondered.

I heard Gregory's thrashing. But his moans had grown weaker. The pool of blood under his head dripped through the slats of the truck's bed and onto the garage floor.

No one spoke. All eyes studied Foley. Conflict contorted his face.

Foley later said his struggle was that of every person who had lost loved ones because of Gregory's treachery. It was the struggle to forgive. Three long years of his people's suffering rose like a wave to drown out the core message of the Cross and to smother, if possible, all reminders of the mercy and grace of God.

And while Foley battled against the avalanche of his resentments and sought to put forgiveness in its proper place in his heart, Gregory cried out, "Jesus!" and breathed no more.

Silence descended on the garage.

Reverend Beech's people bowed their heads and murmured inaudible prayers, and I wondered what Foley would do.

At first, Foley did nothing. But then he stepped forward.

Foley looked down into the bloody face of the pitiful soul he had hated. Moments passed. At last, with solemn resolve, Foley removed his ragged jacket. With it, he covered Gregory's face and wounded forehead, and with the deepest of sighs, Foley declared, "Our brother is now in Heaven."

Several in Reverend Beech's party fell to their knees, and Reverend Beech embraced Foley.

"I am sorry for my anger," Foley said. "You are all welcome here. God has led you to us, and we cannot turn you out. You are now our brothers and sisters. Together, we will wait for Jesus and celebrate when He comes."

"Thank you," murmured Reverend Beech. "Praise God!"

With the crisis resolved, even the youngest among us felt relief. Foley's son, Joey, pulled on his father's sleeve, and when Foley bent down, Joey asked, "Does this mean, I can give Brandon a cookie now?" He pointed to a boy his own age from Reverend Beech's group.

"From the mouths of children," Foley sighed, and he drew Joey close. "Of course, son. In fact, I think we could all use a moment to settle ourselves. Sabrina, could we, perhaps, prepare lunch? And then our friends can tend to Gregory."

~ ~ ~

During lunch, Reverend Beech explained his people's escape from the earthquake and how they had ended up outside our door.

"We feared our hiding place in the church catacombs would

collapse and kill us, but we had nowhere else to go," said Reverend Beech. "We prayed and waited to be buried. And somehow, by the grace of God, the ceiling of our prayer room held. We remained in hiding until every skyscraper above us had to have fallen.

"When we emerged in the rain, we stared in shock. Not a building stood, not even the church above us. And while we stood surveying the rubble, we heard our catacombs collapse below us. We had miraculously survived. But where would we find shelter now?

"We felt drawn to the park. There was no rubble at the park—just grass and mud and the maintenance garage. We hurried to the building, hoping to get out of the pelting rain. And that's when we heard your singing! It was like hearing voices from Heaven."

A woman in Reverend Beech's group sobbed, and Foley's wife comforted her. "You're safe now," Sabrina insisted. "God has been gracious to us all."

As the meal ended, Eli, the young man who shadowed Foley, opened the garage door and set out his water pails. Then Eli remained with the buckets and let the rainwater shower him, from his scarred face to his dusty sneakers.

What a wonderful idea! Everyone left the building to shower in the rain. Although it chilled us, it felt good to remove quake dust from our hair and clothes. I also noticed how the rain had cleared the air. I decided that was how Reverend Beech's group had not faced the suffocating pollution we had run through.

When we returned inside, Foley was relating for Reverend Beech our group's history. We dried ourselves and listened. Reverend Beech and his people remarked on the similarities in our experiences.

"I'm surprised," said Reverend Beech, "that we haven't run into each other at some dumpster."

Foley assured him that we were careful to steer clear if others were spotted. "We've had our share of trouble with robbers," he said, and he glanced at me.

I shuddered at the memory. But then I jumped! And I was not alone in my surprise.

Everyone jumped when the engine of one of the maintenance trucks roared to life. Over the roar, a panicked Eli shouted, "I didn't mean to do it! Really! It was an accident. I just turned a key!"

Foley rose to turn off the motor, chuckling as he went. "Eli, you'll suffocate the lot of us with carbon monoxide poisoning."

But before Foley could kill the engine, the vehicle's radio crackled to life.

"...and the earthquakes will not defeat us," we heard.

"It's Tannin," Foley declared with a sigh. "He's still alive."

Tannin's voice reverberated. "We are surveying the damage, and I can attest that it is possible to recover, no matter where you are. Take heart! And for those who can join us, please know that we continue to gather in the East for battle. We have food and supplies for everyone who is willing to fight the rebellious God-people who still refuse the implant. We will prevail against these criminals! I will address you, again, in the coming days. Listen for my messages. We have put down trouble makers, before, and have solved world problems. And we will do it, again!"

The broadcast ended, and Foley turned off the engine.

As the group discussed this turn of events, Josh pulled me aside. "We need to go," he said.

"Will we come again?" I asked.

Josh did not answer.

CHAPTER FOURTEEN

SIGHT

"Lord Almighty!" Marlene Grace cried when she swept into the room in the morning. "What has happened to you, child?"

Startled awake by her cry, I opened my eyes—and screamed. Aides from up and down the hall flooded into my room.

I kept screaming. In the midst of my screaming, I also coughed. And with each spasm I tasted dust. Marlene Grace hovered over my face in panic. "What's wrong? What's wrong, baby?" she cried.

Through a flood of tears, I sobbed. "I can see!"

My friend passed a hand before my eyes.

"Yes, I see your hand," I cried. "And I see the people at the door."

Marlene Grace drew back and shouted to heaven, "Praise God! A miracle!" And she ran to the door. "I'm going to call Dr. Ellerman right now!" she yelled over her shoulder.

After she left, I heard one of the aides at the door whisper, "Not only can she see, but it's happened again." The girl approached the bed and laid a hesitant hand on my arm. "Can you move?" she asked.

"No," I said. "But I can see!"

The aide's wan smile said she would rather have heard that I could walk. There was no other explanation for my disheveled appearance. My hair was wet, and I could see my T-shirt sleeves and dirty arms resting above the covers.

Wait until you peek under the covers and see my blue jeans and tennis shoes, I thought.

Considering what I had been through, and from all I was able to see of me, I thought I looked pretty good. But there was no logical explanation for my clothes and the wetness. And on top of it all, I couldn't stop coughing.

"How do I explain this to Mrs. Crouch?" the night aide wailed. "I swear that no one entered or left this room last night!"

Her fear made sense the moment a severe-looking woman stalked into the room. The aides parted like the waters before Moses, and in strode Mrs. Crouch. Like a pharaoh advancing, she marched to my bedside. There, the supervisor gasped sharply. "What on earth?"

Now she demanded, "Christine, what has been going on here?"

"Nothing," I replied with wide-eyed innocence.

"Nothing?" Mrs. Crouch snorted. "This is not nothing. You did not get soaked this way while sleeping in your bed! And where did you get these clothes? Is this a stunt? Who's involved in this? Kathryn? Cynthia?"

The girls she named drew back in horror. "No, ma'am! We had nothing to do with this."

Now, Mrs. Crouch peered into my face. "Kids in a nursing home," she spat. "Nothing but games!"

Then she growled, "Someone said you woke up screaming and saying you can see. I wonder, have you been able to see and walk, all along? Is this some sort of sham, Missy?"

Now, in front of the horrified aides, the indignant woman snatched a thumbtack from the bulletin board above my bed and stabbed me with it. My arm did not move.

When I didn't flinch, Mrs. Crouch stabbed me again—this time through my dirty blue jeans, in the leg.

Marlene Grace returned in time to see the second stab, and in a fury, she gripped Mrs. Crouch's hand. "You touch that child one more time and I'm going to deck you!" she said. "What do you think you're doing?"

Marlene Grace was not a small person. With her hands on her hips and fire in her eyes, she posed a formidable adversary. Mrs. Crouch took an involuntary step back before she regained her composure. The other aides stood frozen, mesmerized by the encounter.

"Just what did you think you were doing?" Marlene Grace demanded. "This baby can't feel or move a muscle, and your unsterilized thumbtack could introduce infection. You leave this girl alone!"

Mrs. Crouch stood her ground and said, "Something fishy is going on here, and I'm going to get to the bottom of it. For all I know, you're in on it!"

"Hardly!" Marlene Grace countered. "I discovered this at the same time everyone else did. I don't know the answers, but I'm certainly not going to harm Cricket to find out."

My champion bent over me and patted my forehead as she

informed Mrs. Crouch, "I've called Dr. Ellerman. He'll be here soon. In the meantime, I'm going to clean up this girl. You can stay or you can leave."

"Very well," Mrs. Crouch snarled. "But I WILL find out what's going on with this child."

I doubt it, I told myself.

"Sheila! My office!" Mrs. Crouch commanded, and the terrified hall monitor slunk after her superior.

Marlene Grace stared until the rest of the aides returned to their duties.

"Now, honey," Marlene Grace said, "let's get you cleaned up and dried off. I've never seen such a mess."

Still driven by the force of her anger at Mrs. Crouch, Marlene Grace yanked back my covers to get started. She put her hands on her hips and wagged her head at the sight of my blue jeans and muddy tennis shoes.

That's when I murmured, "I can see you. You're beautiful, Marlene Grace."

"Now, now. No use adding lying to all of this," Marlene Grace chided. "I may be pleasant to the eyes, but I'm no beauty."

"You are to me," I said. "Thank you for standing up for me."

Marlene Grace's face softened, and she stripped off my muddy clothes with less force than she had taken in yanking off my covers.

"Humph!" she said. "I may have lost my job. But nobody messes with my girl!"

Now, Marlene Grace brought a pan of water, soap, and a towel to my bedside.

"Gracious, child!" she scolded. "You are a mess! I don't know if

I can get all this off in one washing. And then I have to change these sheets!"

I knew she wasn't angry with me.

"Muddy tennis shoes in bed," she snorted. "And what are all these muddy paw prints?"

~ ~ ~

By the time Dr. Ellerman arrived, I had been sponged, shampooed, and redressed in a clean and dry nightgown and bed socks. My bedding had been changed, and the holes Mrs. Crouch had punched in me with her thumbtack had been medicated. ("Nasty woman!" Marlene Grace had muttered when she'd applied the Band-Aids.)

Marlene Grace stepped aside to let Dr. Ellerman check my eyes. I gawked at his ponytail—a thing I hadn't imagined when I was blind.

"Your sight," Dr. Ellerman asked, "did it come on slowly or all at once?"

I told him I had simply opened my eyes this morning and found I could see. "It's like I was never blind," I said.

Dr. Ellerman shined his little flashlight into each eye and watched my pupils contract. Satisfied, he smiled and put his flashlight back into his pocket.

"Well, this was a possibility after your swelling and head trauma went away. I'm very pleased to see it has happened."

I suppressed a cough, and Dr. Ellerman quickly asked, "When did the coughing begin? Is this new?"

Marlene Grace confirmed that I had been fine the night before but had awakened with a nasty cough this morning.

Dr. Ellerman made me cough into a tissue, and he examined the sputum. "This is a puzzle," he said. "If I didn't know better, I'd swear this girl has been through a dust storm! We need to get this taken care of. I'm sending her to the hospital."

Now, Dr. Ellerman noticed the Band-Aid on my arm and frowned. "And what's this?"

Marlene Grace answered before I could. "That," she spat, "is a misguided attempt by Mrs. Crouch to verify that Miss Dalton is still paralyzed. The stupid woman stabbed her with a thumbtack."

"A thumbtack?" Dr. Ellerman's eyes widened in disbelief. "Is the woman crazy? That's a good way to introduce infection."

"I know," asserted Marlene Grace. "I told her so. And I put antiseptic and a Band-Aid on it."

"I'm ordering a tetanus shot, too," Dr. Ellerman prescribed, "to be administered at the hospital." He added, "I hope Mrs. Crouch isn't in the habit of using thumbtacks on other residents."

His frown remained when he said goodbye, and Marlene Grace lifted her chin in triumph.

"That woman will no doubt hear about this and start mending her ways," Marlene Grace said.

Then Marlene Grace excused herself to pick up my breakfast tray from the trolley in the hallway. "Let's try to get some breakfast into you before the emergency vehicle arrives to cart you away."

Emergency vehicle. Hospital. I didn't want to go to the hospital. I didn't want to be alone with strangers. I wanted my Marlene Grace.

I studied my friend's face as she lifted forkfuls of eggs and toast to my lips. It was a good face, soft, brown, and round. Dark curls gathered in a knot on the top of her head, and she wore a small gold cross at her throat.

Her confident attitude showed in the way she carried herself. Marlene Grace was comfortable with herself and with being in charge of me. I was glad she was. She had stood up to Mrs. Crouch. I believed that Marlene Grace would face down a tiger, if one would dare come after me.

But I worried. *Would Mrs. Crouch fire Marlene Grace? Would she make life more difficult for the rest of the staff because of me?* The aides in the room this morning had obviously suffered under her tyranny, already.

Marlene Grace wiped my mouth at the end of breakfast. Then, before she removed my plate, she cocked her head and looked me in the eye. "Cricket," she said, "do you know what happened to you?"

I looked away. I didn't want to lie, but I didn't want to explain about Josh and the onyx stones and Foley's planet. It was too far-fetched, too fantastic. I feared I wouldn't be able to convince her, and I didn't want to live with that.

When I didn't answer, Marlene Grace didn't press.

~ ~ ~

With my eyes open at the hospital, I could see the machines and watch the activity that buzzed around me. One person took samples, another pressed and probed, and still another jotted notes on a key-board in the corner. My gray spit puzzled everyone but me.

When at last the testers left, my intensive care nurse bent to lay her cheek on mine, and she whispered, "How's my old friend, Cricket?"

"Oh, Lucy!" I cried.

"Yes, it's me, honey," she said. "And I hear you are no longer blind! How wonderful!"

"Yes!" I exclaimed. "I can see you!"

My eyes took in a young, slender woman with a blue clip the color of her eyes drawing back long, blonde hair in a soft wave. I treasured the image.

Lucy smiled and held up a syringe. "Tetanus shot," she explained. "Dr. Ellerman said you had a fight with a thumbtack."

That's one way of putting it. It would be difficult to explain the story to Lucy, so I didn't.

After Lucy gave me the shot, she warned, "I'm to sit you up now. Are you ready?" The head of the bed rose, and a moment of dizziness swept over me.

"Whoa!" I cried, and Lucy slowed the rise.

"Can't have you passing out on me," she said.

With my head finally raised, I noticed two visitors at the break in my curtain. Two men.

Lucy acknowledged them and said to me, "I'll leave you to talk with your company, but I'll be back."

The men smiled as if we were old friends. I frowned until they spoke and I recognized their voices.

"Good morning, Cricket," my Children's Protective Services representative said. "We hear you've had a bit of excitement."

Mr. Gilson's eyes reflected kindness, and his gray hair and beard reminded me of Grandpa Noffer, but I hadn't expected an older man. His voice didn't match his age.

"Yes," echoed the other man who I now recognized as Mr. Tipple. He was well dressed and clean-shaven, with rusty-colored hair.

"What's been happening?" Mr. Tipple asked. "We got a call from a woman named Marlene Grace. What can you tell us?"

Oh, oh, I thought. Then, since I had to say something, I started with the easy stuff.

"I woke up this morning and I could see!" I said.

"Yes, that's wonderful news!" said Mr. Tipple. "And I notice that you're sitting up. Great signs of progress!"

I smiled. Then I waited. I was not volunteering anything more.

Mr. Tipple tried again. He said, "We, uh, heard stories of unusual things happening at the nursing home. Can you tell us about them?"

I pretended not to know what he was talking about, and Mr. Gilson intervened. "According to staff, they found you, for a second time, in an unusual state for someone who cannot get out of bed."

My mind raced. How could I answer but say nothing? Finally, I said, "I guess the staff found me, this morning, in a kind of messed-up condition."

Mr. Tipple nodded. "Yes. And they tell us that you had on tennis shoes and street clothes over your gown. Since you can't move, it would seem that someone dressed you. Do you recall who?"

With my most innocent look, I shook my head. "Nobody's dressed me that I can think of," I said, "except for my gown and bed socks."

Mr. Tipple frowned, and I couldn't read his face.

Mr. Gilson asked, "And how did you end up muddy? Did some-one take you away from the nursing home?"

"As far as I know, nobody's moved me from that bed in all the time I've been at The Arches," I insisted.

Mr. Gilson raised a brow. "So, you're saying you've gotten dressed and dirty all by yourself?"

I wanted to say yes, but if I did, it would be impossible to explain. So, I just gave the men a confused look. Then, I went on the offensive. I asked, "Has anyone else at the nursing home had similar unexplained happenings?" The men glanced at each other in surprise.

"No, I don't believe so," Mr. Gilson said. "But we haven't asked that."

Mr. Tipple changed the subject. "I hear that Mrs. Crouch attacked you with a thumbtack. Is that right?"

I nodded. "I think she was trying to confirm that I couldn't walk, which, of course, I can't."

Mr. Gilson hurried to say, "Of course. We've had that confirmed by Dr. Ellerman."

Mr. Tipple knit his brows. "And Ellerman said you have cement dust in your lungs."

Again, I hid that I knew how that had happened. I simply said, "Is that why I've been coughing so much?"

By their looks, I could tell that my guardians didn't know what to think. They stood fidgeting in an awkward silence until Mr. Tipple said, "Well, young lady, I hope you're better soon. We'll check on you, again, in a day or two. For now, you just rest up and get better."

"Yes. Get better," Mr. Gilson echoed.

I thanked them.

When they left, I heaved a sigh. It was getting harder and harder not to tell about my adventures.

Then I coughed and tasted the dust. I would be glad when I could breathe, again, the way I used to breathe.

CHAPTER FIFTEEN

NO MORE MRS. CROUCH!

One of the best things about being able to see was that I no longer had to rely on sound for everything. For example, I didn't have to put up with the constant noise of the television in order to have entertainment. I often watched TV, now, with closed captions—captions that also let me tune out Mrs. Jamieson. Today, the more the counselor probed about the mud incident, the more I concentrated on the posted words on the hospital television screen above her head. Mr. Gilson and Mr. Tipple had passed on their report to her, and Mrs. Jamieson was trying her best to get me to open up.

"Cricket," Mrs. Jamieson repeated, "what can you tell me about the unusual incidents the nursing staff has reported?"

When my evasive answers shed no light on her inquiry, the persistent woman reverted to poking and prodding into my hurts and losses. I wanted to throw things at her—*if only I could!*

Before she left, Mrs. Jamieson broached the nursing home incident one more time, and once more I played innocent. "I go to sleep and things are normal," I said, "and then I awaken and I have on dirty clothes."

In a moment of brilliance, I asked, "Mrs. Jamieson, what do you think it is?"

Caught off guard, the counselor frowned. "I'm sure I couldn't say," she said. "But surely you remember something about what has happened, don't you? The nursing staff tells me you aren't a particularly sound sleeper."

I cocked my head as if trying to think, and I said, "I wish I could tell you, but I just can't."

Mrs. Jamieson's look said she didn't believe me, but she *really* wouldn't believe me if I told her the truth.

~ ~ ~

Intensive breathing sessions and antibiotics were clearing my lungs, and Lucy tended me with the greatest care. But while Lucy's care was comforting, it was also poignant. Because she had been my grief partner in the past, I found myself reliving many of those early moments.

And yet, I could see that my grief was changing. I could now recall happy times with my family. I pictured the love on my dad's face as he watched Mom sing hymns in church. And I remembered sharing hot chocolate with Scooter after a sledding party. Unlike before, I didn't push these memories away. I let them come, and I cried through them.

Whenever Lucy noticed my tears, she hugged my cheek without a word. And I loved her for that.

~ ~ ~

At the end of two weeks, my release drew near. I both dreaded and looked forward to leaving the hospital. I hoped things had settled at The Arches, and I hoped Mrs. Crouch would stay away and leave me and Marlene Grace alone.

I floated in and out of a nap until I heard, "Good morning, child."

"Marlene Grace!" My broken spirit leaped, even though my body could not.

My special friend swept into the room with a breeze of perfume I had never smelled before. I drank in her kiss on my forehead, and I kissed her chin.

Now she said, with a twinkle in her eye, "I've got my fella here. Is it okay if William comes in?"

Aha! I thought. *That's why the perfume. You have a boyfriend!*

Flashing a smile as big as the sun, a well-dressed William strolled through the door. "How do you do, young lady?" he sang.

I liked his voice. And I loved the way he looked at Marlene Grace.

Marlene Grace brushed a stray hair from my face and said, "William and I have been out for lunch, and I told him we had to stop and visit my Cricket so I could tell her my news."

My heart skipped. Was Marlene Grace getting married?

And then I became frightened. *Is she going to leave me?*

My fear grew when Marlene Grace said, "My news is that I've quit the nursing home."

At sight of the panic in my eyes, Marlene Grace hurried to say, "But I start work tomorrow at a new job—and you'll be there with me."

I clung to her words.

"You see," she said, "I learned there's a new rehabilitation facility in Heatherton, only forty miles away. It's a place just for kids—no old folks allowed. And I imagined how wonderful it could be for my

Cricket. Nobody there would poke you with a thumbtack or let you get messed up. I invited your Mr. Tipple and Mr. Gilson to tour the place with me, and they highly approved. So, I interviewed there and explained about you and me. And they hired me. I start work, tomorrow, and you're my special assignment."

"A new place?" I murmured, as I let her words sink in. "I'm going to be in a new place with you?"

"That's right, my precious one. You and me. Wild horses couldn't keep me from taking care of my special girl."

Tears coursed down my cheeks. I was going to be with Marlene Grace in a new place—a place for kids. Marlene Grace would still be bending over me with her kisses.

My friend's tears mingled with mine, and she bent over and kissed my forehead.

William exclaimed, "I've never seen so many tears in my life!" and he pulled out a handkerchief.

He dried my tears and muttered, "God went overboard and gave women an extra bladder behind their eyes. I've never wrung out so many soggy hankies. You two are the crying-est women I've ever known—especially this woman of mine. I swear she has the biggest heart God created."

I couldn't have said it better. After all, Marlene Grace had made room in her heart for both of us.

~ ~ ~

As she had promised, Marlene Grace met me at the front door of The Treehouse Children's Rehabilitation Center when my transport arrived. As the staff wheeled my gurney into the building, I heard music and children laughing in the gymnasium on the left and saw an ice cream counter and party room on the right. An arrow in the hallway pointed to a swimming pool.

We passed dozens of young people carrying books and insulated cups. I smelled warm cookies. Cell phones flashed within a huddle of bandaged girls playing an online game. And I saw two boys in wheelchairs passing a basketball between them on their way to the gym.

I loved my room. The bright-yellow walls bore stenciled butterflies in flight above a field of flowers. From my pillow and matching powder-blue coverlet, I could peek through a window into a real garden. Everything breathed life.

And hovering over it all with her love was Marlene Grace.

"Now, things are complete," she purred. "My favorite girl is back with me, at last."

~ ~ ~

It seemed I was always being introduced to a new doctor. The Treehouse's Dr. Bolger, a pudgy, red-faced, jolly man, reminded me of Santa Claus on holiday from the North Pole. Although he had no beard and his hair was dark, Dr. Bolger could have substituted, any day, for the old elf. The doctor asked me the usual questions, asked Marlene Grace more questions, and did a quick exam. Then he scribbled notes.

"You'll be starting physical therapy later this morning," he said. "I've added you to the schedule for Crystal. Be sure you *do* everything she tells you."

He was teasing, of course. Dr. Bolger knew full well that I couldn't do or not do one thing Crystal might tell me to do. But I didn't mind his joke.

"Anything else you want to tell me before next week's visit?" Dr. Bolger asked. "I've got you on my schedule for every Wednesday at ten. And if something comes up in between, you can have Marlene Grace call me."

I had nothing more for him, and he said, "Okay then, have a wonderful day, Miss Cricket!" and he passed through the door to continue his rounds.

"I like him," said Marlene Grace. "Don't you?"

I agreed. "He's nice—and kind of funny."

Marlene Grace leaned in and whispered, "And in December he heads for the North Pole, don't you imagine?"

I laughed. Everyone must think the same thing of him.

~ ~ ~

Between Marlene Grace's attention and visits from Dr. Bolger, Crystal, and various children, my life at The Treehouse stayed busy.

I also learned that I could follow the Treehouse activities on my television. Marlene Grace split the big screen to show a movie or television on one side and a closed-circuit relay of the gymnasium or the swimming pool on the other side. Via the closed-circuit coverage, I could watch children playing wheelchair volleyball or *swimnastics*. I could listen in on a creative writing lesson and hear the essays and poems the students wrote. I could request to have the visiting baby possums stop by my room before they left the building in the afternoon. And I could order a snack at any hour of the day. Best of all, Marlene Grace could switch the programming to suit my mood.

At first, I relished every moment of life being lived around me. But little by little, my depression returned. I found I was jealous of the children moving throughout the building and interacting as they chose.

Oh, I was thankful that I could hear and see and talk. And I loved my beautiful room. But I longed to get up and move with everyone else—like Diana did.

A wheelchair-bound girl of my age, Diana often rolled herself into my room to show me something she had made in art class. Her talent lay in sketching and painting. But today, she brought an origami swan she had folded in a lesson with Mrs. Shimoda.

I admired it, and after a few minutes, Diana said, "Well, I have to go now. My mom's coming for me. Catch you, later!"

Diana's escape to the outside world underscored that even among those who had disabilities, I was still different. I could not go home at night. I had no family. And I could not leave my room or use my hands to fold origami swans.

I resented my quadriplegia, and I aimed my anger, once again, at God. *What's the point to life if I'm stuck here and can't do anything?* I demanded.

I hadn't realized that I sometimes spoke those words out loud until one day Marlene Grace put her hands on her hips and said, "You got no business talking to God like that! You tell Him you're sorry, right now. Say it."

I didn't want to say it. And I didn't. Marlene Grace stood over me clucking her tongue.

"Don't you know what a glorious creature you are, child? There's not a creature on this earth as glorious as you are. You're a human being! That means you're made in the image of God, Himself. And you have a mind and a soul that surpasses any other living thing.

"Even if you can't move—even if you were blind, even if you couldn't talk, even if you couldn't hear, even if your mind was damaged—you're still a testimony to the power of God to create a human being. Don't you toss that back in God's face!"

The intensity of Marlene Grace's anger surprised me. But she underestimated the intensity of mine. I said nothing while she worked over me and got me ready for bed.

CHAPTER SIXTEEN

THE MARK

In my sleep that night, I dreamed I was falling and could not stop. Was there a bottom? Or would I fall forever? It was a relief when a voice awakened me.

"Hey, sleepyhead! Are you awake?"

Because it was Josh's voice, I thought it might be morning, but the room was dark. I grumbled in a groggy slur, "What time is it, anyway?"

"It's just after midnight," Josh said.

"Oh, midnight," I said with my eyes closed, as if to say, *Of course, it's midnight. Why ever would I be asleep at midnight?*

I finally opened my eyes and blinked, but it was too dark to see Josh. I sighed. I shouldn't be angry. I said, "It's good to see you. I've missed you."

Josh laughed. "No, you haven't. You've been busy. You've hardly given me a thought."

I chuckled. I had to admit he was right. I had been busy every day, and when I wasn't busy, I was feeling sorry for myself. Josh plopped down on the edge of my bed, and I groaned. I needed to sleep.

Then Josh asked, "Are you interested in a quick trip?"

I forced my eyelids open. "Now?" I asked.

"Sure, sleepyhead, if you're ready."

I needed an adventure, and although I could barely think for want of sleep, I nodded. And before I could blink again, Josh had clicked the stones.

~ ~ ~

The minute my body began to float, my sleepiness left. Up and up we rose, past the butterflies on my walls, through the roof of The Treehouse, and into the star-spangled night. My gown floated gracefully about me, and I spread my arms as if to aid my flying, as I always had.

Then, I remembered, "Don't I need my jeans and tennis shoes?"

"Hopefully, you'll keep clean, this time, and won't need them," Josh called back. He was trailing food boxes, as he had on our last trip. The floating freight told me we were going to Foley's planet. I was glad. After our last visit, I had wondered if we would ever return.

"Say," I said, when I realized I had no satchel, "where's Hero?"

"Sleeping in his dog bed," Josh said.

"Oh," I replied. "He gets to sleep."

Josh chuckled. "Want to go back?"

"No way!" I said.

Then, as we'd done so many times, we soared without a sound from our solar system and into a wash of galaxies that I couldn't name. I watched for the strange planet to appear ahead of us and grow as we approached it.

This time, however, the planet seemed hidden. I couldn't pick it out until we were nearly there. The globe looked darker than before, and the clouds shrouding it were deeper. I wondered if any light reached the surface, at all.

As I contemplated the clouds, we descended through the darkness and aimed for the maintenance garage in the city park. We landed softly and silently outside the familiar door. In the darkness, I had to guess that the boxes had settled in the grass. I could see nothing. Josh knocked and announced us.

Immediately, the door raised and a shadowed Foley in dim candlelight stepped forward to welcome us. When we entered, it felt as if the outer darkness followed us. If the company in the garage had not been lit by their tin-can candles, Josh and I would not have been able to see them. Everything appeared darker and gloomier than I had remembered.

Even so, the group's greeting warmed us, and eager hands helped unpack the food from Josh's boxes.

"We've been praying you would come," Foley said. "Our food supplies have just run out, and we no longer have the resources to replenish them. The restaurants have all been demolished and so have the dumpsters. We can get water when it rains. And we sometimes find blankets, gas, or thermoses left in the remains of crushed cars, but there is no food in all the city. We've looked carefully—which we can do now in the open. All the city survivors have gone to the country. There's no one left to arrest us or to report us for dumping our toilet material into the sewer. The only troubles we have are the rats and the feral cats that have taken over the ruins."

I shuddered at the mention of rats. Would I ever forget them?

"Come. Sit down and eat with us," Foley said, and he offered thanks.

As we ate, I learned that this was the group's first meal in two days. In alarm, I realized that the children must be famished. It made sense for Sabrina to warn her son, Joey, and the other children to go slowly so they wouldn't get sick. "There's plenty of food for tomorrow," she reminded them.

"It's grown darker outside," Josh observed, and Foley agreed. "There is no sun or moon or stars. It's as if God has snuffed them out."

Foley said, "The radio reports from the countryside mention the darkness, too. We still listen to the news on the truck radio every so often. Tannin says it's even dark in other countries. But it hasn't stopped him from continuing to amass his army in the East."

"An army?" I asked. "What army is prepared to fight Tannin?"

Foley sighed. "No army. But evidently, there are large pockets of Jesus-followers in the East among the ancient God-worshippers, and Tannin is intent on wiping them out. He's going to destroy the rebuilt city and the Temple where the worship of God once flourished.

"He's also pledged to kill two prophets who have stood in the Temple city for more than three years warning people to turn from Tannin and turn to God. No one, so far, has been able to touch the men. God sends fire out of their mouths to destroy any attackers."

"But," Reverend Beech interrupted in excitement, "Tannin is simply playing into the prophecy."

"Yes," said Foley. "Tannin may eventually kill the prophets, but that will not stop the coming of Jesus. When Tannin kills the prophets and attacks the God-people, Jesus will intervene. He will return to the planet, and Tannin and his forces will be the ones to be crushed."

The teenager, Eli, interjected. "I wish we were in the East with the resistance; I'd love to fight Tannin."

Foley patted him on the back. "I know, son. But it seems that we will not be in that fight. We *will*, however, see Jesus. The moment He comes, we will know the fight is over."

"Amen!" echoed voices all around us.

"With that happy thought," Josh said, "let's break out the cookies!"

In the flickering light, I watched the children eagerly reach for a cookie. One youngster nearest me stretched over the table for his treat, and when he did, his face lit up in the tin-can candle. His eyes gleamed in anticipation. Then, as the boy sat back, I thought I saw, for a split second, a lingering glow on his forehead.

Perhaps the glow was an illusion. But Foley saw my stare and smiled.

"Yes," he said. "You've seen it, too: the mark that has appeared. See mine?" He bent over a candle, and for a moment, a glowing symbol appeared on his forehead.

As if in a rehearsed move, the entire group now leaned over the candles, and for a brief moment, the symbol glowed on every forehead throughout the garage.

"It's beautiful!" I said. "And nothing like Tannin's mark. Whatever is it?"

Reverend Beech explained: "We first noticed the symbol on Gregory. You'll remember him as the man who tore Tannin's implant from his forehead before he died. When you two left us, we prepared Gregory's body for burial. While washing the blood from his face, we held up a candle to see better, and we were astonished to see that the wound from Tannin's implant had healed and a new mark glowed in its place. At the same time, we noticed that others among us had the same glowing mark. And it comforts us to recall the Scripture that says, *'His name shall be in their foreheads.'"*

Foley said, "We believe the glowing mark is an encouragement from God to show He hasn't forgotten us. He has confirmed we are His and that Jesus is coming, soon."

"And soon, all the darkness will be gone," added Reverend Beech. "I think much of our current darkness is the fog of evil. The darkness has grown deeper because Evil thinks it is going to win. But it will not."

~ ~ ~

As those who had finished eating left the table, Foley called for Eli to come and sit with us.

"Cricket and Josh, I want you to know more about Eli," Foley said. "He's a remarkable young man and has been through a lot more than many of us." Foley patted the boy's shoulder. "Do you mind if I share about you, son?"

Eli shook his head and cast his eyes to the floor. "No. It's all right."

I examined Eli and wondered what had drawn this boy and Foley together. It was obvious the two shared a bond.

I tried not to stare at the lanky teenager's missing fingers and the burn on the side of his face. Would his story explain them?

Foley began, "I first saw Eli when he burst through the door of the church with a boxed pizza gripped tightly in his hands. Eli raced past me and slid, in one fluid motion, under the pews and out of sight. Within seconds, two muscular men—one brandishing a club—crashed in through the same door.

"'Did you see a street kid come through here?' the man with the club demanded.

"'A street kid, huh?' I hedged.

"'Yeah. A kid with a pizza,' the other man growled.

"'A pizza, huh? How could a street kid afford a pizza?' Although I stalled, I worried because I could smell the pizza. I wondered how long it would be before the boy's pursuers smelled it, too.

"Exasperated with me, the first man asked, 'Did you see him, or not?'

"I answered, 'I hope I see him, because I could use a slice of pizza.'

"The men rolled their eyes. 'Come on, Joe,' one said to the other. 'He's getting away.'

"The two men stormed out the door, and I watched them head down the street and turn the corner. When I was sure it was safe, I called quietly, 'You can come out now. They're gone.'

"The boy with the pizza slowly emerged. It was clear he didn't know if he could trust me, even after I had covered for him. 'Take your food downstairs,' I said. 'You can eat in peace. Here's a candle so you can see where you're going.' I lit a taper and handed it to him.

"I watched the boy struggle with whether or not this was a trap. 'You can leave, if you prefer,' I said. 'But I promise you'll be safe here.'

"Eli's eyes did not leave me as he approached the doorway to the basement. At the top step, he hesitated. But then he started down, and I turned back to the office to finish some reading.

"After a half hour, I looked up to see Eli standing in front of the desk. 'Can I help you?' I offered.

"'Who are you?' Eli asked.

"'Nobody,' I said. 'A nobody, just like you.'

"I watched as Eli's eyes roamed the shelves of Peter's books behind me. 'Why are you reading?' Eli asked.

"'Because this is where I found the truth,' I answered."

Josh and I were surprised now to hear Eli laugh. Foley smiled at the interruption. The until-now silent teenager rested his head against the wall and said, "I didn't know what to think that day. The only *truth* I had ever known was who was bigger than me."

Foley urged, "Go on, son. You tell it. It's your story."

Eli sat forward now.

"You have to know," Eli said, "I was the youngest in a family of seven boys. That meant I had to fight for every bite I ate, every shred of clothing I possessed, and every corner of the floor I slept on. And my parents never interfered.

"'He'll toughen up,' my dad always said, and my mother never crossed him.

"Then, Tannin announced his plan for people to get the implant and receive an annual credit balance. My dad at once saw the possibilities.

"'Seven kids!' he cried out. 'Seven times the income! Imagine it, Maggie. We're rich!'

"My heart sank. I understood, too. I knew that the implant meant I would still have nothing. My dad and brothers would use my credit to serve them. I would be their credit slave.

"That night, I ran away. I vowed to never get the implant. That way, no one could take advantage of me.

"But I hadn't counted on the extent to which my father would go to find me and force me to get the implant. He posted my picture on every light pole and building, and he promised a reward.

"Ironically, my dad's pursuit of me backfired, because when he boasted to others about how rich I would help make him, others saw the possibilities, too. They hunted for me, all right, but it was to find me first and register me at the implant center as *their* credit slave. As luck would have it, I overheard the plots and concluded I wasn't safe anywhere.

"I hid during the day and frequented garbage cans and dumpsters at night. For a while, I managed to avoid everyone. But one day, my oldest brother happened to see me, and before I knew it, I was gagged and bound. Amon dragged me home and threw me at my father's feet. 'Do I get the reward?' Amon asked. In response, my dad cursed and kicked him. Then my dad stripped off his belt and beat me with it.

"I lay on the floor for two days, still bound and gagged—and now bleeding and bruised. I saw the pain in my mother's eyes, but she could do nothing. Then, in the middle of the third night, my mother awakened me. 'Don't make a sound,' she whispered, and she removed my gag. 'Here, eat this,' she said.

"She had reheated leftovers from supper and spooned the warm food into my mouth. I cried. And so did she. 'Let me go,' I begged, but she was too afraid. And that fear was realized.

"'What are you doing?' my father's voice thundered as he entered the kitchen and discovered us. He slammed my mother against the wall and kicked me in the face. Then, he grabbed the hot pan from the stove and pressed it, hard, against my cheek. He laughed when I screamed, and he threatened to do the same to my mother, but I tripped him. In his fury, he kicked me repeatedly until I passed out.

"When I came to, everyone was eating breakfast around the table above me. And my brothers kicked me throughout the meal. Otherwise, they carried on as if I didn't exist.

"When they finished eating, my mother cleared the table and ignored me—or so I thought. In one unobserved moment, she set a paring knife on the floor and kicked it under the table. A moment later, my father collected her, and I was left alone.

"I heard my dad announce in the other room that we would be leaving soon for the implant center. 'Today's the day I get rich!' he bragged. I knew I had to get away before that happened. If I got the implant, I could be tracked. I would never get away then.

"I don't know how I managed it, but I twisted myself around so that my hands could reach the knife my mother had risked sliding to me. And I grit my teeth as I cut into my flesh in my attempts to slice my bindings. I nearly cut off two of my fingers, but I didn't care. I would gladly give two fingers for my freedom.

"I tested my cramped legs and finally managed to creep out the back door. To keep from leaving a bloody trail, I wrapped my cut hands in my shirt and fled bare-chested into the alley. For some reason, no one saw me, and I kept running.

"Soon, I was down by the river, and I washed my bloody hands and shirt. I hid under a bridge until night set in, and then I ran some more.

"I finally sought shelter in an underground area. And I scavenged whatever I could find from the trash and dumpsters. My hand didn't heal well, and I took a chance and robbed a veterinary clinic. If I hadn't, I might have died. The medicines cleared up the infection.

"On the day Foley saw me run into the church, I had robbed a pizza from a delivery car as the driver carried another order to an apartment door. I smashed the car's window and grabbed the pizza from the seat. Then I dashed into the church.

"I saw Foley when I sped by and slid under the pews. And when the two men burst in looking for me, I thought I was done for. But Foley didn't give me away. All I could think was that Foley wanted the pizza for himself. I resolved to give it to him if he would let me go. But Foley encouraged me to go downstairs and eat.

"When I had eaten and Foley had not come after me, I came back up the stairs and offered him the last two slices of the pizza.

"At first, he wouldn't take them. But I finally convinced him to. And as we talked, I saw that Foley didn't have the implant. I asked him about it, and he told me how he had become a Jesus-follower after the Great Disappearance, and how he planned to never get Tannin's mark.

"Before I knew it, I had shared my story and told Foley why I was never getting the implant. And Foley convinced me to stay at the church. 'There are others,' he said. And I stayed.

"And I came to learn about Jesus, and I asked Him into my heart. And now, I have two bounties on my head: one from my family and one from Tannin as a Jesus-follower.

"But I have a real family now. One that loves me! And I have the hope of the prophecies about Jesus' return. That's more than I have ever had in my whole life."

Foley put his arm around Eli. "And," said Foley, "I have gained a second son."

It had seemed impossible to me, as Eli had shared about his childhood, that parents could betray their children. I had never known anything but a loving family. Even though all I had were memories, they were precious memories. Even my disabilities could not compare with the torture this young man had suffered. After all, I had been cared for, every moment.

I murmured to Eli, "I'm glad God brought you to Foley."

Eli smiled. "And we're glad God has sent you and Josh with the very things we've needed in order to survive."

"Yes!" Foley exclaimed. "And, who knows? Jesus might come today, and we may not need your food deliveries anymore."

Eli replied, "Amen!"

~ ~ ~

When I opened my eyes in the morning, Foley and his people were gone. The darkness of the garage was gone. And Josh was gone.

Sunshine streamed through the curtains of my window at The Treehouse, and Marlene Grace had breakfast ready for me.

Marlene Grace asked, "Nice dreams?"

"Beautiful dreams," I said. *Beautiful because in them I could walk and run and fly.*

Marlene Grace put a straw in my orange juice and held it to my lips. After a few sips, she began to cut my bacon.

Suddenly, Marlene Grace said, "What's happened to your beautiful necklace?"

Her question startled me. But she was right. I hadn't realized I could not feel the stone at my throat. Its weight and coolness were gone.

Had the necklace fallen off?

I watched as Marlene Grace felt all around the bed. When she didn't find the necklace, she checked under the pillows and way down under the covers. She even checked beneath the bed.

"It can't be far," she reassured me. "You don't go anywhere."

I bit my tongue. *If only you knew!*

I did wonder how the necklace could be lost. I had to have had it on when we left the planet, or I wouldn't have been able to return to Earth.

Did Josh remove it after we returned? I didn't remember, but I supposed it was possible. But why would he take it? What could that mean?

As Marlene Grace grew frustrated in her search, I decided the only logical explanation was that Josh had the necklace and Marlene Grace would never find it.

I found myself saying, "It's okay. It'll probably turn up. But if it doesn't, it's all right. It's just a stone. I have another like it in my rock collection at home."

Even as I said it, however, I knew the onyx in my collection was not the same. No one but me would know the difference. No one else would know that Josh's stone was magic!

If Josh had taken the stone, I wondered if it meant he would not be returning. I didn't like that thought. I hoped it wasn't true.

Marlene Grace cleared up my empty breakfast tray and went to return it to the kitchen.

~ ~ ~

The minute Marlene Grace left, the door to my room opened and Josh stepped in.

"So, she's got you eating pancakes now, I see."

I refused to answer. If Josh had taken the necklace, I was angry with him.

"Does she bring you strawberry syrup, too?" he asked.

Still, I refused to acknowledge him. I turned my face to the wall.

"You have to talk to me, sometime," Josh said, "or it's going to be a long day with me sitting here, staring at you." He plopped on the edge of my bed, and my head shook on my pillow.

I was going to say, *go away, I'll spend my Saturday however I like,* when I felt a wet, little tongue wash my ear. I turned from the wall, and Hero wagged his tail and licked my nose.

"He missed you," Josh said. "I finally had to bring him so he wouldn't think you had died."

I remembered that I was angry with Josh. "I might as well be dead," I said. "You don't visit me anymore, and I can't do anything but lie here while everybody else is out having fun."

"Oh, poor me!" Josh mocked. "I'm in a beautiful room with an exceptional caregiver, and I can see, but I want more or I'm going to sulk for the rest of my life!"

I felt heat rise in my cheeks. "What do you know about it? You've never had to say goodbye to your family and friends and be stuck in places you don't want to be stuck in."

"So," Josh said, "you're the only person in the world who has it so bad? What a pity!"

Then he jumped off the bed and shouted, *"Snap out of it!"*

I expected Marlene Grace to come running; she had to have heard his shout. But no one came to the door.

"That's easy for you to say!" I shouted back. "You can just wander around and click your stones together whenever you want and do anything in all the universe. But I can't!"

Then, I added, "And where is my stone, by the way? Did you take it back?"

"*Your* stone? Did you say it was *your* stone? I thought it was *my* stone. Don't you have things a little mixed up?"

"Well, didn't you give it to me?"

Josh stood over my face now. "I let you use it. But it's not *your* stone," he said emphatically.

Now I sighed. "So, I suppose there won't be any more adventures in my future?"

"You really are in a funk, aren't you?" Josh retorted.

"So, why do you care?" I snapped back.

"Whoa! Who was it who brought you pancakes at that awful nursing home when you couldn't see or eat or sit up? Who was it who visited you and shared stories? Who was it who took you to your house and took you on adventures?"

Now I felt ashamed. "Sorry," I mumbled. "I didn't mean that." I turned to look at Josh.

"I should hope not," Josh said. "Not that I'm expecting any big thanks, or anything…"

Tears threatened, and I said quietly, "I am thankful. I really am. I just miss all that we did. I miss being able to go places, and I miss helping Foley's people."

Then a thought came, and I asked, "Did Jesus ever come?"

Josh smiled. "What do you think?"

I replied, "I think He did."

Josh pulled a bone from his pocket and set it on the floor. Hero promptly jumped from the bed to gnaw on it on the rug.

Josh plopped again on the edge of my bed. "I've been thinking," he said.

He left such a long pause that I finally asked, "What have you been thinking?"

"I think I'm going to leave Hero here, with you."

I protested in surprise. "I can't take care of Hero! You can't leave him here."

"Too late!" Josh said, and he disappeared.

~ ~ ~

Marlene Grace would be back at any moment. What would she think when she found Hero on my rug, gnawing on a bone?

In a panic, I thought, *she'll shoo him outside! He'll be on the streets, again!*

And before I could think further, Marlene Grace pushed open the door.

I saw her slowly turn her head to eye the little dog on my rug. Then she looked at me. Then she looked back at Hero. From my angle on the bed, I couldn't see what Hero was doing. From Marlene Grace's half-smile, I assumed the little terrier had stood and was wagging his tail in his most winning form.

"Well," uttered Marlene Grace, "what have we here? A stray Jack Russell?"

Marlene Grace walked over to the rug. When she bent down, Hero stood on his hind legs. He was just tall enough now that I could see him lick her face. I held my breath.

I let it out when Marlene Grace began to laugh. "I don't know where you came from, but you sure are a cute one," she said. She picked up Hero and looked into his face.

Before I thought, I blurted out, "He's mine. He's my dog."

Too late I realized that statement made no sense. How could Hero be my dog? Surely, Marlene Grace would demand an explanation.

Instead, she simply said, "I assumed as much since he's in your room."

I couldn't tell if she was teasing me or humoring me. Either way, she couldn't possibly believe Hero was my dog. What would she do now?

To my surprise, she did nothing. She put Hero back on the rug and picked up my hairbrush from the dresser.

"Excuse us," she said to the terrier, "but we have some beautifying to take care of here." Then she proceeded to brush the night twists out of my hair.

Hero put his paws on my bed and watched.

"Well, what do you think?" Marlene Grace asked him when she finished.

Hero yipped once and panted a happy grin.

"I agree," said Marlene Grace, and she returned the brush to the dresser.

I expected Marlene Grace to quiz me now about where Hero had come from. But instead, she said to the dog, "I have to leave for a few minutes. Will you keep Cricket company for me?"

As if he understood perfectly what she had said, Hero jumped onto the bed and lay down. Marlene Grace laughed and left the room.

A few minutes later, I heard a knock on the door. Diana, the girl who had shown me her origami swan, wheeled slowly into the room. Diana barely said hello before she asked, "Marlene Grace said you have a dog. Can I see him?"

Has Marlene Grace reported Hero? Somehow, Diana had overheard Marlene Grace telling someone about him. *Are staff members going to come now and remove him?*

Hero greeted Diana by jumping into her lap. With tail wagging and an excited squirm, he licked her chin, and Diana giggled. "He's so friendly!" she cried. "What's his name?"

"His name is Hero," I said. "He's my hero. He saved me once, from a bunch of rats."

Diana's eyes widened. "How exciting! You will tell me the story, won't you?"

Before I could decide what to tell her, Ian, another Treehouse friend, peered around the corner. "Did I hear you have a dog?"

"Yes," I said. "This is Hero."

On his crutches, Ian edged his way to Diana's wheelchair. Hero lifted his nose to sniff Ian's hand. With a wide grin, Ian stroked Hero's ears and scratched his back. "What a neat dog!" Ian exclaimed.

Within seconds, two other children showed up at my door, and then two more. Soon, there were ten children in my room, with Hero as the center of their attention. The laughter I had heard on my first day at The Treehouse now filled my room, and this time, I was a part of it.

When I looked up, Marlene Grace stood at the door, smiling. I knew she was going to let me keep Hero.

~ ~ ~

Marlene Grace added Hero to her routine. Each night after she let him out, Marlene Grace tucked me in and set Hero next to my pillow. In the morning, she let him outside to do his business, and when he came back in, Hero and I had our pancakes. At lunchtime, Hero visited the lawn again, and Marlene Grace supplemented his diet with dog food in a bowl next to my dresser.

"Someday," she winked, "you're going to have to tell me where this little terrier really came from."

I smiled but said nothing. My story would be too far-fetched. But I did begin to tell stories to the children who gathered each day to play with Hero. I told them about the magic onyx stones and flying to another planet. I told them about the first time I had seen Hero. I knew the children would accept the stories as stories, and I could tell about my adventures as if I were weaving tall tales.

The boys loved the scary part about the rats, and the girls shuddered. But everyone demanded more stories each day.

What I didn't realize was that Marlene Grace stood at the door and listened to my tales. One day she asked how many people lived in Foley's labyrinth.

"I ask," she said, "because my family was from a poor section of New York City. As children, my brothers and I explored every alley and old building. I remember sneaking, once, through a broken cellar window and finding several levels of underground rooms and hallways. So, I can picture the labyrinth you describe. I'm just surprised that you know about such things."

As she waited for my explanation, my mind whirled with what to say. I couldn't tell her of my adventures; she would never understand. It was better that Marlene Grace thought I was making it all up.

I chose an alternative approach and shifted attention. "Did you ever have to hide underground?" I asked.

Marlene Grace's response sobered me. Looking at the floor with a shadowed expression, she replied, "Yes. Once."

She fluffed my pillow and said, "I was about your age when my dad's brother, who lived with us, got picked up for drug trafficking. The police thought the whole family was in on it and came to take everyone to the police station for questioning. I ran away, and I hid in an underground hallway until they left. Then I came out and went to a friend's house. I went back home after the police released my parents.

"My dad was a minister. And I guess the police decided he wasn't involved in the drugs. Our only mistake had been to take in Danny. Danny was on parole for stealing, and keeping him had been difficult. We suspected he was involved in something illicit, and he was. And after this arrest, Danny went back to prison."

I tried to imagine Marlene Grace as a little girl in such a household. "It must have been hard," I said.

Marlene Grace smiled. "It was, child. It was hard. But Jesus always helped us."

"How did you end up in Ohio? You said you grew up in New York."

"Well, that's a long story. But the short of it is that I had an elderly aunt who lived here. After my nursing training, she asked if I would consider coming to care for her. And I did. Then, after she died, I stayed here."

"Do you still have family in New York?" I asked.

"Of course," Marlene Grace said. "My father still preaches from time to time at the church he retired from, and I visit whenever I can. Here, I'll show you."

Marlene Grace input a password into her phone and pulled up a dozen family photos.

"These are my parents," she said. "And here is my sister, Alice. And that's me when I was younger."

In the older photos, Marlene Grace looked like Lorna. And

Marlene Grace's parents wore hats and dress coats. It must have been a wintry Sunday morning.

Now Marlene Grace scrolled to another set of photos. As she did, I stopped her.

"Can you go back one?" I asked. "Go back to the picture of the church." When she did, I asked, "What church is that?"

"That was my father's church, the one he pastored," she said. "St. Andrew's."

When she said the name, a chill tickled the back of my neck. *What a coincidence! Marlene Grace's church, although in better condition, could be the church I had seen on Foley's planet. And the further coincidence was that it bore the same name.*

"We lived a few blocks from the church," Marlene Grace said, "in a tall apartment building."

"But," she added, "nearly every building in that part of New York City is tall."

I had to ask. "Was everything concrete and skyscrapers, or were there any trees or grass near you?"

"Oh," said Marlene Grace, "there are scores of parks in New York City. The one nearest my home was just a small park. Only locals visited it. If you wanted a big park, you had to go to Central Park. Central Park is huge!"

I wondered if Marlene Grace's home and park were anything like Foley's park and the buildings near the abandoned church. And I pictured Marlene Grace's underground hiding place. She had said my description of the labyrinth was surprisingly similar.

How strange, I thought. *Two worlds. Two stories. But similar settings. What were the chances of that?*

CHAPTER SEVENTEEN

IT'S AMAZING WHAT
A CHIN CAN DO

D r. Bolger arrived unexpectedly one Saturday in the company of Mr. Tipple and Mr. Gilson. All three seemed eager to share something.

"We have news," Dr. Bolger said. "There's been a development."

Mr. Tipple rocked on his toes with his hands in his pockets. He was proud of something, and I wondered what he had done.

Dr. Bolger explained. "Mr. Tipple has ordered for you a specially equipped, motorized wheelchair designed for quadriplegics like yourself."

"The money came from your trust," Mr. Tipple explained.

"And," called Marlene Grace from the hallway, "here it is!"

With a flourish, Marlene Grace wheeled in a curious-looking wheelchair with Hero in the seat. The little dog rolled in like a tiny king.

"Wow!" I cried. "A wheelchair! For me! A way for me to go somewhere besides this room?"

162

Before I could cry, Marlene Grace said, "Here you go!" She whipped back my coverlet, slipped her arms under my useless legs, and lifted me. Cradling my head to keep it from wobbling, she transferred me to the chair.

The chair's back was molded to support my body, and a special headrest formed around my head—but not so tightly that I couldn't move my neck. A buckle and belt kept me from sliding down or off to one side, and each foot, arm, and hand sat in a specially formed mold. All of my paraphernalia (catheter, etc.) fit into a space in the back.

"Come," Marlene Grace called after she smoothed a blanket over my lap. Hero didn't need a second invitation. He jumped up for another ride.

"Let's go!" Marlene Grace called out, and she wheeled me at a rapid pace to the door and down the hallway to the gymnasium.

"It's Cricket! She's got a new chair!" my friends shouted, and they explored the chair's design.

"Have you tried the controls yet?" Ian asked.

And I started to say, "I can't move any controls." But Marlene Grace stopped me.

"This," she said, "is your control."

A rig appeared from behind my head. When Marlene Grace lowered it to sit in front of my face, a funny-looking *finger* pointed at my chin.

Marlene Grace explained: "When you touch the end of this control with your chin, or grip it with your teeth, you can decide whether the chair goes forward or backward or right or left. And you can adjust the speed by how much force you put on the stick. To stop, you simply lift your chin away from the control. Shall we try it?"

The children watched and cheered as I practiced, sometimes successfully and sometimes not. Diana teased that she was jealous; she had to move her arms to wheel herself around. "You only have to move your chin."

It was a wonder. I could hardly believe that such a vehicle existed and that I was going to be free. I would now be able to go anywhere and join The Treehouse kids in their activities.

"We'll follow you," Diana suggested. "You lead us, okay? It'll be like a game."

"Are you sure?" I asked. "I'm not very good at this."

"We're sure!" the others yelled. "Lead the way!"

True to their suggestion, the kids followed me like Simon Says, in circles and squares and all around the edge of the gym. They laughed and tried to do the same mess-ups I did when I got confused with the controls. Hero barked with their laughter and moved his paws from my right armrest to the left armrest as I spun and changed direction. Hero enjoyed the game as much as I did.

After I had taken us around the gym several times and had performed an unknown number of figure eights and S curves and spirals, I ran out of ideas. But then, I had a thought.

"I want an ice cream cone," I announced.

"Great idea!" Marlene Grace said. "Anybody want to join Cricket?"

A chorus of yeses answered her.

"Okay, then. Follow Cricket!" Marlene Grace cried. And after several hesitations and some unintended starts and stops, I led everyone to the ice cream counter near The Treehouse entrance. There, two servers dished up the dessert for our party.

Mr. Tipple stayed and watched our game in the gym, and he joined us at the ice cream counter. I was glad for the chance to speak to him.

"Thank you, Mr. Tipple," I said. "I must admit that I haven't appreciated you until now. Thank you for looking out for me and my interests. My parents would be happy with what you've done."

"It's what I'm supposed to do," Mr. Tipple said. "I'm glad to do it."

After the party ended and the usual day's routine of the children resumed, my guardian said goodbye.

Marlene Grace cleared away my empty dish and spoon and asked, "Happy?"

"Yes," I answered. "Happy, and afraid I may be dreaming."

Marlene Grace assured me it was no dream. She bent to touch my cheek and kiss my forehead.

"I still can't believe it," I said.

With a happy sigh and a sheepish grin, I asked, "I know I can move myself. But would you wheel me back to my room?"

Marlene Grace chuckled. "Still like to be waited on, huh?" Then she insisted, "Honey, I'd be delighted to take you to your room. I would wheel you to the moon and back, if you wanted."

"I know," I replied. And I swallowed a smile. Little did she know that I had already been there.

~ ~ ~

"Why, look at you!" exclaimed Pastor Howard with round eyes. He had not seen me in a couple of weeks and hadn't any idea I was now in a wheelchair.

"Would you look at that, Lorna!" he repeated to my Sunday school classmate. To me, he said, "When did this happen?"

"It's brand-new," I said. "And it's motorized. See?" I wheeled a couple of feet backwards and then returned.

Lorna, half-hidden behind Pastor Howard (I had never met anyone so shy), peered at my steering finger. "That's amazing," she whispered.

"It is, isn't it?" I replied. "It's a miracle to me to be able to do things and go places."

Pastor Howard had petted Hero, who sat in my lap, but Lorna had held back. Now, Hero jumped down to brace his front paws on Lorna's knees. She giggled, and Hero licked her hand until she petted him.

"That's Hero," I said, and the little dog returned to my lap and wagged his tail.

"It's good to see you, Lorna," I offered.

I knew it had taken a lot of willpower for her to visit me. Lorna's backward ways left her out of many circles and conversations. In Sunday school, Lorna might have been invisible, except that I had always made a point of saying hello to her.

Pastor Howard helped move things along. He pulled up a chair for my friend. "Lorna's brought your Sunday school book," he said. "She's offered to read the lesson to you, if you want."

I smiled. "Of course. That would be nice."

Lorna remained motionless, fingering the booklet she clutched in her hands.

Pastor Howard invented an excuse to leave—at least I recognized it as an excuse to leave us alone. "I need gas in my car," he said, "or we're not going to get home. I'll just slip over to the gas station and be back in a few minutes."

After he left, Lorna still didn't budge. Short black curls framed her pretty tan face, and her eyes burned a hole in a spot on the floor.

I knew she wouldn't talk until I spoke, so I said, "I'm glad you've come, Lorna. You're the only visitor from church I've had, besides Pastor Howard."

Lorna looked up and murmured, "I didn't want you to be alone. And I thought you might like to hear the Sunday school lesson." She added, "Pastor Howard says you can see now, but it must be hard to read when you can't hold the book." Her eyes rested on my motionless arms set in the arm-grooves of the wheelchair.

How remarkable that Lorna has thought about what it must be like for me. It's as if she has put herself in my place. It's marvelous. She seems to feel things differently than most people.

"You're right," I said. "I can't hold a book. And I do like to read. It's very thoughtful of you to bring the Sunday school lesson. What's the topic for this week?"

Lorna focused now on her mission and turned several pages. "We're studying in Acts," she said. "We're on the last part of chapter seven and the first part of chapter eight, about the death of the apostle Stephen."

I knew the general story, and I prepared to listen. "Go on," I urged, and Lorna began.

"Acts 7:54–8:3," Lorna read.

"The Jewish leaders were infuriated by Stephen's accusation, and they shook their fists in rage. But Stephen, full of the Holy Spirit, gazed steadily upward into heaven and saw the glory of God, and he saw Jesus standing in the place of honor at God's right hand. And he told them, 'Look, I see the heavens opened and the Son of Man standing in the place of honor at God's right hand!'

"Then they put their hands over their ears, and drowning out his voice with their shouts, they rushed at him. They dragged him out of the city and began to stone him. The

*official witnesses took off their coats and laid them at the feet
of a young man named Saul.*

*"And as they stoned him, Stephen prayed, 'Lord Jesus,
receive my spirit.' And he fell to his knees, shouting, 'Lord,
don't charge them with this sin!' And with that, he died.*

*"Saul was one of the official witnesses at the killing of
Stephen.*

*"A great wave of persecution began that day, sweeping
over the church in Jerusalem, and all the believers except the
apostles fled into Judea and Samaria. (Some godly people
came and buried Stephen with loud weeping.) Saul was going
everywhere to devastate the church. He went from house to
house, dragging out both men and women to throw them
into jail."*

Lorna was an excellent reader and didn't stumble over a single
difficult word. And as she read, I was amazed that although I had heard
this story before, it seemed different to me, today. It was Foley and his
people I pictured being imprisoned, killed, and driven underground.
Instead of dismissing Stephen as a vague figure from two thousand
years ago, I felt his story come alive. I could visualize what it meant to
be persecuted for believing in Jesus.

When Lorna finished, she and I discussed the questions printed in
the lesson book, and I found my thoughts wandering to a planet so different and yet so like our own.

Lorna mistook my preoccupation for tiredness, and she said, "I
think you're getting sleepy. It's okay if you want to close your eyes
and take a nap. I don't mind. I'll just wait here until Pastor Howard
returns."

What a sweet spirit my friend has! But before I could object and give my full concentration to the last question of the lesson, Pastor Howard returned. Lorna closed her book and withdrew into her quiet world.

"Thank you, Lorna," I told her. "I hope you'll come again."

And I thought how, one day, I could maybe tell her how her reading of the lesson had affected me and why. I would have told her now, but at this moment she would not understand.

CHAPTER EIGHTEEN

LIKE A GENIE

Marlene Grace did not appear until after breakfast; someone else brought my tray and served my food. It was unusual for Marlene Grace to be absent, and I hoped everything was all right. Perhaps she and William had made a late night of it, and seven o'clock had come too early. She would, no doubt, arrive apologizing and yawning.

The aide helped me into my chair to wait for her.

When Marlene Grace did arrive, around noon, she was not subdued. Bearing a package, she danced into the room ahead of Mr. Tipple. "I'm so excited!" she cried. "I can't wait for you to see what Mr. Tipple and I picked up this morning."

Her eager fingers tugged under the cardboard flaps and yanked the box open. Mr. Tipple rocked on his toes with his hands in his pockets, as he had on the day of my wheelchair delivery. I wondered what he and Marlene Grace had brought for me this time.

With a squeal of "See!" Marlene Grace extracted a new-generation ItsA-Phone-and-More and a flexible harness.

My mouth flew open and I cried "Oh!" even before I learned the full extent of what I was seeing.

"Wait until you see how this works!" Marlene Grace exclaimed. Mr. Tipple rocked faster on his toes, and his eyes formed little smiles to match his lips.

Marlene Grace expertly pinched the new harness into shape and fit it around my neck. Then she attached the IAPM phone to special clips on the harness so that its screen hung at reading distance from my face. A stylus, parked in a special grip beside the screen, pointed at my chin.

I was prepared to act amazed at the wonders of the World Wide Web (with which I had been well versed long before my accident), but Marlene Grace didn't turn on the phone. Instead, she stepped back and said, "Now, pick up the stylus in your teeth and press the round dot at the bottom of the screen."

Okay, I thought, *she's letting me turn on the phone. Then she'll scroll to something wonderful.*

I bit the end of the stylus and pulled it from its grip. I poked it at the round dot on the phone, hitting it on the first try. The screen lit up, as I expected.

Marlene Grace now punched in several codes to activate the phone and set its password. Then she backed away.

"Now," said Marlene Grace, "choose the app symbol on the far right."

Surely, she's joking, I frowned. *I'll end up cross-eyed trying to hit that little symbol with this stylus between my teeth.*

"You can do it," Marlene Grace encouraged. And after a couple of tries, I did manage to hit the app symbol. When I did, a list of books appeared—books I recognized and had long wanted to read.

"Great!" I cried, with the stylus still between my teeth. "Now you can read to me."

"Wrong!" Marlene Grace laughed. "There's more."

Now she instructed, "Pick a book you like, and tap it twice."

How easily I had whipped through such commands with my thumbs on my phone before the accident. But that phone was gone, along with my thumbs. I shook my head at the long list and small type. The lines were too close together.

"Just try it," Marlene Grace encouraged.

I sighed and aimed, and my jaw tensed. And on the third try, I managed to hit *Prince Caspian* by C. S. Lewis.

The book cover filled the screen. I had read *The Lion, the Witch, and the Wardrobe,* the first of Lewis's classic Narnia adventures, and I looked forward to having Marlene Grace read me this follow-up story. But Marlene Grace had other ideas.

"Now," Marlene Grace said, "swipe the screen from right to left to turn the page."

No problem, I thought. *This is familiar. I can do this, just like I used to with my fingers.* I swiped with the stylus and read, "Chapter One. The Island."

In a delayed reaction, I realized what I had done—and what more I could do. "No hands!" I crowed. "I can read this entire book without having to bother you."

"Or if you prefer," Marlene Grace said, "you can *listen* to it. Let's wake up Luxor."

I could have tapped the app, but Marlene Grace reached over and did it for me. Instantly, Luxor came alive. "How may I assist you?" a surprisingly human-sounding voice asked.

"Luxor," said Marlene Grace, "turn on the movie *The BFG.*"

"Thank you," said Luxor. "I will turn on *The BFG*."

Like an obedient genie from a bottle, Luxor turned on the movie already in progress. *The BFG* had just been seated at Buckingham Palace with the Queen and was shaking a bottle of green liquid. I laughed because I knew what was coming next. But before the fun could play out, Marlene Grace said, "Luxor, turn off the movie," and the screen reverted to the app selections display.

"Is there anything else I can do for you?" Luxor asked.

"Yes," said Marlene Grace. "Go to the email app."

"Very well," said Luxor. "Accessing the email app."

A blank email appeared on the screen that read *From Cricket,* and a blinking cursor sat on the TO line. Luxor asked for the recipient's name, and Marlene Grace whispered, "Tell Luxor to address the message to me." I did as she suggested, and Marlene Grace's email address appeared.

Now Luxor asked, "What message do you wish to send?"

Marlene Grace whispered again, "You don't need your stylus. Luxor will type in any message you want. Just remember to give him punctuation instructions as you go."

At once, I told Luxor to say, "Marlene Grace comma I love my new ItsA-Phone exclamation point exclamation point exclamation point."

Luxor thought my triple exclamation point was overkill, because he asked if I was sure I wanted three exclamation points. Marlene Grace and I laughed. "Yes, Luxor," I said, "I want three exclamation points."

"Very well," said Luxor, and all three exclamation points appeared on the screen.

"Is there more to your message?" Luxor asked, and when I told him no, he asked if I was ready to send.

I told him yes, and the message disappeared, replaced by the word *Sent.*

Luxor asked if I needed anything else, and I told him, "No, thank you."

Luxor politely responded with, "Goodbye," and the Luxor image on the screen turned dark.

I punched the stylus back into its holder so I could cry out, "Oh, Marlene Grace! I had thought my life was over! Days ago, I could do nothing on my own. And now, I can move and read and write and choose my own television shows and movies. I can even do research!"

"Yes!" replied Marlene Grace. "And Luxor can help you. You can use your stylus, or you can ask Luxor to open apps, open books, turn pages, and even read out loud."

"It's a miracle!" I cried. "It's almost like being *me* again!"

That drew a near sob from Marlene Grace. "I know, my precious girl. You have been a prisoner far too long!"

Although I couldn't be sure, I suspected there were tears in Mr. Tipple's eyes, too. He was no longer rocking on his toes, and he cleared his throat several times.

"Thank you!" I told him and Marlene Grace.

Mr. Tipple nodded and said, "You're welcome, Cricket." Hero jumped from my lap and stretched up for a scratch on his ears from the man. It was the first time I'd ever seen Hero go to my guardian. Mr. Tipple bent, patted Hero, and said, "Good dog!"

"That's right, Hero," Marlene Grace said. "We need to thank Mr. Tipple." Then she said, "And there's one more surprise."

I couldn't imagine anything more, but the last surprise brought my gift full circle.

"Today," said Marlene Grace, "we're all going to eat in the dining hall. You can take your phone with you, Cricket, and show it to the others."

Now, for some crazy reason, I sobbed, and Marlene Grace had to wipe my nose before she could move my chin rig into place.

Hero jumped into my lap. But Marlene Grace removed him.

"Everyone but you, Hero," she said. "Dogs aren't allowed in the dining room. But we'll be back before long."

I marveled that Hero understood. He remained on the rug while Marlene Grace wheeled me through the door.

"Okay, now," Marlene Grace said, "you drive."

And I did.

~ ~ ~

Lunch and dinner in the dining room, each day, drew me closer to the other children. While Marlene Grace cut and served my every bite, I chatted with those at my table. And because Hero was used to sharing my meals, I made sure Marlene Grace saved a few bites to take back to the room for him.

"You keep spoiling him," Marlene Grace said, "and one of these days he won't eat his own food."

I wanted to say, *Hero deserves every treat he gets.* But I couldn't tell Marlene Grace how Hero's ribs had shown when I had first met him. Hero had barely survived on the streets before he saved me from the rats. I imagined that if Josh had not inadvertently (or was it on purpose?) brought Hero back, the little Jack Russell terrier might have starved to death. It made me glad to think that perhaps we had saved Hero, just as he had saved me.

~ ~ ~

The next day I heard, "Since you've now got the hang of your chair and your phone, would you and Luxor like to begin classes?"

I had never known Mrs. Jamieson to be interested in anything except how I felt about my past and how I was coping with my present. Her question about school caught me by surprise.

"I-I... Of course, I would like to go to school," I stammered.

"Good," said Mrs. Jamieson. "Your tutor comes Monday."

Oh, I sighed.

A tutor was fine, but a tutor was not really *school*. I had hoped to join others in a classroom. But that was unrealistic, of course. I realized the drawbacks. Even though I now possessed a remarkable phone and the services of Luxor, I couldn't use them in a classroom. Spoken commands and responses would be too disruptive. A tutor made more sense.

"We can't have you wasting that mind of yours," said Mrs. Jamieson. I gave her a half-smile.

Because I had missed most of the previous school year, I wondered what grade I would begin with my tutor. Would I be allowed to catch up to where I should be? I didn't want to be kept behind.

"Personally," Mrs. Jamieson now said, "I think you'll blow Mr. Murray's tests out of the park."

"Thanks, Mrs. Jamieson," I said. And I meant it. I did look forward to proving myself in a learning setting again.

CHAPTER NINETEEN

THIRTEEN

It tickled me that Marlene Grace was growing increasingly preoccupied with someone besides me.

On Friday, I watched Marlene Grace answer her phone as she walked into my room. She hurriedly set my breakfast tray on the dresser and turned her back to take the call—as if I couldn't hear her conversation with her back turned.

I heard everything, of course, and I smiled. It was obviously a call from William. Marlene Grace's voice turned soft with pleasure. "Yes," she said, "I'll be ready. See you soon."

When she hung up, Marlene Grace apologized for taking the call during work hours, and I teased, "Do you and William have a date tonight?"

Marlene Grace blushed. "Yes, Missy," she said. "William and I are going to Leonardo's for dinner and then we're taking in a play."

I smiled. "I like William."

Marlene Grace's face grew radiant. "I like him, too, Cricket! He's a good man."

"Do you think you'll get married?" I asked.

At that, Marlene Grace grew dreamy. "I hope so," she said, and then she sighed, "but he hasn't asked me yet, so I just wait. God will let us know when it is time."

Then, abruptly changing the subject, Marlene Grace whipped from her pocket a card that she added to my breakfast tray. "Happy birthday!"

"You didn't forget!" I cried. "Thank you!"

"Well, it's a pretty special birthday today," Marlene Grace crowed. "Thirteen years old!"

She cut my waffles and gave me a bite to chew. Then she opened and read the card to me: "Roses are red, violets are blue, sugar is sweet, and so are donuts! (Ha! Ha! So are you!) Happy Birthday to a New Teenager! From Marlene Grace and William."

Then Marlene Grace pressed one of her wonderful kisses into my forehead.

I laughed. "I'm surprised I don't have a permanent indentation there, from all of your kisses."

"And there will always be more," Marlene Grace promised.

Then, Marlene Grace cut a bite of waffle for Hero and declared, "You need to wish Cricket a happy birthday, too, Hero!"

Hero gave a happy yip.

"I like your little dog," Marlene Grace said. "He's got good manners, he's good with the children, and he understands English!"

I giggled and murmured quietly, "Thank you for letting me keep him."

Just then, Diana wheeled into my room and called out, "Happy birthday, Cricket! I've made you a card!"

Then Diana looked at her lap and down at the floor. "Oh, dear!"

she said. "I seem to have dropped it somewhere. Will you come with me while I hunt for it?"

"Sure," I said, and Marlene Grace pulled my steering rig into place. "We'll be right back," I told Marlene Grace. And Hero jumped into my lap.

Diana chatted as we retraced her path to my room, and she kept saying, "I can't believe I dropped it."

When we drew close to the front door, I thought I saw it. "Is it bright pink?" I asked.

"Yes! That's it! I see it, too."

Diana pulled out her long-handled grabber stick so she could collect the card.

"Let's go in here, and I'll open the card for you," Diana suggested, and she rolled forward and pushed open the ice cream party room door.

At once, a roar greeted us. "SURPRISE!"

My mouth flew open. The Treehouse staff and my student friends were all sitting around the party tables, amid balloons and streamers. And Marlene Grace and William stood front and center.

William flashed several pictures on his cell phone of me stupefied in surprise.

And while I was still recovering, The Treehouse cook wheeled in a lit birthday cake to set in front of me.

"Happy birthday to you! Happy birthday to you!" everyone sang, and I began to cry.

I know that everyone thought my tears were in response to their lovely surprise, but in truth, my tears came when I realized that this should be my mom's special angel food cake and my dad's boisterous singing. And Scooter should be trying to beat me at blowing out my candles.

William pulled out his hanky. "I knew it!" he said. And he gently dried my cheeks.

I tried to stop crying. I didn't want to be sad. I had friends, I had Marlene Grace and her William, and I had Hero.

And I was now officially a teenager.

~ ~ ~

On Monday, Marlene Grace tossed a pair of blue jeans and a T-shirt onto my bed.

"Okay, child," Marlene Grace said in her take-charge voice, "we've got to get you out of that nightgown and into real clothes."

Real clothes. The last time I had been in *real clothes* I had been through an earthquake! I wondered if Marlene Grace ever thought about the day that she and staff had found me at The Arches in my blue jeans and all messed up. My answer came when she said, "These clothes are the same size as the ones you got muddy in, a few months ago."

I glanced up, but Marlene Grace was not staring at me. She was digging for a pair of socks from my dresser.

"Let's get this outfit on," she said, and she set about making it happen.

The shirt went over my head easily, but getting the blue jeans over my uncooperative jelly legs was another matter. I felt sorry as Marlene Grace struggled to pull up the jeans. But once I was dressed and she had combed my hair, she nodded in approval.

"Now," she said, "you look like a thirteen-year-old. And you can go to school like a real seventh grader—maybe even an eighth grader. In any event, you're a young lady now!"

~ ~ ~

"Are you sure you're only twelve?" Mr. Murray asked, after my oral tutoring test.

"Just turned thirteen," I corrected him proudly.

Mr. Murray announced, "Well, happy belated birthday. And you'll be pleased to know I'm starting you in the eighth grade where you would have been if your accident had not interrupted your schooling. I can see why you were at the top of your class."

"Thank you," I breathed. *Thank you for not holding me back a grade!*

"And," Mr. Murray said, "I'm recommending that you sit in on the regular classes here at The Treehouse."

What? Did I hear him right? Am I going to be in a regular class-room? But how will that work?

Mr. Murray explained: "I realize you will not have access to Luxor and your phone in class. It would be a disruption. But Miss Briggs makes good use of a SMART Board, which can allow you to read along with the others. And although you cannot use Luxor to take class notes, I think you are capable of recalling and recording your notes after class. At the end of each day, you and I can follow up on homework and lesson review."

Mr. Murray added, "Classes have already started, but you will not be far behind. Miss Briggs is expecting you tomorrow at nine. Don't be late."

"I won't," I promised. "I won't be late!"

~ ~ ~

Ian and Hero sat next to me in class. As the morning passed, I relished every second. We covered math and then started on English. On the SMART Board, Miss Briggs wrote two words: *simile* and *metaphor*.

Now she asked, "Can anyone explain for us the difference between a simile and a metaphor?"

No one raised their hand. Since I couldn't raise my hand, I cleared my throat, and Miss Briggs called on me.

"Yes, Miss Dalton?" she said.

I said, "A simile is a comparison introduced with the words 'like' or 'as.' A metaphor, however, doesn't bother with the words 'like' or 'as.' Instead, it dives right in with a description as if the thing described were what it resembled. For example, instead of saying a curved stick on a path was *like* a snake, a metaphor might say 'a serpentine stick lay in waiting on the path.'"

Miss Briggs's eyebrows rose, and she looked at me over her glasses. "Excellent, Miss Dalton," she said. "Excellent."

Then, using my example as a starting point, she asked the class to offer more examples of similes versus metaphors. Each sample was added to the SMART Board.

When class ended before lunch, Ian leaned over and said, "How did you get to be so smart? English is my poorest subject, but maybe I'll have a chance if you help me."

"I can try," I said, "if you'll give me pointers in math."

Ian grinned. "Now math is a subject I know something about. It's a deal."

CHAPTER TWENTY

HERO GOES TO CHURCH

"I 'm not particularly fond of Ohio winters," Marlene Grace said. The weather had turned cold, and she had arrived with rosy cheeks and purple mittens. "But then, I was never particularly fond of winters in New York, either." (Marlene Grace had gone to visit her family for Thanksgiving and had been caught in a New York snow-storm.) "On the whole," she said, "I guess I'm not a winter person."

That seemed evident in the way she was suffocating me in a coat, muffler, hat, and mittens. Over it all, she spread a blanket that covered me from neck to toe in my wheelchair. When I asked where we were going, Marlene Grace said I was going to church. "It's time you got back to church," she declared.

Church. I hadn't expected my first outing to be church. But then, Marlene Grace was a minister's daughter. And I knew she had definite ideas of the importance of God in our lives. I knew she wasn't giving me a choice.

"Whose church are we going to?" I asked.

"Yours," she said. "We'll visit mine another time." Then, Marlene Grace said, "And William and Hero are coming with us."

I had never taken a dog to church, and I wouldn't be taking one now, except that Marlene Grace had enrolled Hero in a service dog class and he had passed. Hero pranced around my room this morning in the new vest that signaled he was on duty.

I had thought it odd for Hero to be a service dog. I had always thought of service dogs as large breeds that could lead the blind across busy streets and retrieve dropped items. Hero was undersized for both tasks—tasks that were useless to me, anyway. I never crossed streets and I could not accept any items he might retrieve. Hero's only *service* to me was to keep me company. And he was my protector. He had proven his worth in that role in ways I couldn't recount to anyone— beyond my stories to The Treehouse children.

I also couldn't marvel with Marlene Grace or others about how Hero could distinguish between the *me on an adventure* and the *me who couldn't lift a finger*. On our adventures, Hero would come for a scratch behind the ears, but at The Treehouse he never pawed for such attention. Instead, in my disabled state, Hero rubbed or licked my face; he knew I had no feeling below my neck.

How could I explain to anyone how truly smart my little dog was and how much he meant to me? We had been companions on more adventures than anyone might ever know. And today, it seemed right that Hero should go to church with me.

~ ~ ~

Like a sweet-smelling bouquet, a perfumed Marlene Grace and a cologned William sat with me and Hero in The Treehouse's wheel-chair-accessible van. On the way to worship, I drank in familiar sights.

Little had changed, including the approach to Bethel Community Church.

After parking the van, the driver lowered the ramp, and Marlene Grace helped me to the ground. The church entrance loomed before me, and I closed my eyes. I remembered my family and me walking to the door. *Scooter lagged behind, and my mother scolded him to catch up. Dad shook hands with the greeter, and I bent to tie my shoe.*

But when I opened my eyes, I was back with Marlene Grace, William, and Hero.

Greeters welcomed us, and ushers suggested seating. For the first time since I had attended this church, I sat in the back. I tried not to look at the familiar pew farther up on the right.

Lorna, Mrs. Anderson, and others stopped to say hello. And I was grateful that Hero deflected many awkward expressions of sympathy with a wagging invitation to pat his head.

Finally, soft music began and the sanctuary lights faded. My friends took their seats, and I focused on the lighted screen up front.

BE STILL, AND KNOW THAT I AM GOD, the projected words announced.

Knowing God is not that easy, I countered. *And if God is real, is He surprised to find me here, today, with my old anger? What must He think of me?*

The slide changed, and I stared. I HAVE LOVED YOU WITH AN EVERLASTING LOVE.

Foley had quoted those words in his first prayer—the one for garbage! I remember scoffing. But Foley had believed that God loved him. *Did I believe God loved me?* I had believed it at one time and had accepted God as good. But the accident...

In an attempt to block out God's failures *(lies?)*, I squeezed my eyes shut. *(How stupid! This is His house!)* When I looked again, the screen read, DO NOT LET YOUR HEART BE TROUBLED. TRUST IN GOD; TRUST ALSO IN ME.

Trust? I turned my gaze from the screen and let it fall on the pew up front, a pew now filled with strangers. I clamped my jaw. My anger flared. *How can I trust a God who lets death and harm come to me and my family? How can anyone with troubles persist in trusting that kind of God? Pastor Howard says that everyone has troubles and that God is faithful* through *them. Is He? I don't think so. There's too much pain. God!* I challenged, *I want my family and my life back as they were!*

And then, inexplicably, something inside of me broke. No sooner had the demand screamed from my heart than I felt a powerful shame. For the first time I thought, *What am I doing? Who do I think I am?* A new image filled my mind, an image of my family safe within the arms of Jesus. I wept. And I saw myself surrounded by His care. Pastor Howard had been right. God had not abandoned me. My anger had kept my vision small.

"*God!*" I cried, "*I'm so messed up! I need You! Forgive me for shutting You out. I've been so focused on my losses that I haven't allowed myself to see Your faithfulness. I've been blind to Your care. You have provided for me, here, and for my family, in Heaven, and You have provided for Foley and his family in ways I don't begin to understand. You give us all a future and a hope!*"

As I cried out, I felt God's fingers under me, lifting me up. He held me tight. And then He said: AND SURELY, I WILL BE WITH YOU ALWAYS, TO THE VERY END OF THE AGE.

I wept. I could see that God's plan and faithfulness are forever and that they are bigger than I can see—bigger than all of time and space.

Marlene Grace laid her hand on my cheek and whispered, "It's okay, baby. It's okay to cry."

As I cried, I thought of Mom and Dad and Scooter. And I felt Mom saying, *we're proud of you and the progress you've made, Cricket. Jesus is faithful. Don't be angry with Him. Let God love you. And love Him back. His love is forever!* And the words rang true, and I accepted them.

As the service ended, the final hymn was projected on the screen. I realized I could not have sung its words before I entered the sanctuary. But now I let them sing themselves in my heart. I added my voice to Marlene Grace's and the three hundred other voices that swelled this place with worship:

> *What a Friend we have in Jesus,*
> *All our sins and griefs to bear!*
> *What a privilege to carry*
> *Everything to God in prayer!*
> *O what peace we often forfeit,*
> *O what needless pain we bear,*
> *All because we do not carry*
> *Everything to God in prayer.*

~ ~ ~

Pastor Howard shook hands at the door. He remembered having met Marlene Grace, and he greeted her. Then, he shook William's hand. And he grinned and shook Hero's paw. "It was good to have all of you in worship with us today," he said, "including this little fellow."

Pastor Howard said to me, "I hope you know that your new wheelchair and your being here this morning are an answer to prayer."

"Thank you," I said. "Keep those prayers coming, okay?"

"You bet," Pastor Howard said. "We'll all continue to pray for you." He spread his arms to include all the people of the congregation, and I was humbled.

~ ~ ~

"I have a request," I said, once we were in the van.

"Sure," said Marlene Grace. "What do you have in mind?"

"Can you take me to my house?"

In surprise, Marlene Grace relayed my directions to Logan, our driver, and we turned out of the parking lot.

In the van, I experienced the usual route my family had always taken, and I caught myself imagining me in the family car with Mom and Dad and Scooter.

When we arrived, Marlene Grace found the spare key per my instructions. *Josh and I had passed right through the roof and into the living room on our visit, but today we needed the key. It seemed as if this was someone else's house.*

Marlene Grace and William lifted my chair over the threshold. At once, my family's ghosts rose up to greet me. I pictured my dad in the recliner reading the newspaper, and I could hear my mom in the kitchen preparing supper. Scooter and Dodger rolled on the floor in a game of keep-away over some ratty dog toy.

I sighed and closed my eyes. Marlene Grace did not rush me.

Finally, I turned my chair and headed for the stairs. I wanted to go to my room, where the only ghost was myself.

Marlene Grace said, "William and I can get you up there."

"My room's on the left," I called as she went ahead to check things out.

William lifted me from my chair, carried me up, and laid me on the bed that Marlene Grace had prepared. A pile of pillows let me see around the room.

Hero sniffed where Dodger had once ruled, and I saw Marlene Grace examining the books on my bookshelf. William looked out the window. It felt awkward to have them here.

But I had come for a purpose. There were things I wanted to take with me to The Treehouse.

Per my instruction, Marlene Grace gathered up my rock collection.

"Anything else?" she asked. "How about clothes?" She held up a dress-up outfit I couldn't imagine needing, but I let her collect it.

"T-shirts are in the second drawer," I said, "and there are blue jeans in the bottom drawer."

"Great," Marlene Grace said, and she piled the T-shirts next to the rock collection and the dress.

When she opened the blue-jeans drawer, Marlene Grace uttered an "Oh!" of surprise. I was puzzled. What was surprising about a pile of blue jeans?

Marlene Grace turned and exclaimed, "You assured me you had another necklace—and here it is!"

I stared, astonished. I recalled telling Marlene Grace that I had another *onyx stone,* but what she now held up was another *necklace,* a necklace exactly like the one that had gone missing.

But why was the necklace here? I knew I hadn't left it in the drawer. Josh and I had used the necklace long after our visit to my house. And I couldn't imagine why Josh would put it in the drawer, now.

Marlene Grace slipped the necklace over my head, and once again I felt its familiar coolness and weight on my throat. *Josh,* I asked silently, *what are you doing?*

190

"I'm glad we found the other necklace," Marlene Grace said. "It's lovely, and I've missed seeing it around your neck. You look now like you're supposed to."

I felt like I was supposed to, too. With the necklace gone, I had despaired of future adventures. Perhaps the recovery of the necklace was a sign that my adventures were not at an end.

Marlene Grace asked, "Now, my dear, is there anything else we should take with us?"

"Only one thing more," I replied. "Please bring the family photo from my mom's dresser." I had wanted to take it on my last visit, but I wouldn't have been able to explain how I had got it. Now, Marlene Grace could fetch it for me.

William gathered me up, and on my way downstairs and through the living room, I said a silent goodbye to my empty house.

Goodbye, everyone, I whispered to the years of memories that would never age, no matter how often I might visit.

CHAPTER TWENTY-ONE

OH, OH!

B efore I opened my eyes in the morning, I smelled the pancakes. *Today must be Friday.* Marlene Grace had begun to bring me pancakes once a week.

But when I opened my eyes, it was Josh who held the plate under my nose. "Hungry?" he asked.

"Sure," I said, "but aren't you afraid Marlene Grace will catch you here when she brings my other breakfast?"

Josh grinned and aimed a forkful of pancake at my lips. "Open up," he said, "or you'll get syrup all over your chin."

I opened and chewed, which meant that I couldn't talk. But I had questions.

"I see you're wearing the necklace," Josh said.

I swallowed and refused the second bite until I had said, "Yes, and I'm confused."

At that, Josh laughed. "*Now* you're confused?"

"Oh, don't tease," I said. "You are maddening, you know?"

Josh's second bite threatened to smear my face, so I opened my mouth to take it in.

I attempted to talk with my mouth full. "What's the deal with hiding the necklace in my clothes drawer? First, you take the necklace away, and now you stick it someplace where we'll find it. I don't get it."

"You're going to choke," Josh said. "I wouldn't talk and chew if I were you."

"Then explain," I mumbled in mid-chew.

"Actually," Josh said, "this necklace is not the one you had."

His explanation wasn't helping. Was he saying this was *his* necklace? If so, did he now have mine? And what difference did that make?

"I can hear your questions," Josh said, and I wondered if, indeed, he could read my mind.

Then answer my questions, I demanded silently.

Josh laughed. "You'll get answers, soon enough." And he practically force-fed me another bite of pancake. In between my bites, Josh made sure that Hero got his pancake treats, too.

I preferred speaking my questions out loud, so I asked, "How did you know we would go to my house? And how did you know we would open the jeans drawer?"

"Who do you think put the idea into your head?" Josh asked.

"So, you're telling me you not only read my thoughts, but you give me thoughts?" I was more confused than ever, now.

Because I had little choice, I finished the pancakes, and Josh wiped my chin. To my surprise, Josh didn't bother to hide the evidence of his breakfast delivery in the trash. He left it sitting on a tray next to my bed. Then, he moved to a chair across the room. There he crossed his legs like someone waiting for his name to be called at the doctor's office, and he began to hum a little tune.

I'm sure I don't know what you're up to, I thought loudly.

And in surprise, I heard in my head, *you don't have to shout. I can hear you, just fine.*

My mouth still hung open when Marlene Grace pushed open the door. In her hands was a breakfast tray. I couldn't see if it was pancakes, but I did see the surprise on her face when she spied the empty plate by my bed.

"Well," she said, "has someone already brought your breakfast?"

Unsure what to say, I stammered for a moment.

Tell her the truth, I heard in my head. I stared at Josh who seemed to be invisible, except to me.

"Uh, yes, someone brought my breakfast," I said.

"Oh," Marlene Grace replied. "Who?"

"Uh, a friend," I said.

Marlene Grace narrowed her eyes. "Cricket, what's going on?"

"Uh, someone stopped by and brought me pancakes," I said.

Marlene Grace bit her lip. "I can see that," she said. "But you haven't answered my question: who?"

Tell her the truth, I heard, again, in my head.

"Uh, it's a friend named Josh."

"I see," said Marlene Grace. "I hope I get to meet him, sometime."

"Uh, it's possible," I said.

"Where does Josh live?" Marlene Grace asked.

And now I was stymied. Unless Josh put an answer into my head, I had nothing to tell her. When nothing came to me, I said, "Uh, I'm not sure."

In the middle of our conversation, Hero jumped from the bed and scampered over to Josh. I saw Josh put something into the dog's mouth, and Hero pranced back to the bed and jumped up.

"Well, look at that!" Marlene Grace exclaimed. "Hero has found your other necklace!"

I stared at Josh. He was still sitting with his legs crossed and his chair tipped back on two legs.

Josh eyed the ceiling as if to avoid my gaze.

What's going on? I asked, so that Josh could read my thoughts.

Marlene Grace held the other necklace in her fingers and was comparing it to the one around my neck.

"These necklaces are so unusual," she murmured. "Where did they come from?"

Before I could stop her, Marlene Grace moved the necklace in her hand to within inches of the one at my throat. "See how the stones are so identical?" she was saying.

And before I knew it, she had clicked the stones together.

~ ~ ~

Instantly, Marlene Grace and I rose into the air, passed through the ceiling of The Treehouse, and soared upward, into the morning clouds.

And we didn't stop. Up and up we flew, past the sun and past the solar system and out and out through the glittering galaxy and into the broader panoply of stars.

I had not heard a sound from Marlene Grace, and I was worried. I looked back to make sure she was all right. Like a scaredy-cat on a roller coaster for the first time, her eyes were tightly closed.

"Open your eyes, Marlene Grace!" I called.

And when she did, she cried, "Oh, child! What's happening to me?"

"An adventure," I called back. "An adventure!"

~ ~ ~

195

I wondered where the stones were taking us. Were we going to Foley's planet? I wondered if we would see Jesus there. Had He come? If so, I wondered if the planet had been transformed, as the prophecy had said would happen.

I peered through the stars and looked everywhere for the planet that should be ahead. But the object of my search eluded me. I was blinded, instead, by a wash of bright light that blotted out the familiar landmarks. Perhaps the planet would appear after we passed through the light.

But instead of passing through the light, Marlene Grace and I circled it. And as we did, I realized that this glorious expanse of light *was* Foley's planet! No longer the small and dingy globe Josh and I had visited, and no longer densely shrouded, the planet had become a glorious shining orb. And as much as I longed to pass through to the surface to see the wonders of life that had come to this place, it was not to be. I did not control the stones. Our adventure took us on one orbit around the transformed sphere and then shot us out of its circle and back toward home.

Back we went through the mass of stars, back through the Milky Way galaxy, and back into our solar system. We descended toward the Earth at a blinding speed and then shot through the atmosphere and hurtled toward the surface.

"We're going to die!" I heard Marlene Grace cry out.

"No," I assured her. "We will not die."

Down we plummeted. Down through the roof of The Treehouse. Down to the stenciled butterflies and flowers on my wall. And in that instant, we were cushioned in the curious way that always surprised me. And we landed as softly as snowflakes, I in my bed with covers that had risen to receive me, and Marlene Grace on her feet beside me.

Hero barked a welcome and wagged himself nearly silly.

"Yes, Hero," I said, "we're back." I had no doubt that Hero knew we had gone on an adventure and left him behind. His bark held a note of scolding.

Still lightheaded from her flight through space, Marlene Grace staggered toward the chair occupied earlier by Josh. "Oh!" she cried with her head in her hands. "What *was* that?"

"You did it," I said. "You didn't realize it, but you made it happen."

"I didn't do anything," Marlene Grace protested.

"Oh, but you did," I said. "You clicked the necklace stones together."

In her confusion, Marlene Grace looked at the necklace she still clutched in her hand. "It's just a necklace," she said.

"Not exactly. It's a magic necklace," I replied. "And it takes two stones to make it work."

I could see the thoughts whirling in Marlene Grace's mind. A widening of her eyes let me know when she made a connection to my other adventures. "Cricket, this is what's been happening to you, isn't it?" she said.

I smiled. "Yes. And until now, you never would have understood."

She started to rise from her chair. "So, what would happen if I clicked the stones, again?"

"Don't!" I cried. "You mustn't!"

She backed off but still stood next to my bed. She asked, "Where did we go?"

"You've heard some of the story," I told her. "It's like the stories I've been telling the children about me and Hero."

"Ah!" I saw light dawn in her eyes.

"But where did the stones come from?" she asked.

"From Josh," I said.

"Josh? The one you said brought your breakfast?"

"The same," I answered. "When I was blind and left lying for days at The Arches, I despaired of dying, until one morning Josh brought me pancakes. He's a funny boy, around my age, and he gave me something besides myself to think about. And then, one day, he brought the necklace."

"Who is he?" Marlene Grace asked, and I couldn't tell her because I didn't know, myself.

"He's just a friend, someone who knows me better than I know me. And someone who knew I needed an adventure." I added: "And he used to hide the evidence of his daily pancake delivery in the bottom of the trash."

Marlene Grace began to laugh. "So, it wasn't Lynette, after all! We blamed the housekeeping staff for sneaking a breakfast in your room and hiding the plates in your trash. Lynette nearly lost her job over it, but we couldn't prove it was her."

"Oh! I'm glad she wasn't fired," I said. "It was Josh, not Lynette."

"Hmm," said Marlene Grace. "And when you turned up all messed up, was that Josh, too?"

"It was because of the adventures," I said. I told her, again, the story of my first visit to Foley's planet and how I had been robbed and tied up on the street.

"And that's when Hero saved you, right?"

"Yes, Hero saved me from the rats."

"So," said Marlene Grace, "why didn't we see Hero when you first returned?"

"Because Josh kept him. Josh didn't leave Hero here until the day you first saw him. And I was certain you would turn Hero out. I'll love you forever for letting me keep him!"

Marlene Grace murmured, "It was the oddest thing. The day I saw him, all I could think of was that he belonged here. That thought wouldn't leave my head."

Josh, I thought. *Josh put that thought into your head!*

"And," said Marlene Grace, "I couldn't turn him out if I tried. Everyone, here, loved him. And he's such a good dog."

Hero knew we were talking about him, and he padded over to Marlene Grace and put his paws on her knees.

Finally, Marlene Grace sighed. "I don't understand it all, but something really happened this morning. And I'm putting this necklace in the drawer so it won't accidentally happen again."

"Maybe," she added, "we'll use the stones another time. But for now, I think it's safer to keep them apart."

"Agreed," I said.

"And, it's time to get you ready for school," Marlene Grace announced, as if to remind herself that she couldn't spend more time untangling the mystery. She turned very businesslike and began dressing me. It must have been hard for her to not ask more questions, but she refrained.

When Marlene Grace had moved me, in my blue jeans and T-shirt, into my wheelchair, she said, "We'll talk later."

~ ~ ~

Marlene Grace wasn't the only one with questions. Instead of paying attention in my classes, I puzzled all morning about why Josh had orchestrated today's adventure with Marlene Grace. He had obviously set it up. But for what purpose? Just so I would have someone to talk to about our trips?

In truth, I was glad it had happened. I was glad I could finally tell my experiences to someone. Only a person who had experienced one of these trips would understand my story and not think I was crazy. And who better than my Marlene Grace?

Marlene Grace had taken it well. I know she had been frightened nearly out of her wits when we were flying, but she had recovered.

So, was that all Josh was trying to do—give me someone to share my adventure stories with? Or was there more?

CHAPTER TWENTY-TWO

CHRISTMAS SURPRISE

M arlene Grace draped my family photo with a sprig of greenery and a red bow. She hung a birdfeeder outside my window, and she sat me up to watch the children build a snowman in the garden.

I ventured out to The Treehouse lobby when the magnificent *Christmas* tree arrived, and I watched as the staff and children decorated it. Everything glittered and sparkled and shouted *Christmas*.

And Marlene Grace and I went shopping.

I bought Christmas cards for Mr. Tipple, Mr. Gilson, Mrs. Jamieson, and others. And I wanted to see what might catch Marlene Grace's eye so that I could recruit Pastor Howard's help to buy her a present. For Hero, I picked out a dog bed.

As we made our purchases, Marlene Grace kept asking, "And what do you want for Christmas?" I couldn't think of anything. I finally said, "A box of chocolates. Not milk chocolate, but dark chocolate," and she stopped asking. I assumed I would find chocolates among my gifts under the tree.

~ ~ ~

Marlene Grace and William took me to Bethel Community Church on Christmas Eve. Wrapped all in white, Marlene Grace looked like an angel. William told her so. And I wondered if he was ever going to propose.

Lights in the sanctuary had been turned low to give the candles at the windows and the roping lights around the ceiling a chance to shine. Soft carols on the piano whispered *What Child Is This?* and *Away in a Manger*. In the foreground, a spotlight bathed a *baby* in a bed of straw. And Pastor Howard's first words were, "For unto you is born this day in the city of David, a Savior, who is Christ the Lord."

"*Savior*. Such an important word," Pastor Howard said. "If Jesus wasn't Savior, His birth would have been no more exceptional than yours or mine. We would not be celebrating His coming, and there would be no Christmas."

That's true, I thought. *Jesus IS Christmas.*

"Without the birth of our Savior," Pastor Howard continued, "we and our world would be doomed forever. Humanity fell prey to a lie that twisted us in sin and separated us from Our Creator. And no advances in technology, no brilliantly crafted laws, no attempts to eradicate hate could undo what was done.

"But God made a way. God sent His Son, Jesus, to become a man—a perfect man—who would take our sins to the Cross and bury them. Then when Jesus rose from the dead, He opened the door of life for us and offered a new relationship with God. Now we wait for Jesus to come again and set the universe right. At that time, all troubles and hurts and difficulties will disappear. Jesus will make the Earth blossom under His care, and He will fulfill every promise and prophecy of God's love for us."

Pastor Howard continued. "The writer of the carol *Joy to the World* says it this way: *'No more let sins and sorrows grow, nor thorns infest the ground; He comes to make His blessings flow far as the curse is found.'"*

The congregation joined Pastor Howard in singing every verse of the inspired song, and I tried to imagine our Earth, one day, without sin and sorrow.

~ ~ ~

"Rise and shine!" Marlene Grace sang out. "It's Christmas, Cricket! And you're coming to my house."

In surprise, I mumbled, "I am?"

I shook off my sleep.

"Yes," said Marlene Grace. "We're having breakfast and are spending Christmas day at my house. So, let's get dressed and ready to go."

How odd it felt to dress before breakfast. But the promise of biscuits and gravy at Marlene Grace's home trumped anything at The Treehouse. I only wished we could hurry faster. After all, it was Christmas!

When Marlene Grace finally transferred me to my chair, Hero jumped into my lap to make sure he wouldn't be left.

"Oh, yes, Hero," Marlene Grace reassured him. "You're coming, too."

"Wait!" I called, as Marlene Grace wheeled me to the door. "I almost forgot. We need to take something with us. Go to the back of the closet. See that little box? Bring it." Marlene Grace retrieved the package that Pastor Howard had stashed for me, and her smile told me she had read the tag.

At the curb, instead of Logan and the white Treehouse van, I saw

William next to a brand-new, bronze-colored, specially equipped vehicle.

"Wow!" I said. "Whose van is this?"

"Mine," William announced proudly. "Do you like it?"

Marlene Grace guided my chair up the ramp, and I wondered at the car. Why had William bought such an expensive vehicle, equipped for a wheelchair? It seemed an extravagant expenditure for the few times he might transport me. Plus, I had thought only Logan was qualified to transport residents of The Treehouse.

As if reading my mind, Marlene Grace said, "We're giving Logan the day off for Christmas."

Her comment answered only part of my question, but I waited to pursue it later.

When we arrived at Marlene Grace's house on the outskirts of town, William turned the key in the front-door lock below a giant wreath. Hero slipped inside, and, my dog's and my nose took in the aroma of biscuits already done and a ham still roasting for dinner.

Marlene Grace's tree glittered, and a grand, red poinsettia dominated the coffee table. Christmas carols floated in the background.

William stooped to light the logs in the fireplace, and then he moseyed into the kitchen to ask if he could help. Whenever it grew quiet, I suspected there might be some kissing going on.

When William emerged to wheel me into the dining room, I smiled to see that Marlene Grace had wrapped a girlie-looking apron around his neck. William shot me a look that said, "I wouldn't mention it, if I were you." And before we ate, he tore it off. When I grinned, he glowered at me.

Marlene Grace couldn't stuff my mouth fast enough. Everything was delicious! Marlene Grace's eggs, sausage, biscuits, and gravy were nothing like The Treehouse food.

"You can't beat homemade," declared William as he patted his stomach. "Do we do dishes, now?"

"Nope," said Marlene Grace. "We open presents!"

William and I cheered, and William wheeled me into the living room.

In the glow of the tree lights, Marlene Grace set three gifts in my lap. "Let's open this one first," she said. "It's for Hero."

At the mention of his name, Hero sniffed the package she held.

"No fair," Marlene Grace said. "You can't smell it before I get it unwrapped!"

Hero already knew its contents, however, and he bounced on his hind legs until Marlene Grace extracted his treats. "Merry Christmas, Hero!" she cried.

Next, Marlene Grace opened my box of chocolates and popped one into my mouth.

"Delicious!" I pronounced. "Just what I wanted." Even with my full tummy, I savored the sweetness melting on my tongue. I politely offered one to William and Marlene Grace, and I was secretly glad when they declined. That left more for me! I would ration them, so I could have one each day until they were gone.

My next gift was a gift card so I could order more online books. "One can never have too many books," I declared. Marlene Grace had known that I had devoured most of the books in the list on my phone and was ready for more.

The third package intrigued me. What had Marlene Grace bought? I couldn't imagine anything I needed.

I liked the way Marlene Grace made short work of the packaging—just like I would have done. Torn paper flew in every direction. And then she waved the contents: seven pairs of wildly colored socks. Since I seldom wore shoes (who needs them when you can't walk?), my feet were usually dressed in socks. Every pair I owned were an uninteresting white or gray. But the new pairs were more than socks: they were fashion statements! Gold thread for Sunday, polka dots for Monday, neon for Tuesday, kitty-cat eyes for Wednesday, puppy paws for Thursday, fuzzy tops for Friday, and bold stripes for Saturday.

"People will definitely see you coming!" exclaimed William.

Marlene Grace pulled on a pair and lifted my legs so I could see my feet. She had put on the wildly fuzzy pair.

"I love them!" I giggled.

William teased about the socks and then said, "We have one more present." From his pocket he pulled a small packet wrapped in green foil, tied with a braid of silver.

"You open this one for her, William," suggested Marlene Grace.

"With pleasure!" William exclaimed, and he slid off the braid and slipped his thumb under the flap of the packet. William drew himself up in his chair for the grand reveal. Like a magician on stage, William waved the blank back of the box before my eyes. Then he called out "Voila!" and turned the box so I could see the contents—a dainty pair of gold earrings.

"Earrings!" I cried. And when I realized what they were, I gasped, "For pierced ears!"

Marlene Grace beamed. "Yes. And Dr. Bolger will do the piercing next week."

I couldn't wait to show the earrings off at school. Not even Diana had pierced ears!

I had not expected such perfect gifts, and I thanked Marlene Grace and William.

Now I could hardly wait for Marlene Grace to open my present for her. "It's there," I said, "under the tree."

"I know," said Marlene Grace. "I suspect you thought I might find it in your room before Christmas, because you had someone hide it way in the back of your closet!"

I laughed.

Marlene Grace held my box on her lap for a moment before she began tearing away the paper—not with the festive abandon she had exhibited with my socks, but not with picky fussiness, either.

After discarding the ribbon and wrapping, Marlene Grace held up the small, flat box and shook it. I grinned.

When she removed the top from the box and peered inside, her eyes rewarded me. "Oh, how beautiful!" she exclaimed.

She lifted out the delicate, silver-worked butterfly necklace, and William offered to fasten it for her.

Marlene Grace clasped it to her neck and kissed my forehead. "It's lovely, Cricket!" she whispered, "I will always treasure it."

"A beautiful gift for a beautiful woman," William declared.

Instantly, I realized my failure to get a present for William! I announced, "I'm so sorry, William! I didn't know we would all be opening presents, together, or I would have got you something. But if you'll bend close, I'll give you a Christmas kiss."

"Perfect!" William boomed, and he bent to claim his gift. "One can never have too many Christmas kisses!" he said with a glance and a grin at Marlene Grace.

Before I could wonder what gifts William and Marlene Grace might have bought for each other, William pointed to a box under the tree. "That one has my name on it," he said. "Do I get to open it now?"

Marlene Grace shushed him. "Just like a little kid," she said. "Can't wait, can you?"

William grinned at her. "Just a little boy at heart," he declared.

Marlene Grace placed the present in his lap. And, whether to tease her or because it was his nature (I was unsure which), William meticulously peeled back every piece of tape to avoid tearing the paper. Marlene Grace finally cried out in exasperation, "For Pete's sake, William, just open it! The paper isn't that expensive, and I'm dying to see if you like it!"

William guffawed and now ripped the wrapping to shreds. When he had lifted the top from a long, thin box, he drew back in surprise. Inside was an elegant, hand-turned, burl-wood-barreled fountain pen with a matching cap. (At least, that's how William described it.)

"It's the one you admired at the woodworker's shop we passed last month," Marlene Grace said. "At least, I hope I got the right one."

"You certainly did, my love..." William murmured. He lifted the pen and lightly ran his fingers over the smoothly polished wood. He turned it over and over so that the gold band and clip glistened in the tree lights. Then, he dug a business card from his pocket, jotted his name, and admired the fluid signature.

"Rich," he declared with satisfaction. Then he slipped the pen into his shirt pocket, patted it, and kept looking at it resting there.

Marlene Grace sat back, satisfied that he was pleased.

At last, it was William's turn to fetch the final package from under the tree. He presented it solemnly to Marlene Grace and made much of saying, with a shrug, "Just a little something."

In contrast to William's careful peeling back of the tape on his present, Marlene Grace yanked off the ribbons and tore away the wrapping, only to find another wrapped box inside, and then another. William stifled a grin at her frustration.

"Are you sure there's something inside?" Marlene Grace cried, until she came to a tiny velvet box, only an inch high and wide.

Now, her hands shook. William took the box from her and bent on one knee.

I drew in a breath as William asked: "Marlene Grace, will you marry me?"

Marlene Grace sobbed a "yes" through fingers that covered her mouth. William pulled her right hand away from her face and slipped the ring onto her finger. Marlene Grace fell into his embrace, and William kissed her hair, her tear-stained cheeks, and finally her lips.

"I love you," he said.

"It's about time!" I blubbered, and we all laughed.

Like magic, Marlene Grace was transformed. The ring turned her into a queen. And the queen served the ham for dinner and frosted cutout cookies for dessert. And William threatened to devour them all. I had never seen a man eat so much. It was as if before the proposal he had been starved.

Love is strange, I decided. *Wonderful, but strange.*

~ ~ ~

The next day over breakfast at The Treehouse, I asked Marlene Grace if she had told William of our adventure with the stones.

"It's interesting you should ask," she said. "I have started to tell him on several occasions, but something has always stopped me. I think it's because I'm afraid he won't believe me, and I don't want to take that chance."

"I understand," I said. "That's how I felt before you clicked the stones."

Marlene Grace shook her head. "I'm still not sure what I experienced, that day. For example, where did we go? What was that shining thing we flew past?"

"That," I said, "was Foley's planet."

In surprise, Marlene Grace exclaimed, "Really?! In your stories you always described that planet as dark and depressing. But what I saw was glorious and shining."

"That's because," I said, "what you and I circled on our adventure was a changed planet."

I had not gone into all the prophecies of Foley's planet in my stories to the children, so Marlene Grace had not heard how Foley's people had come to live underground or how they had looked forward to the coming of Jesus.

I told her now, and she listened with deep interest. But her face held a strange expression that I wondered about.

"From our previous visits," I said, "Josh and I knew that Jesus' return would be soon. Then when you and I flew past the planet, I knew we were seeing proof that Jesus had come."

Marlene Grace pursed her lips. "Cricket, you and I should talk more about this," she said. "There are some things I think you should check out. But right now, I have to get you ready for class."

~ ~ ~

All day, I wondered what Marlene Grace wanted to talk about. Something about Foley's story had disturbed her. I wanted to learn more, but we had no chance to talk. There were too many obligations in the way, including her date with William after supper.

We would have to talk tomorrow.

~ ~ ~

In the morning, it was Hero who awakened me. His tongue left my cheeks wet, and I wondered if Marlene Grace had forgotten to take him outdoors.

"Don't worry. I'll do it." Josh's voice surprised me.

"Where's Marlene Grace?" I asked.

"She's coming. She's going to be late," Josh said. He opened the door and walked Hero to the garden. From the garden, Josh tapped on my window and waved a silly wave.

When Josh and Hero returned, Josh placed my phone harness around my neck and set the stylus between my teeth.

"Give Marlene Grace a call," he suggested.

Why? I wondered. *What's wrong?*

I turned on the phone and woke up Luxor. "Call, Marlene Grace," I said. At once, the phone rang.

When Marlene Grace answered, she sounded harried. "Cricket? How did you know to call me?"

"Josh suggested it," I said.

"Ah," she murmured, and I knew she was puzzled by my answer.

"Where are you, Marlene Grace?" I asked.

"I don't want you to worry," she said, "but I'm at the emergency room. William fell down some stairs this morning and broke his leg. I thought I could check on him in the ER and still have time to be there for you, but you seem to have awakened early. I'll be there in a few minutes, okay?"

"Is William all right?" I asked.

"Yes. They've taken him to X-ray and have a hospital room set for him when he comes out. I'm leaving, right now, and I'll visit him in his room this afternoon."

"Marlene Grace, don't rush to get back here," I protested. "Josh can get my pancakes."

There was silence on the end of the line before Marlene Grace said, "That's good, Cricket."

I told her to tell William to get well fast. And I said goodbye.

After my call, Josh stood. "Pancakes, coming up!" he declared. And with a bow, he turned and left for the dining room—or wherever he went to pick up my breakfast.

By the time Marlene Grace arrived, I had eaten Josh's pancakes, and Hero was still licking syrup from his whiskers. My empty plate remained on the tray, but Josh had not stayed.

I wondered where Josh always disappeared to, and I wondered if he would ever be visible to Marlene Grace.

~ ~ ~

Marlene Grace quickly and efficiently sent me off to classes with a kiss on the forehead. She promised, "I'll be back for your lunch." And she was. Then, as I headed for my afternoon classes, she called, "I'll be back for your supper." After supper, she prepared me for bed and set my reading harness so I could entertain myself until another aide tucked me in.

I worried over how Marlene Grace was being torn between tending William and me, and I prayed for her.

As I lay in my nightgown reading, I saw that Marlene Grace had sent me an email. It read:

Cricket, we haven't had a chance to talk, but I think you should look up these prophecies in your Bible. (By the way, a Bible is loaded in your book app.) Look up these verses: Matthew 24:4–14. I may have more for you to read, later. I'll see you in the morning, dear. Love, Marlene Grace.

Hmm. What is so special about these verses? I pointed the stylus to the book list and opened the Bible on my screen. I would have tapped until I found the verse, but it was easier to tell Luxor to find it.

I also asked Luxor to read it to me, and I listened to Jesus' prediction of wars, famines, and earthquakes. And I heard His warning about deceivers and the persecution of those who followed Jesus. I was drawn to verse 13: *But he who stands firm to the end will be saved.*

How similar these warnings were to those quoted by Foley and Reverend Beech. It was chilling to read the same words from Jesus about Earth.

I wondered, *could the same things happen here?*

Foley said that when he was a child, he and his family had lived much like we are living now. And Foley said it had taken less than fifty years for all the changes on his planet to take place. *Could a mere fifty years change the Earth, too?* I wondered. The thought disturbed me.

I went to sleep thinking of the hungry eyes of Foley's children. Three years and more, underground! Three and a half years of waiting for the fulfillment of a promise that Jesus would return. It seemed so improbable and desperate. And, yet, it had happened.

I awakened to hear myself calling out for Josh to "click the stones, I have to warn and prepare my planet!"

"Take me home!" I was crying in my dream.

CHAPTER TWENTY-THREE

NOTHING IS THE SAME

"Try pancakes," I heard Josh say over my head in the morning, as if pancakes were a cure-all for my agitation.

I said, "Josh, we need to talk."

"After pancakes," he said. Then, in that maddening way of his, he mashed a forkful of sticky pancakes against my lips.

I sighed and opened my mouth.

As I chewed, Josh retrieved the second stone necklace from the dresser drawer where Marlene Grace had put it for safekeeping. I watched as Josh put it around his neck.

"I suppose you want my necklace, too?" I said. (I hoped he would say no.)

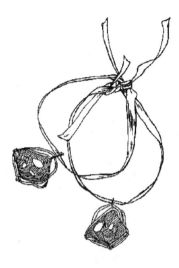

"Not yet," he said, and I was relieved for now.

Bite after bite of pancake disappeared, and when I finished, Josh left the plate on the tray. He leaned against my bed.

"Want to take a trip?" he asked.

"Is that why you've been stuffing me?" I asked. "Will I need the energy?"

Josh grinned, and he pushed a T-shirt and a pair of blue jeans into the bottom of his bag. Hero sniffed the bag and whined until Josh let him climb inside my satchel.

"Looks like we're ready," I said.

I saw Josh take my hand. It was something he rarely did. Now, he clicked the stones, and we started to rise. We rose to the ceiling and dissolved through the roof and into the sky. Floating like a breeze, we left the atmosphere and moved in a still silence toward the object of our journey.

"Are we going to Foley's planet?" I asked.

"Yes, and no," Josh said. (I should have known I wouldn't get a simple answer.)

"When Marlene Grace and I traveled," I said, "the planet was bright. It shone like the sun." It was a hint for Josh to explain what we had seen, but he only murmured, "Mm-hum."

The stars glistened around us, and as we passed through them, there seemed to be no end. I began to search for Foley's planet. We should soon reach its galaxy and solar system. I looked for the bright light, but it was gone.

And then, I saw the planet. But it was not exploding in light as it had been on the day Marlene Grace and I had approached it. Instead, the whitest of white clouds encircled it, and I saw no hint of darkness anywhere on its surface. "What's happened to the light?" I asked, but Josh did not answer.

We approached rapidly, now. Down, down we hurtled toward an open green space, and we stopped only inches above a field of grass that gently received us.

As far as I could see, blades of green rustled in the breeze. "Where are the people?" I asked.

"Just over that rise," Josh said.

Josh pulled Hero from the satchel, and I pulled on my blue jeans, T-shirt, and shoes. Then we followed Hero as he scampered ahead of us.

I welcomed the soft sun on our faces. And birds sang as if caroling us on our way. The expanse and freshness of the country expanded my spirit. Josh and I had never been outside of the planet's city. Here, hills of green and distant lavender rolled on without end. What a change from the earthquake-ravaged metropolis of our earlier visits.

The minute we reached the top of the green rise, I heard voices and saw hundreds of people at work erecting the framework for an entire neighborhood of homes. Below the workers, swarms of children played tag and soccer. Hero raced ahead of us to be in the middle of the fun.

When Josh and I approached, a voice from above called out, "Don't I know you?" Foley flew down the ladder to embrace us. "Josh! Cricket!" he cried. Eli also hurried to greet us.

Foley waved his hand. "See our new town? Isn't it going to be beautiful?"

As we talked, another man I felt I should know joined us and shook hands. "Good to see you again," he said. Before I could ask for a jog of my memory, several children broke away from their games and surrounded us.

"I remember you," an older girl said. "You brought us cookies! And I remember your dog, too. He warned us when it was time to leave the underground."

Foley nodded. "That was a long time ago, but you are right, Beth. This dog has a perfect name: *Hero*."

"Come," said Foley to Josh and me, "and see what we're doing."

Along the smooth, graded streets, Foley and the man I couldn't place meandered with us through the little development. The bare frames of homes rose like skeletons ready for roofs and walls. The pounding of nails followed us as we walked.

"Are we keeping you from your work?" I asked.

"No, no," Foley assured me. "We have all the time in the world. Deadlines mean little now. We can take as long as we want…"

Eli interrupted, almost under his breath, to say, "Speak for yourself, Foley. Some of us are in a hurry."

Foley laughed. "Don't mind Eli. He's in love with a girl from the next settlement and plans to marry her as soon as his house is done."

Foley slapped Eli on the back in a fatherly fashion, and Eli blushed.

Foley continued. "What I was saying was that, except for special circumstances,"—he eyed Eli—"we can move at our own pace. There are no masters or bosses to drive us at a furious pace for their profit. Everything here is ours, and ours alone. The old system of doing things is gone."

"Where do you get your supplies?" My eyes swept the vast fields in every direction. There were no stores or businesses in sight. "And where did you city dwellers learn to build like this?"

"Ah," said Foley. "Our lumber is easy to come by. See that copse of trees? We planted those last week, and although it seems impossible, they have already matured for felling and cutting and planing. And we dig iron from the earth to smelt and pound into nails or whatever shape we need. And when we don't know how to do something, we send for one of the elders from the capital city. They come and teach us whatever new skills we need to know. Amazingly, our brains grasp things easily. I've even conquered the math needed for our building project! Our God has blessed whatever we put our hands to do."

Foley added, "Plus, worries and problems no longer take up our attention. You can't imagine how freeing that is!"

I thought it sounded like *living happily ever after.*

"And this will be my house," Foley said proudly. "And this will be my garden. No more darkness and scavenging. Our children can be in the open air and run and play. And we have plenty of nourishing food. We will never go hungry again."

"Come," Foley said, "and sit with my family." Sabrina had set a table, and I guessed it must be lunchtime.

At the table were Eli, the man I didn't know, an older Joey, and two young children.

I wondered how much time had elapsed since our last visit. Joey had last been perhaps five, as young as these children. *Are these little ones Foley's, too? And am I right that Sabrina is pregnant?*

Sabrina served apple juice and salad and honey cakes, and I contrasted this fare with the scavenged food and canned goods her family had eaten in the past.

As we lunched, I realized that I hadn't seen Jesus. Wasn't He supposed to be here? Or was I mistaken? Had He not come? I blurted out my question. "Where's Jesus? Didn't He come?"

Foley's laugh trilled like music. "Ah, yes!" he exclaimed. "You haven't seen us since Tannin was still amassing his army. He was boasting of his plans to kill the fire-breathing prophets and to attack the mountain of the God-people and crush them out of existence. Then he planned to sweep over the entire continent.

"Well," said Foley, "in his arrogance, Tannin broadcast his success in killing the two prophets and leaving them to lie in the streets. But"—Foley giggled—"the news media couldn't resist saying that at the end of three days, the bodies had returned to life and been taken up into Heaven!"

Wow! I thought. *I wonder what Tannin thought, then!*

"And," said Foley, "The resurrection of the prophets profoundly affected the God-people. Even those who had resisted becoming Jesus-followers suddenly believed.

"Millions emerged from hiding and lined the streets leading into the Temple City. 'God forgive us for rejecting Your Messiah,' they shouted. 'Hosanna! Lord, save us!'

"And they chanted, 'Come, now, Lord Jesus! Blessed are You who comes in the Name of our God!'

"There was no ignoring their cries. We heard them clearly over the airwaves.

"And Tannin mocked them.

"In our little garage we fell to our knees to plead for God's deliverance of His people, even as we heard the sound of troops hewing down the helpless people.

"Tannin boasted of his invincibility.

"Suddenly, in the middle of Tannin's cruel invasion, our radio crackled and hummed loudly, and, instead of the screams of dying victims, we heard a different commotion over the airwaves. And at the same time, here, in the maintenance garage, a radiance—a supernaturally bright light—shot through the cracks and made the windowless interior shine like day. And the light *sang*; there's no other way to describe it than to say that the light was also *music*. Immediately, we knew what it was!

"We threw open the garage door and ran into the light that permeated every atom of everything. Glorious melodies and powerful sounds of marching shook our bones. We knew it was Jesus and His army! He had come, at last! We had no doubt that as Tannin had swarmed over the ancient city, shaking his fist at God, the skies had exploded in a flash of glory, and the noise of heavenly troops had overwhelmed him.

"And as we stood by the shed cheering and shouting our praise to Jesus, we were startled to be lifted up from the park and swept into the air.

"In the blink of an eye, our little band found ourselves before a Throne of even purer Light in the heavens. And we were settled with thousands of others on the right hand of the Shining One on the Throne. Facing us, to the left, were Tannin and his startled army of millions. As far as the eye could see, the dark mark of Tannin's implant smoldered on their foreheads. In contrast, the mark of Jesus glowed like fiery diamonds in the foreheads of those with us.

"And the Voice from within the Light on the Throne said to us on the right, 'Come, take your inheritance.' And to those on the left, He thundered, 'Depart from me, into the fire of punishment.'

"Before our eyes, the millions on the left of the Throne cried out in agony and were swept away. Like smoke, they disappeared from our sight.

"But we found ourselves miraculously immersed in light and set back on the ground of the battlefield Tannin had left. Somehow, the battlefield had become a vast and lush garden."

~ ~ ~

Foley's eyes glittered, now.

"Above us, a celestial dance commenced. And, as we watched, the transformed ancient city, made new despite Tannin's destruction, came down from Heaven as a radiant *bride* for her wedding feast. I can't explain it, but Jesus, as the *bridegroom*, received her. And her *bones and flesh* were ancient but beautiful, filled with thrones and the lives of billions of saints. Among them were believers from every age of our history, including ancients, prophets, and disciples whose stories have populated the Scriptures. And all were given seats at the wedding feast.

"And at the banquet, while Reverend Beech and his people ate and drank with us, the most amazing thing happened. You'll remember Gregory, the man who tore the mark from his forehead? He called us to join him at his table! And that was the beginning of millions of reunions all over the banquet hall. We cried and laughed every minute to meet a family member or a friend from our past and to rejoice in our discoveries. And we didn't want the celebration to end. And, in the middle of it all, I saw the one person I had most wanted to see.

"As I waded through a tangle of people toward him, Pastor Peter pressed through another crowd toward me. With tears, we met and clasped each other in joy.

"'Foley!' Peter cried. 'I knew you had found my letter! I thanked Jesus for it.'

"'Yes,' I replied with tears, 'I got your letter. And I want you to meet the people who became Jesus-followers after you left. None of us would be here if you hadn't written your letter!'

"Peter rejoiced with our group. And he introduced us to many saints we had read about in the Scriptures, including Adam, Eve, Abraham, Moses, and Paul.

"And so," continued Foley, "it seemed as if the banquet celebration might go on forever. But, in fact, the feast lasted only for several decades."

When my eyes registered astonishment, Foley said, "I know it doesn't sound possible, but it did happen!"

And I said, "But you look no different from when we last visited you. If the celebration lasted for decades as you have said, you should be beyond old!"

Foley's laugh rose from his toes. "You are a perceptive child," he said. "And you need to know that I *am* old. But somehow, with the lifting of the curse of evil, the deteriorating effects of life have been reversed. I feel like I could live a thousand years! And Sabrina and I may have dozens of children before we're done!"

~ ~ ~

Sabrina grinned self-consciously as Foley guffawed, and I sat in amazement as Foley resumed his story. "At last," he said, "the feast drew to a close. We had hugged every believer we had ever known, and we had met every notable person we had ever read or heard of. The time had come for us to pay our respects to the Host of the banquet."

Foley's voice caught with emotion. When he recovered, he said, "About those next moments, I scarcely have words. How do you explain a face-to-face meeting with your God, the most intimate friend of your soul?"

Foley closed his eyes in a bliss of remembrance. And I leaned forward to hear every detail.

"In the presence of Jesus," Foley murmured, "my entire being reverberated with His life and love. No part of me missed His enveloping touch. And it was the same for everyone. No one left the banquet without His blessing and renewal. And we heard Him say, 'Go now. Fill the land. Be fruitful and multiply.'

"In that instant, we found ourselves transported again. This time, we floated over the landscape of the planet. We watched in wonder as, below us, a great change took place. The ugliness of Tannin's wars and the scars of the many earthquakes and fires folded, as if by unseen hands, into the earth, like kneaded bread dough. Then, the newly exposed surface pushed out green grasses and grains. Trees sprang up and passed from blossom to fruit in rapid succession. Springs and rivers bubbled from the ground, and lakes teemed with fish. Animals passed before us in mass migration, with all of them eating grass and not meat, as some had eaten before the renewal. And the animals chose where to settle.

"The sun that had been darkened as we had hidden in the maintenance garage had regained its light and raced across the sky and set, and the moon and stars overtook the night. And only when the sun had risen again did we begin our descent to the ground.

"We found ourselves settled in groups on vast tracts of land. And only after we had taken a head count did we realize that Gregory was with us!"

Aha! I thought. Now, I recognized the man with Foley. It was Gregory! I had never seen him apart from his agony and without blood covering his face.

"Yes, Cricket, it's me," Gregory said when he saw the flash of recognition in my eyes. He said, "I chose to come here with Reverend Beech and Foley and their people. I had to come so I could tell them the wonders I have seen in Heaven—and what will happen, here, over the next thousand years and beyond!"

Oh! I breathed. *Of course! Gregory has been in Heaven!* Gregory had died before Jesus came to the planet. And since Jesus promised that everyone would be with Him forever, it made sense that Gregory—and millions of others who had died—would have followed Jesus back to the planet when He returned here.

"And so," Foley said, "our little band, in the company of Gregory, stood in wonder at the restored world around us. We were Adams and Eves in a new garden. And we ate of the fruits and grains, and we drank from the springs. And like people on vacation after long years of hard work, we did nothing for months but bask and eat. We slept under the stars and played under the sun.

"And," said Foley, with a twinkle in his eye, "we set about *multiplying!*"

I giggled. Yes, Sabrina was pregnant!

"And, yes," Foley said, "these two young children are ours, too."

As before, I could not pin down a timeframe for how long Foley and his people had been on the renewed planet. Joey seemed older by perhaps four or five years. But adults were the same as I remembered them—as if aging had slowed to a trickle and years had become days. When life had been so difficult for Foley and the others in the underground shelter, dreary days had seemed like years. But I observed that, now, as part of a renewed planet, each day flowed with a renewing richness.

I remembered from Sunday school a man named Methuselah who had lived to be 969 years old, and I wondered, now, if such a thing could be happening here. *Could Foley live a thousand years—the time span given in the prophecies for the current renewed planet? Would he live to see the final end to evil? Would he be alive to see Jesus create an entirely new planet? What would it be like to live that long?*

Grandpa Noffer had once said that he didn't want to live to be more than a hundred years old, because there was too much sorrow and trouble. But here, trouble was gone. Jesus ruled. *And living to be a thousand would be a joy!*

~ ~ ~

"Can you stay for a while?" Foley's wife, Sabrina, interrupted.

I wanted to say yes, but I looked at Josh for the answer. *Won't we have to get back before my school day begins?* I asked silently.

For once, Josh gave me a direct answer. He replied in my head, *time is different here. You and I will not be missed.*

"We can stay," Josh said, out loud, and Foley cheered.

CHAPTER TWENTY-FOUR

ONE DAY OF THE THOUSAND YEARS

F oley tinkered with a wobbly wheel on a child's wooden wagon as I marveled at the softness and clarity of the air. The distant hills appeared close enough to touch with a stretch of my hand.

No pollution, Josh said in my head, and I knew he had been reading my mind.

And, yes, he said, *you aren't imagining things. Those creatures near the trees on that far hill are dinosaurs.*

Really? Dinosaurs? I said. *Didn't dinosaurs die out on this planet, like they did on Earth?*

Josh assumed a little grin and said, *Yes.*

I decided that when the transformation Foley described had overtaken the planet, the dinosaurs and other extinct creatures had been restored to the animal population. I wondered at the wisdom of that, because I held a vivid recollection of the *Jurassic Park* disaster.

That was a movie, Josh reminded me.

Exasperated, I asked, *Do you have to listen to everything I think?*

Yes, Josh said. Then he informed me (in a loose quote of Tim from the *Jurassic Park* movie), *These dinosaurs all eat grass. They're veg-gie-sauruses—even the T-Rex.*

I rolled my eyes. It was unnerving to have someone read your every thought.

I always could, you know, Josh said, *and it never bothered you before.*

Silently, but loudly, I protested, *But I didn't know about it then. It's very different when you know someone is reading your mind!*

Josh shrugged and said, *what's the big deal? God does it all the time.*

That stopped me. Josh had a point. But somehow this was different—or was it?

Then, I tried the impossible—to think *nothing.*

Instead, I found myself focused on the dinosaur hill. And this time, I noticed a farther distant hill that glowed like sunshine.

"What is that hill?" I asked, out loud.

Eli, who had joined us, answered. "That's The City, the Capital City of the whole planet. And it shines because Jesus is there."

"Oh!" I breathed. "Can you visit Him, there?"

"Of course!" said Eli. "We often do."

I ventured, "What is He like?"

Eli seemed puzzled. "Just like He's always been—only more."

I waited. Would Eli tell me *more?*

Finally, I asked, "More?"

Eli's brows furrowed. "You're an angel, and you don't know?"

Foley intervened.

"Our friends here have never said they are angels, Eli. I'm still unsure where they come from, but I sense that Cricket has not seen what we have seen: the face of our Lord!"

"But how do I describe Him?" Eli insisted. "Except to say that His presence is love and peace and wisdom and joy! It isn't so much something you *see* as it is what He makes you *feel*."

"Well said, my boy," said Foley. "I remember fearing to come before Him the first time, because I feared He would see my weakness and my sin. And He would hear the struggle of my mind and heart to be perfect, good, and worthy of His slightest consideration.

"I entered the Throne Room on my knees, with my eyes clamped shut and my forehead bent to the floor. I thought I would burst in my shame, and I waited to hear His condemnation and feel the angels drag me from the room. You see, I was ready for *judgment*. I understood *judgment*. But what I didn't understand was the extent of His *grace!* I had never wrapped my arms around the size and scope of His *love!*

"As I mourned my failures in a puddle at His feet, I felt a touch on my shoulder and head. 'Yes,' I thought, 'they have come to throw me out.' What I didn't know was that it was Jesus' hand!

"And as His hand lay warmly on my head, I felt my shame dissolve. Joy percolated through my fear. And my mind rang with the words: *You are not worthy, but I Am Worthy. And You are Mine!*

"And tears, purer than any that have ever fallen from my eyes, washed my face and bathed me all over. And His radiance dried my sobbing flood. The hand of Jesus lifted my chin from the ground, and my eyes met His. There, I saw my reflection. In His eyes I saw a *me* I had always longed to be. And I cried out the most beautiful word ever created: *Jesus!*"

And Foley's baritone voice erupted now in a praise song, as if his spirit had no other choice:

"Holy, holy, holy!"
The seraphim cry;
"Holy, holy, holy,
"O Lord, Most High!"

When I see You *holy*, Lord,
I see me as I am.
And when I see You as You are,
I hide myself in shame.

What hope has one of unclean lips;
What hope has one *undone?*
But when You call me, "Come, my child,"
I see the battle's won!

"Holy, holy, holy!"
With all the angels cry;
"Holy, holy, holy,
"O Lord, Most High!"

Yes, You, My Lord, are a God of love,
But love is only part.
'Tis *holiness* that dreamed of me,
And *holy* cleaned my heart.

Without *holy*, love is dead;
With *holy*, life is Love!
With *holy* as my covering,
I take my place above.

"Holy, holy, holy!"
With angels I now cry;
"Holy, holy, holy,
"O Lord—my Lord—Most High!"

(*HOLY, HOLY, HOLY,* BY DEBBY L. JOHNSTON)

Foley's eyes remained closed. I knew he relived the glory of his meeting with Jesus. His story and song made me ache to see Jesus, too. I thirsted to see in Jesus' eyes my own perfected reflection.

I heard Josh say in my head, *One day, you will see Him.*

Oh, Josh! I cried silently, and I could speak no more.

~ ~ ~

At Foley's suggestion, Eli whistled, and a stir of hooves broke over the rise.

"May we ride?" Eli asked the four horses that appeared. Beautiful, proud Arabians. And I was certain I saw them nod and neigh their assent.

Eli offered his hand to boost me onto the back of a jet-black stallion—and I realized that Eli's hand now had all of its fingers! I had been too preoccupied with everything to notice before. *Jesus did that,* I thought. *And Eli's scar is gone, too.* Josh smiled; I know he heard my astonishment.

"Grab the horse's mane and hug his sides with your knees," Eli instructed. It was good advice. I had ridden little, and always with a saddle. Riding bareback was a new experience.

Josh and Eli expertly flung themselves up and into position, and I admired the chiseled beauty of our steeds.

One horse remained. Foley was busy, and we waited.

When Foley tossed up a blanket for each of us, with a mention that we might need it tonight, I sensed that this was an overnight trip. "I need to call Hero," I said.

Before I could yell, Josh let out a whistle, and I saw Hero's head lift from a crowd of children. When Hero started running toward us, the children thought it was part of the game, and they laughed and came, too. On seeing them up close and all together, I realized how many children belonged to the compound. Until now, I had observed them only at a distance.

It struck me that there were too many children—perhaps three hundred or more who were preschool age, alone. And many of them looked like angels. I know that's an odd way to describe them, considering I have no idea what an angel looks like, but the sense of their otherworldly innocence and contentment outstripped the sweetness of the children I knew from among our underground friends. I wondered why the angelic children were different.

They're beautiful, aren't they? I heard Josh say in my head.

But before I could answer, Joey lifted Hero so I could put him in my satchel. He would be safe there—unless I fell off!

Now, instead of Foley mounting the fourth horse to join us, it was Gregory who threw himself onto the glistening back of the chestnut mare. And Gregory took the lead as we set out.

"Hang on!" Eli advised me, again. But once we started to move, my fingers automatically gripped the horse's mane, and I clung tightly with my knees, for dear life.

With each stretch of the horses' strides, the ground blurred faster beneath us, and the hills that had seemed days away now rushed at us with astonishing speed. The moment we reached the dinosaur field, our horses eased to a walk, and above us, a pod of curious, gentle giants bent down to inspect our company.

Hero never bristled or growled. Instead, he rubbed noses—with a T-Rex!

My heart pounded. Images from the movie leaped to mind. One false move, and we would cease to exist! But despite the thunderous footfalls of apatosauruses, brachiosaurs, and a T-Rex, no one stalked or threatened to eat us. I even managed to lay a trembling hand on the nose of a velociraptor!

Then, when a wooly mammoth and a saber-toothed tiger inched their way through the reptilian crowd, I clapped in delight. If this had been Earth, it would have meant a reversal of the Ice Age.

Did they have an ice age on this planet? I asked.

Of course, Josh said with his enigmatic grin.

I urged my stallion to bring me closer to the mammoth, and I petted his trunk. *Scooter would have loved this,* I thought. As if Scooter could hear from Heaven, I said, *I'm petting him for you!*

The dinosaurs, mammoth, and tiger lost interest in us and wandered back to their feeding. What I wouldn't have given to have had a selfie!

"Time to go," Gregory called. "We have someone to meet." And at his command, our horses followed his lead, east.

As if we crossed multiple time zones, the sky darkened with every hoofbeat. High on the mountaintop where we stopped, at last, it was fully night. For the first time, I saw that Gregory's apparel glowed white and bright in the darkness. And stars here were brighter than any I had seen from the surface of our Earth. Each pinpoint gleamed as a little prism of light, so pure and clear that I had to shield my eyes when I tried to look directly at them. They reminded me of diamonds flashing in the sunlight.

In my absorption with the sky above me, I almost missed that a door was opening at our feet and a figure was beckoning us to climb down into the light of an underground cavern. *Underground* and *cave* usually meant *primitive* and *dark* shelter, but primitive and dark were the farthest thing from what we walked into.

Never had I seen such a mass of scientific equipment and computers than what had been crowded into this room. And dwarfing everything was a massive telescope with its head poking through the ceiling.

"Welcome, Gregory!" a short, bearded man said. And Gregory introduced us to Galileo.

What a perfect name for this little astronomer, I thought. And I shook my head to think how Earth's sixteenth-century star-gazer would envy this man's technological array.

"Come," called Galileo, "see my newest discovery!"

One by one, he sat us at the telescope eyepiece and gave us a peek at what excited him.

"It's the most distant object I've captured so far," he said, and his voice quivered with emotion. "And now that I know it's there, I can make plans for a visit!"

A visit? He made it sound like a trip to Disney World—a nice vacation and then back home, again. But if this object was as distant as he described, a visit would take years of planning and years of travel.

"How will you get there?" I asked, to be polite.

He smiled. "Ah," he said. "You, child, have not yet gained your glorified body and mind. But I will try to explain. It's a matter of quantum physics, you see. Some scientists and mathematicians of old pursued clues to the possibilities, including conjecture and experiments with quantum tangles. But once you grasp it, it is as simple as pinpointing where you are and where you want to be, and bouncing off known locations in a quantum fashion."

Galileo saw the blank look in my eyes and laughed kindly. "I know you can't understand this. But one day you will. Let's just say that it pleases me to explore all I can of God's universe, in the Name of Jesus. And I can assure you that I will soon make my visit to the Emerald Star and its planets."

"Do you have a spaceship?" I asked.

Again, Galileo smiled indulgently. "No, my dear. All I need is a small survival pod—rather like packing a suitcase for a short trip. And that's only because I'm leaving this planet. Trips within the realm of the planet require no provisions and take no time, at all."

"So, your trip to the star won't take you long?" I asked. I found it incomprehensible that one could move in less than a handful of centuries to the outer reaches of the universe.

But then, I stopped. *What had Josh and I been doing?* We had taken our own *quantum leaps,* hadn't we? Were the onyx stones an invention like the one of which Galileo spoke? Were the stones not *magic,* at all?

I noticed Josh staring at me with a Cheshire grin, and I said silently, *Am I on the right track?*

Josh did not reply. I knew he knew the answer. And it frustrated me that he withheld information. *Why did he tease me?*

~ ~ ~

I awakened in the morning in the open air on the hillside next to Galileo's cave. Eli had already called the horses, and Hero stood over me, as if to say, *what took you so long to wake up?*

I must have slept well, but I had no recollection of it.

"Time to head back to our community," Gregory said, and he handed me what looked like a thick plant stem.

I heard Josh say in my head, *It's breakfast.*

Right, I countered silently.

Josh shrugged. *Suit yourself,* he said.

And then Gregory laughed. "You need to know that I can hear you two!"

In shock, I thought, *Is there anybody who can't hear me?*

Eli hasn't a clue, said Josh.

Then Gregory said in my head, *Anyone who didn't die before the planet's transformation cannot hear you. Everyone else can.*

Oh, my! I thought.

Then, I reasoned, *even though Eli can't hear you, can you hear his thoughts like you hear mine?*

Of course, said Gregory.

Eli looked up now. "You've been leaving me out of a conversation, again, haven't you? You do know it's impolite?"

"Of course," Gregory hurried to assure Eli. "We'll keep you in the loop from now on."

I had hundreds of questions now, but felt barred from asking them. For example, *did Gregory know Josh before our introduction, yesterday?*

~ ~ ~

I saw Eli chew a plant stalk similar to the one Gregory had given me. I decided to test the stem. Tentatively, I nipped it with my front teeth. The plant's sap ran onto the tip of my tongue. Not tart. Not sweet. It was … like the juices from a steak!

"It's good, isn't it?" Eli said. "It's called the *plant of renown*. Since we no longer eat meat, this plant, which grows everywhere like a weed, provides the nourishment we miss from meat. We eat it, the animals eat it, and even certain birds eat it. The lazy lions sleep in the middle of it so they don't ever have to hunt!"

"Hero likes it, too," said Josh, and I fed Hero my last bite.

It was true, the plant had satisfied me in a way I had not expected, and Hero begged for more.

~ ~ ~

In their super stride, our horses bore us back to Foley's compound, and I felt like I was coming home from camp. Gregory helped me dismount, and I patted the horse's neck.

"Thank you," I whispered in his ear, and the horse lifted his muzzle for a rub.

Because Hero was restless to be down so he could run and play with the little ones, I reached into my satchel to lift him out. And I screamed!

I yanked Hero out and tossed the satchel into the air.

"Snake!" I cried. "Rattlesnake!"

Sabrina caught the bag in mid-air.

"Look out!" I cried.

But Sabrina smiled and gently emptied the bag onto the ground. The snake slithered into the grass, and I stepped back instinctively. But Sabrina never moved.

To my horror, Joey and a friend stooped to look at the creature.

"He looks scared," said Joey, and he picked up the snake and held it close. The snake twisted itself around Joey's arm and let him and his friend pet it.

Gregory put a hand on my shoulder. "It's okay, child," he said. "There is no danger. In the same way that the wild animals have been tamed in the renewal, the serpents now guard their poison. Joey and his friend are in no danger from this creature. And even if a child were to be bitten, we have the healing of Jesus to make him or her whole again. You will notice that, here, there are no disabilities or lasting injuries. All are covered in Jesus' care."

My mind reeled with *the impossible that had become possible*. A garter snake was one thing. But a fanged rattlesnake was quite another. Would I ever be able to accept the change?

No more harm. No more poison. No more wildness. No more carnivores. No more limits on travel or discovery. No more hunger. No more secrets. No more shame.

My mind dizzied. I wanted to be changed, too. I wanted to never have a thought I didn't want heard by God or anyone else. I wanted innocence. I wanted healing and safety. And what I wanted most was my family and our future together!

And these thoughts conspired to overwhelm me so that Josh and Gregory had to gather me into their arms.

"The time will come, child," Gregory said.

I knew that he and Josh felt my pain. And I knew that God felt it, too. Like Josh and Gregory, He knew my every thought!

And as I fought to stop my free-fall into depression and despair, Gregory reached out and took my stone in one hand and Josh's stone in the other hand.

Then he pulled the stones together.

~ ~ ~

I embraced the rush of wind that now lifted us up. But our transport did not take us into the skies of the universe. We were not going home.

Instead, Josh and Gregory and I now raced across the planet's grasses at a speed faster than the earlier strides of our horses. And when I lifted my head, I saw our destination. And I cried out as the farthest hill drew near—the hill that shone like the sun.

The stones settled us just outside the gates of the Shining City. We stood where we could peer inside.

"I cannot take you further," Gregory said. "But before you go home, this much is allowed."

Through the gates I could see people laughing and talking and mingling. And I heard the play of children as they called to one another in their games. And I heard music, everywhere. And I saw colors richer than those found in any garden.

Why are there so many children? I wondered. *An overabundance of children. Children who look like angels.*

Gregory had heard my question and said, "How many children throughout the ages do you suppose have died? Many in childbirth. Many in war. Many by disease. And, sadly, many snatched from life before they could be born. Children make up more of Heaven than any other age group. And when Jesus brought His followers to the planet, they were not left behind. Some remain here in The City and some have become part of the communities throughout the planet. The children will always be with Him."

I was both saddened to think that so many babies and children had died and gladdened to think that Jesus cared so much for each of them.

And I heard His music—the music that my heart had always been hungry for. Every being and every blade of grass in this place sang the same song. Each had its own harmony, but each contributed to the whole. And I wanted it to never end.

I closed my eyes in my longing, and I heard other sounds—voices whispering, whispering in my ear. And I almost recognized them. And one voice, in particular, calmed me. And when I heard it, I knew it was His!

"I have loved you with an everlasting love," the Voice said.

And I felt many arms holding me. Surely, it was my mother and father and Scooter.

But no. It was more.

HE was more. Just as Eli had said! And I felt the peace of a love greater than any I could have imagined.

CHAPTER TWENTY-FIVE

WHERE I BELONG

B ecause Marlene Grace dressed me each day in blue jeans and T-shirts for school, it might not have been evident to just anyone from The Treehouse that I had been on an adventure—except that my clothes had been *pulled over my nightgown.*

Marlene Grace, of course, knew at once what had happened. She also noted the empty plate of pancakes beside my bed.

And yet, she had to awaken me.

"Cricket!" she whispered. "Are you all right?"

"Yes," I murmured. "I'm all right."

"I couldn't awaken you," she said. And I heard fear in her voice. "I thought I had lost you."

I said to myself, *you almost did.* I almost begged to stay with Jesus on Foley's planet. But I had heard Marlene Grace's voice. And I was also drawn to come back to her.

"I love you, Marlene Grace," I said. Now I cried, and Marlene Grace cradled me.

"Oh, my baby!" she keened softly.

And Hero licked my tears.

~ ~ ~

It was days before I could tell Marlene Grace all that had happened to me.

And when I did, I felt her fear that I might one day go on an adventure and never return.

I reassured her. "Somehow, I doubt that I will ever go to Foley's planet again, and I know I will have to wait to step into the presence of Jesus. But He is there, waiting, for that day."

"Of course, my dear," Marlene Grace said. "Jesus loves us. He has always loved us, and He has a place prepared for us."

Yes, I agreed from the deepest recesses of my heart. *Yes, He has!*

But I also knew that Jesus wanted me to live in this world and not to wish away my todays. I had a purpose here, broken body and all. My disability did not mean I could not have an impact on those around me. I could be a Josh or a Marlene Grace to someone else. There was no limit to love!

~ ~ ~

When William's cast was removed, he ventured forth with a handsome cane. I observed that he did very well until Marlene Grace would appear, and then he would relapse for a moment. I suspected that he pretended to need her help so Marlene Grace would fuss over him.

I told him I liked his cane and that he looked very distinguished.

"And I can drive again," William informed me. "In fact, I'll be driving us to church this morning."

"*My* church," Marlene Grace announced.

"*Your* church? What fun!" I said.

And I rode, again, in William's expensive, bronze-colored van.

~ ~ ~

Marlene Grace's church seemed formal to me, at first. Everyone was dressed in their best, including hats on the women. Marlene Grace wore a hat, and gloves too, and she had dressed me in the dress-up outfit we had picked from my closet. With bows in my hair, I felt a little too fancy for me, but I could see now that Marlene Grace had made a wise choice.

"Is this the Miss Dalton you're always telling us about?" asked a distinguished-looking lady.

"It certainly is," said Marlene Grace, and she introduced me to Reverend Jones's wife.

Marlene Grace referred to Mrs. Jones as "our first lady," and she whispered in my ear, "All of our pastors' wives are called *first ladies.*"

"Ah," I said. "I hope I was polite enough."

Marlene Grace smiled. "Child, you were just right."

With his dapper cane helping him pick the way, William guided us to a pew at the front of the sanctuary. In all the years I had come to church, I had never sat in front, and I felt conspicuous. But I was with Marlene Grace and William, so it was okay.

I wondered which of the gentlemen on the platform was the pastor, and after announcements, singing, and offertory, the man I had chosen stood.

"Today," Reverend Jones began in a rich, commanding voice, "we're going to get down to business! You all know that Jesus is coming."

Amens! rocked the sanctuary. I couldn't help but smile.

"And His trumpet call won't have a warning," Pastor Jones said.

"Amen!" called the congregation, including Marlene Grace and William.

"So, if you aren't right with Jesus, today, you'd better get to it!"

"Amen!"

"There's no reason to be left behind when He calls His saints in the Rapture."

"Amen!"

"And let's be frank," Reverend Jones said, "it's not gonna be pretty here on earth once all the believers are taken away!"

Amen, I whispered. And my thoughts flew to Foley's people in the labyrinth after the Great Disappearance. It would someday be like that, here, I knew.

Now, Reverend Jones quoted Matthew 24:21. "These are Jesus words," he said. "Jesus said, *'Then there will be great distress, unequaled from the beginning of the world until now—and never to be equaled again.'* And verse 29 says, *'Immediately after the distress of those days, the sun will be darkened, and the moon will not give its light; the stars will fall from the sky, and the heavenly bodies will be shaken.'"*

Reverend Jones shouted now. "You don't want to be caught in that!"

"No, sir!"

"You want to be ready before those days come!"

"Yes, sir!"

"Verse 42 says, *'You do not know on what day the Lord will come.'* And first Thessalonians 5:2 says, *'The day of the Lord will come like a thief in the night.'"*

"Amen!"

Reverend Jones expounded now on the many Scriptures that describe the awful tribulation that will befall the Earth when Jesus takes His followers away. "It's a punishment!" Reverend Jones cried out.

"Amen!"

"It's a punishment designed to show that God is who He says He is!"

"Amen!"

"And it's going to be nearly impossible to become a believer during that time and then hang onto your faith!"

"Amen!"

"So," Reverend Jones said loudly, "how can you be ready? How can you be among those who will go with Jesus, before it's too late?"

Yes! How?

"First," he said, "you need to agree with God that you are a sinner. Romans 3:23 says, *'For all have sinned and fall short of the glory of God.'* And Romans 6:23 says, *'The wages of sin is death, but the gift of God is eternal life in Christ Jesus our Lord.'* And Romans 10:9 says, *'If you confess with your mouth, "Jesus is Lord," and believe in your heart that God raised him from the dead, you will be saved.'"*

"Amen!"

"Say it with me," he said. And the congregation knew what verse he wanted them to recite: John 3:16.

For God so loved the world that he gave his one and only Son, that whosoever believes in him shall not perish but have eternal life.

Reverend Jones now said, "When you are *in Christ* and *saved,* you are assured you are no longer under the judgment that will afflict the people who are left behind on this earth."

"Amen!"

"Are you ready, today, to ask Jesus into your heart? If you haven't asked Him yet, are you ready to believe He died and conquered death on your behalf to cover your sin and make you blameless before God? Are you ready to confess your belief publicly, before others, to show your faith is real? If so, I invite you, today, to confirm your salvation publicly by coming up front and saying so!"

The organ began to play, and the pastor stood at the front with his arms spread wide in invitation.

I had already claimed Jesus as my Savior years ago at my church. And after my doubting, I had heard Jesus' declaration of love to me and had renewed my bond with Him. But today's message, coupled with my stone adventures, stirred my heart deeply, so that I wanted to affirm it, again.

As Reverend Jones called for people to come forward, I joined a small group who responded. I had only a short distance to go from the front row in my chair.

Marlene Grace came, too, and knelt beside me. She prayed with me as Reverend Jones led us all in a simple prayer:

Lord Jesus, I confirm that I've asked You into my heart. I know I am a sinner. I know You died to pay for my sins. And I know You rose from the grave to prove You are able to save me. I know You are the Son of God and the Lord of all the universe, and I trust You to count me as one of Your children, forever. Amen.

I added my own *Amen* statement after that: *Thank You, again, that You have loved me with an everlasting love, and thank You for giving me Marlene Grace! Amen.*

~ ~ ~

In the van, after church, I told Marlene Grace that I had already been a Christian but that I had wanted to say it again.

"It is always a good thing to remind ourselves of all that Jesus has done for us and all that He will be doing in our *forever*," Marlene Grace said.

And just like he had in church, William said, "Amen!"

I wanted to say how much the sermon reminded me of Foley's

people and the Great Disappearance, but I would have to wait until later when Marlene Grace and I were alone.

Or so I thought.

As he drove, William said, "Seeing a people in tribulation can bring those Scriptures to life, can't it?"

I looked at Marlene Grace, and she smiled. She said, "Yes, I told William all about our adventure and your journeys with Josh." She added, "And William doesn't think we're nuts."

"By no means!" insisted William. "I only wish I could have gone with you."

Marlene Grace told me, "I decided that since we were going to be married, William needed to know my secret. I wanted to be able to talk with him about it."

Marlene Grace and William exchanged a look, now, that puzzled me. I didn't think they meant to leave me out, but I felt like they had another secret, and this time, it was me who wasn't included. *Oh, well. I imagine that engaged people should be allowed to have secrets.*

Then I heard Marlene Grace say, "Shall we tell her?"

Marlene Grace and William exchanged that look, again. Only this time, William winked.

"Okay," Marlene Grace said, and she sat up straight and rearranged herself in the seat. She cleared her throat and turned to look me full in the face.

"Cricket," she said, "William and I have something to ask you."

She cleared her throat again. I thought she was on the verge of crying. And then she said, "William and I want to know if—if you would like to live with us."

I sat, speechless. It took a minute for the words to sink in.

At last, my mouth flew open. "Live with you? And not live at The Treehouse?"

In the rear-view mirror, William flashed me a grin.

"That's right," said Marlene Grace. "What do you think?"

"I'm all for it," affirmed William. "In fact, it was my idea!"

"Was not!" Marlene Grace jabbed him in the ribs.

William laughed. "But I do think it's a great idea."

And before I started crying, William handed his handkerchief to Marlene Grace.

"Yes!" I sobbed. "Oh, yes!"

~ ~ ~

"Dearly beloved," Reverend Jones said, as two beautiful people stood before him. And this time, it was William who cried.

When the newly pronounced man and wife walked arm in arm to the back of the sanctuary, I followed them slowly in my flower-filled chair. Hero brought up the rear, with the ring pillow still tied to his back. And God joined us all, when, by their vows, God joined William and Marlene Grace as husband and wife.

~ ~ ~

Knowing that I belong somewhere, with people who love me, brings me deep fulfillment. Marlene Grace and William have taken me in as if I have always been family, and my routines fall naturally into the scheme of their lives.

Marlene Grace provides for me from home, now. She has quit her job at The Treehouse. Never again do I have to sleep in a room that is not truly my own. Every morning, William takes me and Hero to The Treehouse for my lessons, and Marlene Grace lunches with me in the dining hall. I keep up my physical therapy with Crystal and meet, on schedule, with Dr. Bolger to make sure I stay in top condition. And every night I come home to supper and to my own bedroom at the back of our house.

Marlene Grace and William have let me choose the paint for my room, and I have kept the color as close as possible to the yellow I loved at The Treehouse. Marlene Grace even found stencils similar to the flowers and the butterflies that cheered me there. I never tire of waking up to my stenciled garden.

CHAPTER TWENTY-SIX

BUTTERFLIES

On Saturday, as usual, I slept in. It was our routine that on Saturdays Marlene Grace would wait until I awakened and called for her. During the week, my last dream of the night was usually interrupted. But on Saturdays that was not so. And if you're like me, the last dream of the morning is always the most wonderful and vivid. So, I treasured my Saturday sleep-ins.

This morning, in my dream, I walked through a beautiful garden, with colors brighter than any I had ever seen. And along the way, a kaleidoscope of butterflies kept me company.

One landed on my nose and made me look at it cross-eyed. Its little feet tickled, and I sneezed.

And then, perhaps because of the power of suggestion, a real sneeze overtook me and I awakened. I attempted to extend the dream by keeping my eyes closed. But it was over.

I yawned and lifted my eyelids to gaze at my flowered walls. And then I smiled. *I must still be dreaming. The butterflies on my wall are moving.*

As I watched, the butterflies exercised their wings. Open and closed, open and closed.

Closed, they looked plain and ordinary, but the minute they laid their wings open, their colors dazzled the eye. I tried to decide what kind of butterflies they were, but they seemed an unusual species.

Now, Hero barked, and at his insistence, Marlene Grace opened the door.

At once, hundreds of butterflies took wing! Marlene Grace gasped and held her chest. And I realized I was not dreaming.

Hero danced on his hind legs trying to reach the exquisite creatures that gracefully winged their way around my ceiling.

"Child, what *is* this?" Marlene Grace called out. "Where did these butterflies come from?"

I didn't know and could only say, "From my dream."

"From an adventure with the stones?" Marlene Grace asked.

"No," I said. *At least I didn't think so.* "Just a dream."

"My! My!" Marlene Grace exclaimed. "They are gorgeous!"

The butterflies settled now, on the walls, as if they had been stenciled there. But they continued to open and close their colors.

William appeared over Marlene Grace's shoulder. "What in the world...?" he cried in astonishment. He hung in the doorway, staring in wonder.

Then, as if on command, the butterflies rose into the air and floated to the window. There, they covered it, en masse.

"I think they want out," I said.

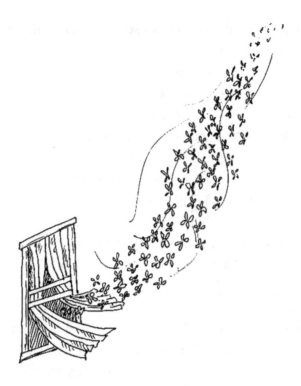

Marlene Grace looked doubtful. "Do you really think so?"

"I agree with Cricket," said William. "Why else would they all congregate at the window? It seems to be a pretty clear sign to me."

Marlene Grace looked at me with a question in her eyes, and I nodded a yes. "Let them go," I said. And Marlene Grace carefully raised the window.

As if following a leader, the butterflies lifted into the air and stole away through the opening. Out they flew in a colorful fluttery cloud, and up, up they went, to disappear into the skies of the morning.

Marlene Grace giggled. "You should see the expression on Miss Bebley's face," she said.

I guessed that our sweet, reclusive neighbor had seen the escape of the cloud of butterflies and had stood with her mouth open in amazement. It wouldn't be long before she quizzed Marlene Grace about what she had seen. I wondered what Marlene Grace would tell her.

But for now, Marlene Grace said, "Well, that was an exciting start to the day!"

William agreed, but he also said, "And it made me hungry!"

Marlene Grace gave him a playful swat. "You're always hungry," she declared. "But you're right. It's time to get breakfast going. Come on, Cricket. Let's get you out of bed and dressed."

The butterflies were the main topic of our breakfast conversation. And no amount of speculation could explain how they got into my room or why they were there.

"I think Josh put them there," said Marlene Grace. And I thought that was the most logical explanation. *But why?*

I hoped Josh would show up soon, and I would be able to ask him.

I added this morning's butterfly visit to my online diary—a book I had begun as a way to document all of my experiences with Josh and the stones.

~ ~ ~

It wasn't until evening, after Marlene Grace had washed and gowned me and set me in my bed, that I discovered one of the butterflies still in my room. The delicate creature had disguised itself on the wall among the painted butterflies.

After Marlene Grace had said good night and shut my door, the butterfly rose in the glow of the dim nightlight and landed on my pillow. I could see Hero's bed, and I could tell that he had watched the creature fly across the room. But Hero did not move from his comfortable spot.

"Pretty, isn't he?" Josh suddenly asked.

Aha! I had wondered if Josh might come tonight, and I was glad I would be able to ask all of my questions.

"Yes," I said. "And I had a feeling you had something to do with his being here, along with all of his friends."

I watched Josh reach out and let the butterfly crawl onto his finger.

"I've never seen one like that," I said.

"They're very common where he's from," Josh said. "He's one in a billion."

"And where is he from?" I asked.

Now Josh played his maddening game. He simply said, "Somewhere very far away."

"Ah," I said, rolling my eyes. I changed the subject. "How do you know it's a *he?*"

Josh shrugged. "I just know these things." But then he said, "See the green dot on his hind wing? Unlike the females of this species, all males have the green dot."

"I see," I said. "Like the black dot on male monarch wings?"

Josh smiled. "I knew you'd know that," he said.

I decided to try again. "So, why were the butterflies here this morning?" I asked.

Josh lazily propped himself against my dresser and played with the butterfly.

Just answer me! I shouted inside.

As if he could hear my frustration, Josh took on a crooked smile.

If I could, I would have tapped my foot or clicked my thumbs. All I could do, however, was give him *the look*. Nothing I did would hurry him along, anyway.

Finally, Josh set the butterfly on the dresser.

"He's going to die soon, you know," he said.

I thought back to what I had read about butterflies, and I assumed that Josh meant that this little guy had mated when the other butterflies were here. I knew that most male butterflies didn't live long after mating. But I also knew that this side discussion was just another of Josh's delays. Why couldn't he simply answer my question about where the butterflies had come from?

I refused to repeat myself.

Josh approached my bed now. "It's the stones," he said.

"The stones?"

"Yes, the stones brought the butterflies here. They're telling you where they're planning to take you, next."

That was an answer I had not expected. "The stones have a plan?"

"In a sense," said Josh. "Actually, they just do what they're told."

"Hmm," I said. "Do you tell them what to do?"

"Hardly," Josh said.

I closed my eyes as I tried to think. My mind flew back to the first time Josh and I had taken flight.

"Will we ever go back to Foley's planet?" I asked.

"Foley's planet?" he repeated. "You do know better than that, don't you?"

I had to admit that I had my suspicions. "You mean, do I know the truth about Foley's planet?" I asked.

Josh raised an eyebrow.

"Yes," I said. "I think our trips were not to faraway places but to faraway times. Am I right?"

Now Josh smiled.

"So," I said, "does that mean the butterflies are not from another planet but from another time in Earth's history?"

Josh shrugged his shoulders as if to say, "Could be."

I had so many questions now. Would Josh answer them? Or would he keep me wondering?

"I need to know something else," I said. I blurted out, "Are you an angel?"

At this, Josh belly-laughed and flapped his arms like wings. I thought he was going to say no, but instead, he said, "Who do you think God sent to Abraham to announce a baby for Sarah? Who do you suppose brought pancakes and water for Elijah after he fled from Jezebel and Ahab? Who do you suppose reminded Peter on his escape from prison to not forget his clothes? And who do you suppose escorted and transported Philip after he had met with the Ethiopian eunuch?"

At last I had an answer! "It figures," I laughed. (But then I thought, *pancakes for Elijah? I'm going to have to check out that story in the Bible, again.*)

Somehow, I knew that Josh had looked very different on each of those Biblical occasions. He was in his present form only for me.

"Why did you come to me?" I asked.

Josh shrugged his usual shrug. "Because I was told you needed me."

At once, I felt a hollow in my stomach. I knew that his answer meant something else.

"You're not going to come back, are you?" I whispered.

"You never know," he said. "Maybe not for a while. You have Marlene Grace and William now."

I couldn't hold back my tears.

Josh set Hero on my bed. "And you have Hero," he said.

The little dog licked my tears.

"Yes, I have Hero," I said. "Thank you for him."

"And you have the One who has loved you with an everlasting love."

Yes, I said fervently from my heart.

Josh crossed the room now, and looked out the window at the dark sky. "You also have the stones," he said. "I'm to leave them, here, with you."

"Is that why you also brought the butterflies?" I asked.

"Yes. And it's why you dreamed about them," said Josh. "You'll dream that dream, again. And, each time, you'll learn more about where the stones will take you. It's up to you to decide when to go."

I tried to imagine taking a trip without Josh. *Would I know what to do if something went wrong, like on our first trip to Foley's planet? Would I be able to make a difference, like we had with the boxes of food? Would I...?*

Josh cut short my questioning. "You don't need me," he said. "By now, you should know that the only person you truly need is Jesus. And He will guide your way."

I knew it was true. I had felt God leading me to Himself with every adventure. Even in my deepest despair, He had never let me go!

The lone butterfly left the dresser now, and flew to land on my forehead.

Butterflies. I wondered where in Earth's history I would find billions of these beautiful creatures. And I wondered what new adventure awaited.

I had only one last question. "How do I know who to take with me?"

But Josh was gone.

~ ~ ~

I lay awake for a long time, reliving my stone adventures, especially the last one. And I pondered what was to come.

Where would God take me, next?

And then I slept. The dream came, again.

And so, it continues . . .

Notes From The Author— For Teen Readers And Adults

Now that you've read the story, I would like to address two points of interest regarding the story.

1 – ANGELS AND MAGIC?

It would be easy to think that angels and magic are the subject of this book, but they are not. God's never-failing love and provision are the bedrock for my story. Magic is not in charge: God is! The stones are simply a device to tell of God's care and transport of the heart for a clearer look and deeper understanding of His love and plans. And Josh does nothing more than what angels have always done: they bring God's aid in unique situations and according to His purposes.

2 – END TIMES

The hope of the underground people lies in a prophecy about the return of their savior. And Cricket begins to understand that the same factors are at work on her planet. The fulfillment of the prophecies I've presented in the book is speculative. Scholars differ on interpretations of the visions and words of the End Times. I have chosen to present a *pre-millennial and pre-tribulation* view, but there are good arguments for other timelines and fulfillments. My purpose in writing this book is not to espouse one End Times doctrine as absolute, but to stir readers to look forward to Jesus' return however God may choose to bring about His promises. Our job, according to the Bible (Hebrews 10:24–25), is "encouraging one another—and all the more as you see the Day approaching." We need to keep our eyes on Christ and our glorious future, scripted by the God who is worthy to bring it to pass. Like Paul (in Philippians 3:13), we need to forget what is behind and strain toward what is ahead. We need to press forward to the goal and the prize in Christ Jesus!

Do NOT take my word for how and what will happen. I will have succeeded if my story drives you to explore God's Word on the subjects presented. To aid in this, I've included some of my Biblical resources in the notes at the end of this book.

ABOUT THE AUTHOR

With four Christian fiction books already published (including a novel trilogy and a collection of short stories), Debby L. Johnston makes her first foray into the Christian teen fiction genre with *The Onyx Stones: Mystery of the Underground People*. A graduate of Judson University in Elgin, Illinois, and a long-time pastor's wife, Debby hopes that young readers will take *The Onyx Stones* adventure with Cricket and Josh and grow in excitement for Jesus' return!

Reader's

Discussion Guide

1 – Cricket experienced tragic events in her life and was tempted to blame God for not taking care of her and her family. She said that God didn't care. Do you think that is true? Do only good things happen to Christians?

2 – When Josh appeared in Cricket's room while she was lying in bed, blind and unable to move, he showed her that she could still enjoy the smell and taste of food, and she could hear and talk. When you have setbacks in life, do you ever take stock of and thank God for what you still possess and can do? Or do you wallow in self-pity over the things you've lost or can't control?

3 – If Josh had come to Cricket's room only once, she might have forgotten him or decided he was just a pretend or one-time friend. But Josh came nearly every day. God doesn't forget us, and we shouldn't forget Him. How important is it for us to connect with God every day in Bible study and prayer?

4 – Cricket got good advice from Pastor Howard, and later from Reverend Jones. Do you respect your pastor's advice and listen to his sermons?

5 – It is not always common for young people to experience the loss of a parent, close relative, or close friend. But it can happen. Has this happened to you? Have you felt any of the grief feelings that Cricket felt? Have you shared those feelings with your pastor, a teacher, or someone else you respect?

6 – Why do you suppose that flying (after the stones are clicked) was such an exhilarating feeling for Cricket? Someone once said that prayer is like riding a flying carpet. Your prayers for missionaries can take you to faraway countries. Your prayers for friends can take you into their homes. Your praises to God can take you into His presence. Have you been flying in prayer, lately?

7 – Cricket is treated badly by the first people she meets on Foley's planet, including a woman who boldly attempts to steal from her. Is it sometimes a good idea to avoid or walk away from people who treat you badly?

8 – As Cricket lay on the street in the dark, all tied up, she prayed for God to send Josh to rescue her, but God sent a little dog, instead. Has God ever answered your prayers in a different way than you expected?

9 – At first, Cricket did not share her *adventures* with anyone. She feared people would laugh and think she was crazy. As Christians, it is easy to keep our spiritual *adventures* to ourselves, but we can miss the opportunities of sharing what we're learning in Christ. When Cricket finally shares (with

the help of the stone necklace Josh has allowed Marlene
Grace to find), it is a blessing to both Cricket and Marlene
Grace. Do you think you can find ways to share your faith and
the things you're learning from God?

10 – You'll notice that Josh did not automatically begin bringing
food to Foley's people. He did it only after Cricket suggested
it. Does God sometimes put ideas into our heads for us to act
on before He steps in and works, too?

11 – Is there anything that happened on Foley's planet, according
to Foley's history account, that could not happen in some
form or other in our world today? For example, do we have
lots of natural disasters (floods, hurricanes, earthquakes,
etc.)? Do people steal from one another? Are there conflicts
and wars?

12 – In the story, Foley tells about the *Great Disappearance*. Many
Christians refer to this event as the *Rapture*. No matter what
you call it, what would our world be like if all Christians were
to vanish suddenly and be taken up into Heaven?

13 – In this story, after the Great Disappearance, many nonbelievers
begin to realize that their Jesus-following friends were telling
the truth about Jesus taking them to Heaven in a surprising
instant. These nonbelievers find notes and Bibles left by their
vanished friends that help them learn about God's promises
and how to become Jesus-followers. Have you witnessed to
your friends about Jesus' salvation and Heaven? And if you
were to be taken up to Heaven, would your friends find your
Bible and other evidences of your faith?

14 – In the book, Tannin begins to persecute the Jesus-followers.
Could that happen in our world today? Would you be willing

to live an outcast's life like Foley did in order to avoid caving in and renouncing your faith?

15 – Marlene Grace becomes Cricket's best friend and helper. Has God ever sent you this kind of helper? Have you ever been this kind of helper to someone else?

16 – Mr. Tipple and Mr. Gilson from Children's Protective Services served as legal guardians of Cricket after her parents were killed. Do you know of any children who have no parents or who are wards of the state?

17 – Do you know anyone who has a wheelchair? Is it like Cricket's (motorized in some way) or like Diana's (fully hand-operated)? Do you slow down to walk and talk with them as they move from place to place?

18 – Do you know anyone with a service dog, like Hero learned to become?

19 – We live in amazing times. It is not uncommon to speak into a handheld phone or laptop and have our words typed in automatically. And we have all the resources of the World Wide Web at our fingertips or voice command. Without these things, the quadriplegic Cricket would not have been able to communicate outside of a face-to-face exchange. And she could not have done homework and school lessons. Do you read your Bible online, sometimes? Do you use your online Bible to help you memorize Scripture during the day?

20 – Are you looking forward to when Jesus returns to wipe evil off the Earth and set up His kingdom? Do you suppose that it will be anything like the way Foley describes it in the book? What do you imagine that time will be like?

21 – Dinosaurs? Among the many Biblically referenced changes

on the Earth during the thousand-year reign of Jesus on Earth (the *Millennium*) are changes in animal behavior (lions eat straw, poisonous asps or snakes are safe for children to play with). I have *speculated* in the story that God *might even* bring back extinct creatures. I include it as a possibility to show God's complete control over nature during this time. Do you think that extinct species might be restored to Earth, or not?

22 – Early in Cricket's experience with Foley's people, she is startled to think that Jesus had brought salvation to Foley's planet in the same way He brought it to Earth. By the end of the book, however, Cricket realizes that Foley's planet *IS* Earth. In case you have been wondering about the possibility of God sending Jesus to other planets, let's consider at least two points in our Bible that argue *against* it. *First:* the grand goal of Jesus providing our salvation is that the Church (His Earthly followers) be finally united *as One* with Him—as a man is to his wife (Revelation 21:9). Since Genesis-ordained marriage is *one* man and *one* woman and we read that human marriage is an example of Jesus and His Church, it would follow that Jesus would not have a second or third wife. So, we can perhaps assume He has no other *Church* on any other planet. *Second:* Jesus is God's *only* begotten son—there is no other *son* of God to send to another planet. We, on this Earth, are a very blessed people: to be created in God's image, to have God send His only Son die for us, and to look forward to our final *marriage (as His Church)* to Jesus, forever!

23 – Time travel is not a new concept. In fact, it is mentioned in the Bible in various forms. In one sense, the *visions* of the

Old Testament prophets (Daniel) and the New Testament prophets (John of Revelation) are a type of mind/time travel. These *travels* are described as *visions*. Cricket and Josh's onyx stone adventures are perhaps somewhat similar. Plus, there are actual *physical transports* mentioned in Scripture. One example is Acts 8, where the apostle Philip is transported by God from one location to another on Earth (and then back again) in order to witness to an Ethiopian eunuch. Cricket and Josh's experiences might be compared to this. And of course, Jesus, in His resurrected body, *appeared and disappeared* in various places to meet with His followers. Since God is in control of time and place, isn't it likely that He would utilize time travel or immediate transport options in the Millennial Earth?

24 – Like Cricket, have you asked Jesus into your heart? Are you willing to ask Him in? If so, you can say the prayer Reverend Jones helped Cricket pray after the church service at Marlene Grace's church (see chapter 25), and then tell someone—perhaps your pastor—about the decision you have made. Remember, you can always ask your pastor to explain whatever you don't understand about becoming a Jesus-follower or about what *asking Jesus into your life* means. or about what asking Jesus into your life means.

25 – Where do you suppose Cricket and Hero might go, next, with the stones? And who might Cricket take with her?

Scriptures Referenced In The Story

CHAPTER EIGHT

Luke 15:3–7—Parable of the lost sheep

CHAPTER NINE

1 Thessalonians 4:16–17—Caught up with Him in the clouds
Matthew 24:40–41—One will be taken and the other left (Great Disappearance)

CHAPTER TWELVE

Matthew 24:29–31—Sign of the Son of Man will appear in the sky

CHAPTER THIRTEEN

Revelation 13:16—The mark of the Beast in the forehead

CHAPTER SIXTEEN

Revelation 22:4—Jesus' Mark on the forehead

CHAPTER SEVENTEEN

Acts 7:54–8:3 (NLT)—The stoning of Stephen and persecution of the early Church

CHAPTER TWENTY

Psalm 46:10a—Be still, and know that I am God
Jeremiah 31:3a—I have loved you with an everlasting love
John 14:1—*Do not let your hearts be troubled. Trust in God; trust also in me.*
Matthew 28:20b—*And surely, I will be with you always, to the very end of the age.*

CHAPTER TWENTY-TWO

Luke 2:11 (KJV)—*For unto us is born this day in the city of David, a Savior, who is Christ the Lord.*
Matthew 24:4–14—Jesus predicts wars, famines, and earthquakes; v. 13—*But he who stands firm to the end will be saved.*

CHAPTER TWENTY-THREE

Revelation 11—Two witnesses
Zechariah 12:8-13:1 & Matthew 23:37-39—Israel is called to repent and to call for the Messiah (Jesus) to return.
Matthew 25:34a—*Come ... take your inheritance.*
Matthew 25:41a—*Depart from me ... into the fire.*
Revelation 19:9—Marriage feast
Isaiah 24:1—Land turned upside down (symbolic or literal?)
Isaiah 11:6–7—Lions will eat grass
Isaiah 11:9—People will no longer fear poisonous snakes
Ezekiel 36:30; Zechariah 8:12—Multiply, fruits, crops
Job 40:15–24—Possible mention of dinosaurs? (also check out mentions of "behemoth," "leviathan," "dragon")

Isaiah 35:7—Natural springs
Revelation 20:4–6—Thousand years
Isaiah 2:2; Zechariah 6:13—Jesus will rule from Jerusalem
Revelation 3:5—Dressed in white

CHAPTER TWENTY-FOUR

Isaiah 11:2–3—Quickness of understanding
Daniel 12:4—Knowledge will be increased
Ezekiel 34:29—Plant of renown
Revelation 21—New Heaven and new Earth

CHAPTER TWENTY-FIVE

Matthew 24:21—*Then there will be great distress, unequaled from the beginning of the world until now—and never to be equaled again.*

Matthew 24:29—*Immediately after the distress of those days, "the sun will be darkened, and the moon will not give its light; the stars will fall from the sky, and the heavenly bodies will be shaken."*

Matthew 24:42b—*You do not know on what day the Lord will come.*

1 Thessalonians 5:2b—*The day of the Lord will come like a thief in the night.*

Romans 3:23—*For all have sinned and fall short of the glory of God.*

Romans 6:23—*The wages of sin in death, but the gift of God is eternal life in Christ Jesus our Lord.*

Romans 10:9—*If you confess with your mouth, "Jesus is Lord," and believe in your heart that God raised him from the dead, you will be saved.*

John 3:16—*For God so loved the world that he gave his one and only Son, that whosoever believes in him shall not perish but have eternal life.*

CHAPTER TWENTY-SIX

Genesis 18:1–15—Angels announce to Abraham and Sarah that they will have a son

1 Kings 19:6—Angel brought Elijah "hot cakes" and water

Acts 12:7–8—Angel releases Peter from prison

Acts 8:26—Angel tells Philip to go where he finds the Ethiopian and witness to him

CPSIA information can be obtained
at www.ICGtesting.com
Printed in the USA
LVHW081938261219
641783LV00003B/18/P